Sawyer's Crossing

A New England Novel

Sharon Snow Sirois

LIGHTHOUSE PUBLISHING

North Haven, Connecticut

LIGHTHOUSE PUBLISHING
P.O. Box 396
North Haven, CT 06473

Design by Peter J. Sirois
Illustration by Beverly Rich
Computer Graphics by Bob Rich

All Scripture quotations are from the Holy Bible,
New International Version ©1978 by N.Y. International Bible
Society, used by permission of Zondervan Publishing House

Library of Congress Control Number 00-090513

International Standard Book Number 0-9679052-9-X

Printed in the United States of America
01 02 03 04 05 06 07 — 10 9 8 7 6 5 4 3 2 1

I would like to thank God, whose faithful guidance has led me through each step of this journey. His unconditional love has made me the person that I am today. It is privileges to love, praise, and serve Him.

"Hope in Him…" ISAIAH 40:31

"Trust in Him…" PROVERBS 3:5-6

"Live a life worthy of the Lord and please Him in every way." COLOSSIANS 1:10

Acknowledgments

I'd like to thank the team of people that have been behind me from the beginning. It's been a long road, but you guys have believed in me, and stuck with me from the very start. I realize that without the Lord, and your support and encouragement, this dream never would have become a reality. Thanks to you all, from the bottom of my heart.

Peter. You are one of the best gifts God ever gave me. You're an incredible husband and father. You are a friend that knows me better then I know myself sometimes. Thanks for all your support, encouragement, advice, and patience! But most of all, thank you for you. I love you!

Jennifer, John, Robert, Michael. God broke the mold when He made you kids! You guys, are without a doubt, the most awesome, coolest kids I know! I receive so much blessing from being your Mom.

Thanks for your encouragement, your big bear hugs, and your extra sticky kisses! I love you!

Mom, Dad, David, Karen, Elizabeth. I never really knew how special our family was until I grew up, and had one of my own. You showed me how to live this life by an example that I will always admire. Thanks for believing in me.

The Sirois Family. You welcomed me into your hearts and homes. Thank you for all the special times we shared together. Your friendship is something that I treasure.

Bob and Gerry Hofmann. You gave of your time and love unselfishly, showing me, by example, what it means to walk with God. Thank you for your love and devotion.

Karol Ann Shalvoy. God knew that I needed an incredible editor and He sent you! You are a great blend of correction and encouragement! Thanks for the long hours, the patience, and the support.

Beverly Rich. Thanks for the beautiful cover illustration. You painted my dreams, and turned them into reality.

Jane Lyman and Bob Rich. Thank you for your expertise in computer graphics and commitment to excellence.

Beverly Kern. Thanks for your help and encouragement.

Richard Shalvoy. Thank you for all your computer expertise. Without your help, I probably would have ditched my computer off the highest mountain!

It's a strange feeling for a writer
to be at a loss for words, but
that is exactly how I feel when I try
to describe just what you mean to me.
You are my husband, and my best friend
in all the world. Our love is deeper
and more powerful than any I've ever known.
I love and cherish you with all my heart.
This one is for you, Peter.

Prologue

"Daddy, please...," the little girl begged earnestly, as she excitedly jumped up and down.

Her father watched her lovingly, as her long, blonde ponytails gently bounced in the air. The young father smiled tenderly at his six-year-old daughter. He knew that he would have a hard time denying that little angel-face much of anything. She was so sweet, and innocent, and almost always cheerful. The little energetic bundle reminded him so much of his wife that his heart couldn't help but overflow with love for the child.

"OK, Kelly," the young father said kissing her quickly on her rosy cheek," you go and hide, and I'll come and look for you in a few minutes."

Kelly ran out of the small kitchen, squealing with delight, as her parents sat at the old wooden table, watching her go. "Jerry," Rachel said as she rubbed her pregnant tummy, "Kelly is the only six-year-old that I know of that thinks the game is called 'Cops and Robbers,' and not 'Hide and Go Seek.'"

Jerry let out a loud, hearty laugh that filled the air. "Rach, don't blame me! Kelly made up the game herself! Actually," he said growing serious, and arching his dark eyebrows upward, "you should really take pity on me."

"Pity?" Rachel said eyeing him suspiciously.

"Yeah, Rach," he said in a sad voice, "because I'm a cop, Kelly always makes me play a cop. I never get to hide and be the robber. Kelly always insists that I find her!"

They both laughed. Jerry's case wasn't very convincing. The love and pride that he felt toward his little girl was spread like a banner across his glowing face. Jerry sighed contentedly. At twenty-eight years old, he felt like he was the luckiest man on earth. He was married to his high school sweetheart, had a wonderful daughter and a baby on the way, and he was doing a job that he loved to do. Life couldn't be better for him. He reached across the table, and tenderly squeezed his wife's hand. "I'm living a dream, Rach. I love you."

As Kelly lay quietly under the old, sagging couch, she was able to watch her parents clearly. She smiled as she saw her Daddy take her Mommy's hand. Then, she looked curiously at her Mommy's belly. She wondered for the hundredth time if God was going to give her a baby brother or a baby sister. She honestly didn't care what she got; she just wanted another kid to play with.

As Kelly intently watched her parents, she saw the back door suddenly fly open. A man dressed in black clothes came running over to her Daddy. Kelly immediately felt frightened by the man's huge size. He was the biggest man that Kelly had ever seen. Kelly's small body lay motionless and rigid, as she listened to angry words tumble from the big man's mouth. Kelly decided instantly that he must be a bad, bad man. Nobody ever talked to her Daddy that way. Everyone loved Daddy...except for this mean, giant, man.

Then Kelly saw it. Flickering in the kitchen light, she could clearly see that the bad man had a gun. Kelly was squeezing her doll so tightly, that her fingers hurt. She wanted to yell, or cry, but she couldn't. She felt too afraid.

"You took away the best years of my life, Douglas!" The big man yelled bitterly at Kelly's Daddy. "And now, Douglas, it's time for me to take away the best years of your life!"

"No, Pitman!" Jerry Douglas yelled right before the shot went off. Kelly watched in horror as Pitman shot her Daddy three times in the head.

Then Pitman spun around quickly and shot Kelly's Mommy twice. As the big man walked slowly out of the kitchen, he said in an evil voice that shook Kelly's small body, "Too bad you married a cop, Lady. I don't believe in leaving any witnesses around."

Kelly rubbed her large blue eyes in disbelief. She watched, waiting for her Daddy and Mommy to get up off the floor, but they didn't. They didn't even move. Finally, in a small, trembling voice, she squeaked out, "Daddy? Mommy?"

Her parents' only response was silence. A paralyzing terror gripped Kelly as her Daddy's words came racing back to her. "Never play with guns, Kelly. Guns can kill." Right then and there, in that sickening moment, Kelly knew the honest truth. Guns had killed...both her Mommy and Daddy. As she stared wide-eyed at the gruesome sight in front of her, a wave of cold, hard fear washed over her. What if the bad man comes back? What if he comes back and finds me!

Quickly Kelly slid out from under the couch. She ran to her parents' bedroom, and dialed 911, just as her Daddy had taught her to do. When a man answered the call, Kelly dropped the phone in fear. Maybe it was the bad man. She felt too frightened and confused to know for sure. She ran to her room, and slid under her bed.

Still clutching her doll, she cried until she heard the sirens. They stopped outside the small Cape, and almost instantly voices filled the tiny kitchen. So many voices...Kelly thought listening carefully. She didn't recognize any of them, until one called her name out.

"Where's Kelly?" The voice asked sounding panicked. "Jerry and Rachel are here, but where's Kelly?"

A moment later, he was shouting her name. "KELLY! KELLY!" She heard the man running through the house. Even as he called to her, she felt completely helpless to move.

A moment later, the man was lying on his stomach, on the floor, and looking at her, under her bed. He gently took her by the arms, and slowly pulled her out. "Oh, Sweetheart... Sweetheart," he said in a choked-up voice, as he held Kelly tightly. For the first time since the shooting, Kelly began to feel a little safe.

"Kelly," the man said in a quiet, tender voice, "it's Uncle Baily. It's OK now, Honey. I won't let anyone hurt you."

The fifty-year-old police chief of Sawyer's Crossing, whom Kelly affectionately called Uncle Baily, rocked the little girl gently. He picked her up, into his strong protective arms, and carried her out the front door to his squad car. "Kelly," Baily said in a voice full of concern, as he slowly began to drive down the road, "I'm going to take you to your Grandma Wheeler's. OK?" Kelly numbly nodded. Her small body was shaking violently. "Bad man...,"

Kelly said in a quiet, but angry voice. "He was a bad, bad man."

Uncle Baily pulled the squad car to the side of the road. "Kelly," he asked in an alarmed voice, "did you see this happen? Did you actually see the bad man?"

Kelly simply nodded. Her voice was suddenly gone.

"Sweetheart," Baily said in a troubled voice, full of warning, "don't tell anyone that you saw that bad man. Whoever did this to your Daddy and Mommy...he's...," Baily shuddered in fear, "he's sick! If the papers or TV get word around that you've seen him…that bad man may come after you! You're the only one who has seen him, Kelly. You're the only witness that can identify him. Oh, dear God…," Baily said in a frightened voice. "Kelly, whatever you do, Honey, don't tell anyone that you've seen him. "Sweetheart," he said protectively covering his large hand over her small one, "right here, right now...you must take an oath of silence. Promise Uncle Baily that you'll never tell anyone, and," he said in a determined voice, "Uncle Baily will promise you that he will personally find that killer. I will find him, Kelly...," he said looking at the small child intently, "I will find the man that killed your Mommy and Daddy if it's the last thing that I do on this earth."

One

As Kelly entered Baily's office at the Sawyer's Crossing police station, she felt as though she were stepping back in time, to her childhood. Baily's office had been a second home for Kelly, complete with special desk drawers that held toys and candy for her. As she scanned the small, crowded office quickly, eyeing the floor-to-ceiling bookcases, and the plants that filled every inch of window space, Kelly began to feel overwhelmed at all the wonderful memories she had in this room. From all kinds of fast-food kid's meals, to endless games of checkers, Baily and Kelly had shared many a special moment and conversation in this very room. As Kelly bent down to pat Amos, Baily's old Golden Retriever, she smiled lovingly at the round, jolly man. Immediately after the death of her parents, Baily had actively stepped into her life as a loving father-figure. Even though Kelly had been brought up officially by her Grandma Wheeler, Baily had made a point to see her or talk to her every day.

Baily and his wife Mel, having no children of their own, welcomed Kelly into their hearts and lives with open arms. They shared birthdays and holidays together, family outings and daily adventures. When Kelly was a teenager and expressed interest in wearing a badge, like he did and her father had, Baily enthusiastically encouraged the girl, knowing that she would be a natural for the job.

As Kelly stood before Baily, at twenty-five, fresh out of college and the Vermont Police Academy, Baily smiled at her proudly. "Well, young lady," he said waving her over to a chair in front of his desk, "now that you're an official officer here at Sawyer's Crossing, tell me how your first week went?"

Kelly's big blue eyes lit up with excitement, as she slowly tucked some strands of blonde hair behind her ear. "Oh, Uncle Baily," Kelly said in a sincere voice, straight from the heart, "I love my job. I love helping the people here at

Sawyer. I feel it's a way that I can really make a difference in my corner of the world."

Baily smiled understandingly at Kelly. At five-eight, the thin, bubbly blonde with the milky white complexion and rosy pink cheeks was not only a knock out on the outside, but on the inside as well. Kelly had a heart of gold, with the confidence and enthusiasm to make a great difference in their small, rural community.

"Well, Kelly," Baily said proudly, "I'm not the least bit surprised. I knew you'd be a great addition to the force."

Kelly smiled back at the old chief, and in a teasing, spunky tone said, "Uncle Baily, I think you're just the slightest bit prejudiced toward me...but, thanks for the compliment anyway."

An unusual sober expression dropped across Baily's round, wrinkled face. "Well, hang onto the compliment Dear," Baily said in a heavy voice, because I'm afraid that you're not going to like what I have to say next."

Kelly stiffened and leaned forward in her chair. She looked intently at Baily, her eyes already narrowing in the anticipation of bad news.

"Kelly," Baily said in a serious voice, filled with regret, "you know this time has been coming for a while...I promised to hang on until you made the force."

Kelly interrupted him, with an urgent, almost accusing tone. "You're not retiring, Baily!" She hastily pushed herself up from the chair. "I've only been here for a week! You can't do it," Kelly said adamantly.

Baily smiled tenderly at Kelly. "Kelly, the Doc says I have to. My heart isn't as strong as it should be..."

"Your heart's fine, Baily!" Kelly shot back angrily. "First you hit me with retiring...then this heart thing! I don't want to hear it!" Kelly was really angry now, and her blue eyes were shooting electric sparks at the old chief.

"You're not even old enough to retire!" Kelly said in a last ditch effort to strengthen her case.

Baily let out a loud, jolly laugh, that to Kelly's annoyance bubbled freely through the small room. "Sweetheart,...I'm pushing seventy."

Kelly swung around, and stared at Baily in shock.

"You've grown up, Sweetheart...," he said as he smiled at her lovingly, "and," he said raising his bushy gray eyebrows, "I've grown old."

Kelly squinted her eyes at Baily in a disapproving way. "You're not old, Baily!" She stated emphatically. Then Kelly let out a loud sigh, filled with turbulent emotions. "Oh, Baily," Kelly said with a heavy heart, as she wiped some tears from her eyes, "no one can ever replace you."

A moment later, alarm covered Kelly's face. "You didn't already hire some jerk to replace you, did you?" Kelly asked urgently, suddenly feeling as though someone had thrown her out of a plane without a parachute. Her small, safe world was abruptly and unexpectedly crumbling to pieces before her eyes.

Baily nodded slightly, and waved a hand at someone behind Kelly. "Officer Kelly Douglas," Baily said in a formal voice, "I'd like you to meet the next Chief of Police at Sawyer's Crossing...Capt. Mark Mitchell."

Kelly spun around in shock, and stared openly at a tall, blonde-haired man, casually walking into Baily's office. He had a friendly face that seemed to break easily into a smile, and an honest and genuine sense about himself. Yet, as Kelly continued to eye him disapprovingly, she thought the young man looked more like a model in a cop's uniform, than a real cop.

As he warmly extended his hand to her, he said in a sincere voice, "It's a pleasure to meet you, Officer Douglas. I'm Mark Mitchell."

Kelly couldn't seem to help it. Her next words just flew out of her mouth. "You seem awfully young, Capt. Mitchell," she said in a disapproving tone.

Baily laughed loudly. "I told you, Mark. Kelly is going to be the toughest one to win over."

Kelly gave Baily a hard, cold scowl that most others would have fainted from, but the old chief just laughed harder. After all the years he known Kelly, he had come to predict her reactions accurately, and anticipate her directness.

Mark's eyes had narrowed slightly, but in a voice that still maintained its friendly tone, he said directly to Kelly, "I guess I do seem young, Officer Douglas, but I'll let my record speak for itself."

An awkward silence was broken by the ever optimistic Baily. "Mark's only thirty-five, but he's done more in his years as a cop down in D.C., than most people have done in a lifetime."

"D.C.!" Kelly practically yelled at Baily. "You hired a city-slicker to replace you, Baily! You know you should have hired a Green Mountain Boy from Vermont."

Mark's body had grown rigid now, and his stance was definitely defensive. He still wore a partial smile plastered to his face, but one look into his stormy blue eyes gave Kelly an accurate indication of the anger mounting inside of him. "I grew up in Bennington, Vermont, Officer Douglas," Mark replied in a firm voice that commanded respect. "I still consider myself a 'Green Mountain Boy.'" He was sounding more like a police chief with every passing moment, and the feeling made Kelly increasingly uneasy.

Kelly looked at Mitchell in surprise. She knew she should apologize to him, but she just couldn't bring herself to do it. "I need to go," Kelly said turning her angry eyes back to Baily. "Gram is expecting me."

With that said, Kelly turned and headed out the door, without so much as even glancing in Mitchell's direction. Kelly had known Mitchell for all of ten minutes, and she already hated him. No one could ever replace Baily, Kelly thought angrily. Especially, she thought grumbling under her breath, not a thirty-five year old city-slicker.

Two

The very next morning, Baily introduced Mark Mitchell to the entire Sawyer's Crossing police department. Baily's pride in the new chief was evident, and everyone seemed genuinely pleased except for Kelly.

"Wipe that smile off your face, Rand," Kelly whispered angrily to her partner, "unless you want me clobbering you in the nose!"

Rand Thompson was a friendly, low-key type of guy, even though his imposing linebacker size implied otherwise. He smiled sadly at Kelly, realizing the transition would be harder on her than anyone else on the force. "Sorry, Kel...," he said in a compassionate voice, "I know this is rough on you."

"Yeah, well," Kelly said in a sarcastic tone, "everyone else seems to be welcoming 'Golden Boy' with open arms."

Just then, Mitchell turned around and looked directly at her. By the amused expression on his face, Kelly was quite sure that he had heard her comment. As Mitchell walked slowly toward her, he looked like a man trying hard to contain his laughter. "Douglas," he said in a firm voice, that was lightly laced with humor, "I'd like to see you in my office immediately."

Kelly should have been concerned, and slightly intimidated, but she wasn't. "Your office?" Kelly demanded in a questioning voice.

Mitchell turned around to face her with an expression that held just a trace of anger. "Yes, Officer Douglas," he said in a commanding tone. "My office. Now."

Kelly followed him, with her temper growing hotter each step of the way. This man is completely impossible, she thought as she bored raging eyes into his back. Even though he appeared friendly on the outside, she was sure he was a power-hungry, commanding jerk on the inside.

As Kelly followed Mitchell into Baily's old office, she stopped abruptly in her tracks. As she surveyed the once cherished room, it appeared as though it had been struck by a tornado. Boxes and boxes of Mitchell's things were piled everywhere, and not one single item of Baily's remained, including the plants. Kelly's eyes dropped to the worn area on the carpet that Amos was always curled up on, and she felt oddly strange inside not seeing the old dog there. How could things change so fast, Kelly thought shaking her head. Literally, overnight, her world had changed, and she knew this change would not be for the better.

Mitchell eyed Kelly understandingly as she continued to take in the changes. "Baily moved his things out last night," he said in a quiet voice. Kelly stared at Mitchell with such a surprised expression, that she couldn't even nod. The full impact of Baily's retirement was just slapping her in the face now. Reality can be so cruel, Kelly thought bitterly. As she continued to stare at the new chief, her eyes narrowed furiously. It was all Mitchell's fault, Kelly decided quickly. She felt as though Chief Mark Mitchell was invading a private place in her life. This old, dusty room was so special to her heart, that she felt as though Mitchell was intruding, by just being in here. As

Mitchell started to speak, Kelly threw her hands on her hips defiantly.

"Douglas," he said in a firm, but quiet tone, "I realize that this is going to be harder on you than most. But," he said in a voice that was growing steadily firmer, "I am your new boss, and I expect to be treated with respect. You don't have to like me," he said in a tone that was clearly indifferent, "but we need to get along well enough to work together professionally."

As Kelly studied the fair-haired model, it suddenly struck her that Mitchell didn't like her any more than she liked him. Everything was changing at this moment. Mitchell was clearly laying the cards on the table for her. He was her new boss. He was the man who could make her life miserable in Sawyer's Crossing. And, Kelly thought dismally, he was the man who could ultimately fire her.

Kelly immediately tried to mask her dislike of the man. "I'm sure we can work together professionally, Chief Mitchell." Kelly knew her voice sounding strained, and it only made her comment less convincing. Mitchell studied her through intense eyes, searching her face for the truth. Then, in a steady voice, he said honestly, "I certainly hope so, Officer Douglas."

Then, Kelly watched as Mitchell dropped down into Baily's old seat, behind Baily's old desk. The sight of him behind Baily's desk angered her all over again.

Kelly watched Mitchell in a rigid, determined way as he gazed at a paper in his hand. "I'm going to be meeting with all the staff one on one, to get to know them." Mitchell stated in a casual tone. "And," he said looking up from his paper and smiling charmingly at Kelly, "you get to be my first victim."

Kelly was fairly sure that he meant victim in a friendly way, but it still made her stiffen, and pull the walls in tighter around her.

"Tell me, Officer Douglas," Mitchell said in a curious voice, "why it is that someone who graduates first in their class in college, and first in their class at the Academy, would want to work in a small town like Sawyer's Crossing?"

OK, Kelly thought, narrowing her heated eyes at him, "victim" is a very accurate word. Her sinking opinion of Chief Mitchell just plummeted. "Why wouldn't I want to work in

Sawyer's Crossing?" Kelly said in a defiant tone, purposely answering his question with one of her own.

Mitchell paused, and studied her for a moment. The intense scrutiny of his gaze made Kelly want to look away, but she forced herself to meet his stare, and hold his eyes with all the courage she could find. After what seemed like an eternity, Mitchell spoke in a firm, but quiet voice, that held just an edge of hardness to it. "You're a tough case, Douglas. I just wanted to know what drew you to a small place like Sawyer? Most kids your age would be running off for the bright lights of the big city."

His statement only piqued Kelly's temper, and for a moment she lost her head. "You mean like you did!" she blurted out in a voice that dripped with resentment. Instantly, she covered her mouth with her hand. She couldn't believe that she had actually said that to his face, and judging from the hard expression on Mitchell's face, neither could he.

He's going to fire me before this interview is over, Kelly thought panicking. "I'm sorry, Sir," Kelly said quickly, in a nervous, almost desperate tone. "That was completely uncalled for. I was out of line."

Mitchell's jaw tightened, and he continued to dissect Kelly through heated, examining eyes of his own. She felt herself practically melting under his inspection.

Kelly continued hastily, "I wanted to work in Sawyer's Crossing, Sir, because this is my home. This is where I grew up. I love this place."

Her honest answer seemed to take some of the wind out of Mitchell's anger. "Do you still have family here?" he asked intently, not taking his investigating eyes off her for an instant.

Kelly turned her eyes away from his probing, penetrating stare. "A grandmother," Kelly replied, in a quiet voice.

"No parents or siblings?" he persisted.

Kelly tensed. There was no way that she was going to explain about her parents to Mitchell. That was too personal an issue, and, as far as she was concerned, completely none of his business. "No, Sir," Kelly replied evenly. "Gram and I are the only ones left in Sawyer." He nodded, but seemed surprised. "That must be difficult for you. I'm sure you must miss your family.

Kelly was completely taken off guard momentarily by Mitchell's sincere, compassionate voice. Something in his voice had hit a nerve deep down. As she looked in Mitchell's eyes, to identify the emotion, whatever she had heard was no longer there. Quickly, Kelly reverted back to her shell. "Yes, Sir," she replied in a masked voice, "I miss my family."

After a few more questions, Mitchell dismissed Kelly. There was something evasive about the young cop, and Mitchell couldn't decide if it was due to Baily's retirement, or something more. He made a note to keep an eye on Kelly Douglas, both professionally, and personally. There was something about the young officer that drew him to her, and yet, at the same time, something that almost haunted him. There was something deep in her eyes, but he couldn't put his finger on it yet. Time will tell, Mitchell finally concluded. And, reluctantly, he knew that time was the only thing on his side as far as Kelly Douglas was concerned.

Three

"I'm supposed to be driving!" Kelly said in an irritated voice to her friend and partner Rand Thompson.

The big man just laughed lightly. "Yeah, I know, Kelly...," he answered in an amused tone, "but with you behind the wheel as angry as you are, I feel like I'd be committing suicide!" Rand let out another laugh, as Kelly poked him in the side.

Kelly tried to act angry, but she couldn't. Rand's observation was correct. She was steamed. "You know," Kelly said defensively, "I was in a good mood until Mitchell laid his pep talk on us this morning."

Rand laughed loudly this time. "Why do you let Mitchell get under your skin, Kel? You need to take things more in stride. Beside...," Rand said looking over at her seriously, "he was right."

Kelly turned quickly in her seat and eyed her partner intently. "You really agree with him?" Kelly said in disgust.

Rand glanced at her and smiled. "Yes, Kel, I do. I think the speeding in Sawyer's Crossing has got to stop. This is a tourist town, and people speeding around it make it dangerous."

Rand paused, and then laughed loudly. "You know," he said in a teasing tone, "if Mitchell really wanted to control the speeding problem, all he'd have to do is take away one license." "Oh yeah, Wise Guy...," Kelly said in her best intimidating voice, "and just whose license are you talking about?"

"Yours!" Rand shot back seriously. "You drive that Celica of yours like it's a rocket." Kelly smiled, and smacked his arm playfully. "Really, Kel," he said looking at his partner with concern, "you need to slow down, and be careful. No one downtown is going to fix your speeding tickets for you anymore since Baily's retired. You're on your own now."

Kelly sighed heavily. "That is a major problem for me, Rand. I hate driving slow!"

"Yeah, well, practice, Kelly," Rand said in a voice that was void of any sympathy. "Mitchell already seems at odds enough with you. You don't need to go looking for trouble."

"Thanks for your concern, Rand," Kelly replied in a sarcastic tone.

Rand just laughed.

"You know," Kelly said in a kinder voice, "you're lucky that you're married to my best friend. If you weren't, I would have clobbered you a long time ago."

"I know!" Rand said laughing loudly. "Becca is my insurance policy!"

Kelly's day ended without so much as a single battle with Mitchell. As she climbed the front porch to Gram's house, she decided that her best plan against the "Golden Boy" would be to avoid him at all costs. Any time she had to talk to him, it only seemed to put her at further odds with the new chief.

Wearily, Kelly skipped the kitchen and headed straight to bed. It was late and she knew that Gram would be in bed already, but even so, as she always had done, she checked in on the old woman. Gram was the sunshine in her life. The old woman loved the Lord so much that it seemed to ripple into every area of her life. Kelly was glad that the old woman had God, but she did not share the same belief. At five years old, Kelly had given her heart to the Lord. At six, after her parents had died, she had taken it back. She still felt that if God was really so good, he would have never allowed her parents to be murdered.

The only reason she went to church on Sundays, was to please Gram. She loved Gram dearly and would never do anything to hurt the woman. If that meant suffering through church once a week, she would. It was a small price to pay for all that Gram had done for her.

That night, the dreams came back in full force. Kelly was six again, and hiding under the couch with her doll. For the millionth time, she watched in horror as the bad man shot her parents. It was all so real that Kelly found herself screaming at the top of her lungs hysterically.

The next thing that she knew was that Gram was at her side holding her and rocking her gently. "Kelly! Kelly!" The old woman said lovingly. "Wake up, Sweetheart. You're having a bad dream."

As Kelly opened her eyes and looked up in the direction of the comforting, reassuring voice, she instantly recognized her grandmother's face. Gram smiled warmly at her, and just continued talking to her frightened granddaughter tenderly. "Precious child, you are all right. You are safe, Kelly, and no one's going to hurt you."

As usual, Kelly buried her face against Gram's chest, and wept uncontrollably. "Oh, Gram," Kelly said in a painful voice, between her heart wrenching sobs, "when will it ever stop? When will the nightmares end?"

"Oh, sweet, sweet Kelly...," Gram said in a tearful voice, "you have suffered so much for someone so young. I wish I could stop them, honey. I wish I could take all your pain away."

They held each other for several more minutes, and then Gram returned to her room. Kelly sat up in bed wiping her damp face. "How long," she whispered fearfully to the darkness in her room, "how long will I have to live through that horrible day? Is it ever going to go away?"

As Gram lay in bed, quietly sobbing and praying, she begged her Heavenly Father for help. "Oh, dear Father, the girl has suffered so much...and these awful nightmares...almost every night for nineteen years...it's too much, dear Lord. It's too much for anyone to go through. Please make them stop, dear God. For Kelly's sake, make them stop. Please give Kelly her life back. She's so young, and she's such a tortured soul. Help her Father. Help her turn to You. I know You're the only one who can give the child back her life."

Four

The next morning arrived too early for Kelly, and she inadvertently slept through her alarm clock. The nightmares had ruined almost every night's sleep she had, and getting up proved to be almost unbearable.

After Gram had gently awakened her, she quickly showered and dressed in her dark navy uniform. One good thing about wearing a uniform, Kelly thought, smiling at her police uniform, was that she never had to worry about what outfit she would wear to work.

As Kelly jumped into her red Toyota Celica, she munched on a piece of toast that Gram had shoved into her hand as she ran out the door. As she drove her little sports car down Tim's Path, she was suddenly reminded of Rand's warning to slow down. Kelly glanced at the clock on her dashboard, and pressed the accelerator a little harder. "If I slow down, Rand," she said in a heated voice, "I'm going to be late for work!"

When Kelly rounded a corner, she instantly saw the black and white cruiser. It was partially hidden behind the pine trees, and its lights went on even before she had passed it. Angrily she jammed the accelerator harder. "Not today, Micky!" she said in a determined voice.

As Kelly glanced in her rearview mirror, Micky was still behind her, but at a distance. As Micky closed the gap between them, Kelly could clearly see two patrolmen in the cruiser. Her mouth dropped open, as her eyes did a quick double take. Her heart almost stopped beating as she noticed the tall, blonde officer next to Micky. It undoubtedly was her worst nightmare...Chief Mitchell.

"I'm dead!" Kelly said completely panicking. "I am so dead that it isn't even funny."

Kelly knew that Mitchell would have her badge for outrunning a cruiser, so immediately her mind went to plan B. "I need to outrun him and lose him," she said in a determined, hopeful voice.

Kelly jammed the accelerator harder, bringing her speed up to 60 in a 35 M.P.H. zone. She downshifted the Celica, and slowed only momentarily, as she skillfully maneuvered a sharp right turn through the industrial section of Sawyer. She weaved her way in and out of buildings, with her tires screeching loudly, and then finally down a long brick alley that led directly to the police station. With no cruiser in sight, Kelly literally ran into the station and flew down the stairs into the morning briefing room.

"Man, Kelly," Rand said in a concerned voice, "you're cutting it too close! You're lucky that Mitchell is late, or he'd have your hide!"

Kelly just smiled up at her partner, as she tried to make her body stop shaking. "What was I thinking!" she silently screamed at herself. "I know he's going to find out! I am so stupid!"

Just then, a very angry Chief Mitchell rapidly came down the stairs into the briefing room. He stared intimidatingly at the group of officers for a solid three minutes while he heatedly paced back and forth in front of them.

Finally, in a tight voice, that was barely controlled, he spoke, eyeing the officers suspiciously. "This morning I went on speed patrol with Micky Bencher. A red Toyota Celica passed us doing 50, in a 35 M.P.H. zone, on Tim's Path Road."

As he paused, Kelly began to intently study the toe of her black boot. Everyone knew that she had a red Toyota Celica, and the town was small enough so that everyone also knew that she lived on Tim's Path.

"As Micky and I pursued the Celica, to pull it over, the driver actually sped up, and proceeded to outrun us, and lose us in the industrial park. Then," Mitchell said, almost yelling now, "Micky and I pull into the station to find the same red Celica parked in my employee parking lot!"

Rand noticeably stiffened beside Kelly. "You're dead, Kel," he quietly whispered.

"Now, this rocket driver has two choices...," Mitchell said in an angry, and still very loud voice. "You can come forward now, and I won't pull your badge...or, I can go upstairs and run the plate numbers." He stared at the crew through angry, narrowed eyes, and then said in a low grumble, "If you choose option B, look for another job."

The tension was so thick in the room that Kelly didn't think that anyone was breathing. She knew that she wasn't. She had never been in so much trouble in her life, and she knew that Baily wouldn't touch this with a ten-foot pole. Kelly knew she had done a stupid thing. And now, she thought sighing heavily, she would have to face Mitchell all on her own.

"Last chance...," Mitchell said eyeing the group with fire in his eyes.

"Sir...," Kelly said in a quiet, trembling voice, "it was me."

A look of surprise, disbelief, and disgust spread across Mitchell's face in a matter of about three seconds. "In my office now, Douglas!" he barked in a threatening way.

As Kelly started for the stairs, she felt every eye in the room boring holes into her back. They knew she was dead, and she knew she was dead.

"Rand," Mitchell said in a firm voice, from behind Kelly, "take over the morning roll for me. "Then, lowering his voice slightly, he said to

Kelly's partner, "You'll be riding with Morton today."

Mitchell ran up the stairs, so that he was directly behind Kelly. He was so close to her that she could feel his hot, angry breath, breathing down the back of her neck. As they walked into Mitchell's office, he firmly shut the door behind them.

"Sit!" Mitchell barked out in a commanding tone. Kelly sat, but she was so afraid that she could scarcely breathe.

As Mitchell stood in front of her, with his hands firmly on his hips, he glared at Kelly with an expression that was nothing short of pure rage. Here he was, the police chief of Sawyer's Crossing, trying to enforce the speed limit in town, when one of his own officers takes the law, and defiantly throws it back in his face. His eyes narrowed, and he continued to watch her with an unforgiving gaze, which only made it harder for Kelly to appear calm and cool. Kelly felt as though she was attending her own funeral, execution style, of course. It was obvious that Mitchell was going to make hers a slow, painful death.

Finally, in a low, tight voice, he said to her, "I can't believe that you did that! I just can't believe it!"

As Kelly watched him start to pace again, with all the fear a small caged animal would have against a roaring lion, she agreed with him whole-heartedly for once. She just couldn't believe that she had done something so stupid.

"You should be thrown off the force for out-running a cruiser. Do you know that?" Each word had increased in volume, so that Mitchell was actually yelling at her at the top of his lungs. The effect was frightening.

Kelly mechanically nodded. She tried to force her eyes away from his, but she couldn't. Mark Mitchell was a man who just naturally commanded attention. And, right now, Kelly was giving him her full attention, completely against her will. She was totally petrified of him at this moment. He held all the cards, and she held none...and they both knew it.

She watched Mitchell's eyes dart down to her lap, and followed them. To her astonishment, her hands were shaking so badly, that they were actually doing little flip-flops in her lap. She tried to control them, but she couldn't. Kelly felt as if someone else were shaking her body. For a second, she wondered if she were having a nervous breakdown. She was definitely breaking down, and she couldn't be more nervous if she tried.

Mitchell's gaze immediately softened, and he said in a quieter voice, "I'll be right back." With that said, he quickly exited the door. Twenty minutes later, Mitchell returned, with Baily in tow. Mitchell's face seemed redder than ever, and Uncle Baily's face looked as though he had eaten something rotten. It was not a good sign.

Like a guilty child, Kelly dropped her eyes from Baily's hard gaze. She knew she had disappointed him, and the shame she felt at him being here, was almost more than she could take.

"Do you know...," Mitchell said in a heated voice, standing directly in front of Kelly, "that when I told Baily what had happened, and mentioned to him that if you were younger...I would be calling your parents right now...do you know what he told me?" Mitchell was so mad that he was stuttering now, and the intensity she saw in his boiling blue eyes made her want to run away and hide. "Do you have any idea what he told me?" He paused long enough to draw a deep breath. "He told me that I couldn't call your parents...and do you know why that is, Douglas?" He was actually leaning over Kelly now, and his face was so red that it looked as if it was going to explode. "Do you?" he persisted, with a confident expression on his angry face, clearly challenging her to defy the truth.

"My parents are both dead," Kelly said speaking to her shoes in a quiet voice.

"That's right!" he said slapping a hand against his leg. "And don't you think that you should have mentioned that to me, when I asked about your family—DOUGLAS!" He was shouting again, and Kelly was shaking again.

"Mark!" Baily said firmly, but quietly. "Kelly's Dad was a police officer for me, here in Sawyer." Mitchell's head snapped up, as though he had been given an electric shock. Baily slowly continued. "Jerry Douglas had just gotten off his shift and gone home, when someone broke into his house and shot him and his pregnant wife to death. Kelly was only six at the time. I found her hiding underneath her bed."

Mitchell's face had paled, and he grabbed the side of the desk for support. "I should have been briefed on this earlier," he said eyeing Baily intently.

Baily heard the wheezing even before Kelly noticed it. She was shaking so violently in her seat, that she didn't even recognize the dreaded sound. Quickly, it was growing louder and louder, and Kelly suddenly became aware of her shortness of breath. She felt as if she had cement in her lungs...she just couldn't get any air. A loud buzzing noise grew to a deafening sound in her ears, as her stomach threatened to empty its contents all over Mitchell's office. Kelly jumped out of her chair, fighting for breath. She tried to grab her inhaler out of her back pocket, but her knees gave out, and she started tumbling to the floor. The blackness danced before her eyes, and threatened to take her away.

Kelly was unaware of who caught her, or who forced her inhaler into her mouth, sending puff after puff of the life-saving medicine down her throat. Her lungs seemed to grab for the medicine greedily.

When Kelly came to, she was surprised to find that Mitchell was holding her in his arms, speaking softly to her, as he tenderly stroked her damp hair.

"Are you OK, Kelly?" he asked in a voice that was mixed with genuine concern and compassion.

Kelly could barely nod. This was the worst asthma attack that she'd had in along time, and she felt completely helpless to do anything but lay docile in Mitchell's arms.

"It's OK, Kelly," Mitchell said softly. "You just rest. Don't worry. I'll take care of you." As he continued talking gently to Kelly, and tenderly stroking her sweat-soaked hair, he never took his compassionate blue eyes off her.

Kelly closed her eyes for a minute. Every time that she had a severe attack, she wondered if it would be the end for her. Even though her asthma was technically under control, she felt as though she had a time bomb inside her, waiting to go off.

As Kelly grew stronger, Mitchell helped her to a chair. "How are you doing?" he asked in a concerned voice, kneeling down in front of her so he could look directly into her eyes.

As she nodded OK, her eyes started to spill over with tears. She turned her face away from Mitchell, but not before he noticed her tears. Still kneeling before her, he took her hands and squeezed them tightly.

"You're OK, Kelly. You're OK." His voice was confidant and comforting, and just what Kelly needed to hear.

She nodded again, as she looked into Mitchell's deep blue eyes. His face radiated care and concern, and Kelly felt deeply moved. A tenderness passed between them that was a new emotion for Kelly. She quickly sought to identify it, but closed her eyes feeling instantly overwhelmed by the deep feeling she saw in Mitchell's eyes.

"Kelly," Mitchell said quietly using her first name as though he did it all the time, "I'm going to bring you home. Do you think that you are strong enough to walk?"

Kelly nodded, and slowly got up. As she tried to walk, her shaking returned. She went to grab a chair for support, but got Mitchell's arm instead. As she started to apologize, she noticed that Mitchell was locking an arm firmly around her slender waist.

"Kelly," he said in a quiet, but determined tone, "I'm going to help you to the car. I don't want you collapsing on me."

"Thank you," Kelly said in a shaky, but appreciative voice.

Mitchell helped Kelly out an exit near his office, and slowly but steadily guided her to his squad car.

"I need to drive home," Kelly said stopping in mid step. "I can't leave my car here."

Mitchell leaned Kelly up against the side of his car. He cast her a totally charming smile, and then said in an amused tone, "Kelly, I'm thinking about having that rocket of yours impounded for good!"

Kelly looked at him in shock, and then Mitchell let out a loud, teasing laugh. "I'm only kidding. You'll get your car back later today. I'll have one of the crew drop it off."

As Mitchell helped her weak body into the car, she took his hand, and said softly, "Thank you. Thank you for helping me."

Mitchell squeezed her hand tenderly, holding it longer than necessary. Then, in a thick, emotional voice, he said softly, "You're welcome, Kelly."

Kelly felt her heart melting toward this man. He was unlike any other man she'd ever met. When she deserved his anger, she got it. Yet, when she needed his help and kindness, she got that, too, in an unbelievably tender way.

They drove in silence until they began to pass the industrial park. "Say, Kelly," Mitchell said laughing quietly, "when you're feeling better, I want you to show me the route that you took through the industrial park to ditch Micky and me. That was quite something!"

"You mean I still have a job?" Kelly asked in a surprised voice.

Mitchell laughed loudly this time. "Oh, you still have a job, Speedy, but you're just going to have a new partner for a week."

"A new partner?" Kelly asked, looking at her boss, and feeling completely confused. "Who?" Kelly was quickly starting to feel off-balance and out-of-control again.

"I'm going to team you up with the one person on the force that I know can keep you in line," Mitchell said in a serious, matter-of-fact voice.

Kelly couldn't imagine who in the world he was referring to. "Who?" she asked again, looking cautiously at her boss.

Mitchell smiled at her with such a charming smile that Kelly felt almost paralyzed. As she continued to look at her boss, she felt her insides turning to mush. "The only person on the force that I'm confident can keep you in line, Officer Douglas, is…me!" As soon as he pulled into her driveway, he jumped out of his seat and ran around the car to open her door and help her out. As he took Kelly's hand, to help her up, he shook it firmly, saying, "Kelly Douglas, I'm Mark Mitchell, and I'll be your new partner for the next week."

Kelly's face clearly revealed the astonished feeling that she could not seem to hide. "You?" she squeaked out.

Mitchell simply nodded and gave her another charming smile. Kelly was sure that this man had no idea how his enchanting smile affected her. As Mitchell helped her up the stairs to the house, he took her keys from her hand, and opened the door for her.

He immediately escorted her over to the couch. "Lie down here," he said sounding like her commander-in-chief again. Kelly had quickly learned that when Mitchell used that determined tone, his request was not to be taken lightly.

Kelly watched, with a surprised expression covering her face, as Mitchell took an afghan off the back of the couch and gently covered her with it. She felt overwhelmed at his kindness, and fought hard to hold her tears inside.

Mitchell knelt down near her head and said in a kind voice, "Rest, Kelly. Your new partner will pick you up at 6:30 a.m." Then he squeezed her hand gently, and left.

Kelly tried to fight the sleep that began to overtake her. "New partner..."she thought, her brain already fogging up, "pick me up tomorrow..." Kelly's eyes suddenly bolted open as the reality of that statement hit her. "Mark Mitchell is my new partner! Mitchell is picking me up tomorrow! Oh, no...," Kelly said in a dreaded tone, as though she were walking to the gallows. "I think I would have been safer handing my badge over to him."

Five

Kelly was nervously waiting for Chief Mitchell as he pulled into her driveway at 6:30. As she approached the car, he jumped out of the driver's seat, and tossed her the keys. "You're driving," he said in a casual tone.

"You sure?" Kelly asked looking at him apprehensively.

"Absolutely," he said smiling that charming, brilliant smile of his. "I insist."

As Kelly climbed into the driver's seat, Mitchell said in a stern tone, "Slow down!"

Kelly turned, and looked at him with a questioning expression. "What?" she asked looking at her boss intently.

Mitchell laughed loudly. "Oh, I'm sorry, Kelly. I'm just practicing!"

Kelly groaned loudly, and narrowed her eyes at him. "Why do I get the feeling that this is going to be a sweet payback for you?"

Mitchell's loud laughter filled the car again. "Not at all, Kelly. But," he said looking at her firmly, "if I need to give you a few driving tips along the way...I won't hesitate to do so."

"I'm sure you won't!" Kelly said sarcastically.

Kelly was a morning person, and her bubbly spirit always brought out the mischievous side in her. As a huge smile danced across her face, Mitchell curiously inquired as to what she was thinking. "Oh," Kelly said in a impish voice, "I was just thinking about how much fun it would be to blow Micky Bencher out of the water again. Are you game, Chief?" Kelly asked wiggling her eyebrows at him.

"No!" Mitchell replied quickly, and in a strict enough voice so that Kelly knew for sure that he wasn't. "I'm sure you were only teasing anyway," he added, in a less rigid voice. When Kelly didn't answer right away, he asked in a commanding tone, "You were teasing, weren't you, Douglas?"

Kelly burst out laughing. "Of course, Chief Mitchell. Of course."

Mitchell visibly relaxed. After a moment, he said to her in a friendly voice, "Kelly, when we are partners, I want you to call me Mark."

Kelly nodded, not revealing the surprise that she felt. "OK. And, by the way, Mark," she said smiling at him widely, "you will soon learn that I love to have fun, and tease my partners. I hope that's all right with you."

Mark smiled and nodded. "That's fine with me, Kelly," he said grinning from ear to ear. "But, just remember," he said waving a finger at her, "you're not the only one who likes to tease." He paused, looked at her speedometer, and then said firmly, "Slow down."

Kelly immediately protested. "I'm only going thirty!"

"Yeah, but the speed limit here is twenty-five," Mark said quickly, maintaining the stern tone in his voice.

"Yeah," Kelly said smiling at him casually, "but since I usually do fifty through here...thirty is a big improvement!"

"Kelly!" Mark said evenly, but with an unmistakable twinkle in his eye, "make things easy on yourself today, and just drive the limit."

Kelly instantly slowed the car down to ten miles per hour. Mark turned his blonde head, and stared at her curiously. "Oh...is this too slow for you...,Mark?" she asked in a teasing, almost obnoxious voice.

"You certainly are a wise guy, Kelly," Mark said shaking his head, and laughing lightly. "If you want to drive around at ten miles per hour all day, that's fine with me, Kelly. I bet I can tolerate it better than you!"

Kelly laughed. "That's true. You're used to driving slow!"

Kelly beeped her horn and waved at Micky Bencher, as she passed him and his squad car that was nicely hidden behind a large pine tree. The surprised expression on Micky's face brought a roar of laughter from both Kelly and Mark.

"Well," Mark said still laughing, "I can tell that today is going to be anything but boring!" Then he paused and glanced at the speedometer again. "Slow down," he said adamantly.

Kelly sighed loudly. "You know," she said in an irritated voice, "I don't know which I'm going to hate more...driving around all day at a snail's pace, or you constantly telling me to drive at a snail's pace."

"Let me know when you decide!" Mark said eyeing her with amusement.

"You are infuriating, Mark Mitchell! Do you know that?" Kelly said in an exasperated tone.

"Thank you, Kelly," he said smiling at her confidently. "It's actually one of my better qualities...I'm glad you noticed it!"

"Don't you have work in the office to do, Chief?" Kelly asked in a voice that held a note of hopefulness.

Mark laughed hard. "You're already sick of me, huh, Kelly."

"No," Kelly said shaking her blonde head slowly, "I'm not sick of you personally, I'm just sick of you telling me to slow down."

Mark laughed again, clearly amused by their banter. "Well, if you drove the posted limit, I wouldn't have to annoy you by telling you to slow down." He paused, and then laughed loudly again. He was enjoying being Kelly's partner more then he thought he would. She was spunky and fun, and knew how to tease and be teased.

"And," he said looking at her impishly, "to answer your question about my office...Baily has agreed to cover for me for the week, or as long as it takes."

"As long as what takes...," Kelly asked in a wary, careful voice. She didn't like where this was going.

Mark simply smiled at her, as his blue eyes danced with delight. After a moment he said, "As long as it takes to break you from speeding. Who knows, I may be riding with you for months!"

"You wouldn't!" Kelly said in a voice that held both alarm and shock.

"Yes. I would." He paused, and then continued in a quiet, but serious tone. "Officer Douglas, I'm an extremely determined country boy. And, if it takes months to break my best cop on the force of her speeding habit...then I'll hang in there for months."

Kelly groaned loudly. "Oh, boy...," she said eyeing Mitchell warily, "I think you might actually mean that."

"I do," he said quickly, in a serious tone.

"I was afraid you did." Kelly sighed deeply. "Let's change the subject, OK?"

"OK, but first slow down," Mark said firmly.

"OH!" Kelly said in a frustrated voice. "This is going to make me nuts!" She turned quickly, and eyed Mitchell hopefully. "You want to drive now?"

"No way!" he said laughing loudly. "Your driver's training course has just begun."

Kelly grumbled at him under her breath, and Mitchell smiled confidently at her, with laughter clearly reflecting out of his blue eyes. He seemed to be enjoying this far too much.

"OK, Kelly, let's change the subject. Tell me which of Sawyer's Crossing's twelve covered bridges is your favorite? In the short time that I've been in this town, I've come to see that most people have a favorite."

"That's true!" Kelly said smiling at Mark genuinely. "Everyone does have a favorite. Mine is Stonewall." Then she looked at him curiously. "Do you have a favorite yet?"

"I haven't seen them all," Mark replied casually.

"Well," Kelly said enthusiastically, "I guarantee that if you're partnered up with me long enough, you will. I always make it a point to take my lunch break at a different covered bridge each day. That way, I get to visit each of them often."

"You make them sound like old friends," Mark said in a thoughtful voice.

"If you hang around Sawyer long enough, Mark, they do become like old friends. There's something very special about these old covered bridges."

After stopping at the station for roll call, Kelly and Mark headed to the downtown area of Sawyer's Crossing to begin their beat. The downtown area was quaint, and filled with all kinds of unique shops. There was everything from antique shops to clothing stores, from old general stores to every kind of restaurant that could temp you off the strictest diet. Kelly loved the downtown beat, and made a point of visiting all the shop-keepers.

As she pulled into a parking lot in front of Uncle Bill's Homemade Ice Cream Shop, she turned to Mark. "Rand and I usually walk this part of the beat. We like the personal contact with the people."

"Sounds great!" Mark said getting out of the car. "Let's go meet some people!"

As they headed for the small cafe called Country Kitchen, Kelly turned to Mark, and in a causal voice said, "I always start here with a strong cup of Mabel's coffee. Want some?"

"Sure, Kelly. That sounds great," Mark said nodding and smiling at her. "By the way, would you mind introducing me to the people you know along the way. I want to get to know as many of the town's folk personally as I can."

"I'd love to," Kelly said in a friendly voice. "This is a great town, Mark, and the people are really special."

As they started to enter the Country Kitchen, Mabel spotted Kelly, and waved to her. "Hey, Sweetie, you want the regular?" Kelly nodded. "And does your cute friend want anything?" the older woman said as she smiled casually at Mark.

Kelly watched Mark blush, and couldn't help but smile at him. "I don't know, Mabel," Kelly answered in an amused voice. "Why don't you ask Chief Mitchell if he wants anything?"

Mabel's mouth swung open in surprise. "You're the new Chief?" she asked in an awed voice. Mabel seemed immediately embarrassed at her earlier comment about Mark's looks.

"Yes, Ma'am," Mark said smiling at her genuinely.

"Well, I'm Mabel Myers, and it's a pleasure to meet you," she said extending her small hand toward Mark's.

"Same here," Mark said kindly.

As Mabel passed by Kelly, she said in a quiet voice, "Well, I still think he's awfully cute."

Kelly laughed, and when Mabel had gone to fix the coffee, Mark asked her in a curious voice what was so funny. "It will make you blush again," Kelly said in a teasing voice. Mark's eyebrows just arched upward.

"She thinks you're cute!" Kelly said smiling at Mark mischievously.

Mark rolled his eyes, and blushed again. "What's on the outside isn't important. People should be more concerned about what someone's heart is like."

"That's true," Kelly said seriously.

As they took their coffee, they slowly started patrolling Main Street.

"You're going to see a lot of people here today, being Saturday and all," Kelly said eyeing the crowds in front of them.

"I'm counting on it, Kelly," Mark said in a friendly, but serious tone. "I want to be known as a chief who is in touch with the town's people."

"You know," Kelly said thoughtfully, "I think that you will, Mark."

"Was that a compliment from Kelly Douglas?" Mark said throwing his arms out wide, pretending to be floored.

Kelly laughed at his dramatics. "It was an observation, and a compliment." She paused and took a sip of her coffee. "I was too hard on you before, Mark. I apologize. I think you're going to fit in well around Sawyer." Kelly's opinion of Mark changed dramatically after he had helped her through her asthma attack. For the first time since they had met, she'd gotten a clear glimpse of his heart...and she could no longer deny that Mark Mitchell was a very nice man.

"Thank you, Kelly," Mark said in a sincere voice. "Coming from you, that means a lot. I was hoping that we'd be able to be friends."

Kelly smiled at Mark. "Well, I just think we might, Mark Mitchell. I'd suspect that you'd be a good friend to have."

"I don't mean just professionally, Kelly," Mark said in a serious, but quiet tone. "I don't want you to just think of me as a 'Get out of Jail Free Card.'" Mark said eyeing her carefully. "I won't eat your speeding tickets like Baily did."

Kelly laughed loudly, almost spilling her coffee. "I think I already know that, Mark. Here you are babysitting me for the week because you wouldn't eat my speeding ticket." Kelly paused thoughtfully for a moment, and then slowly continued, "I didn't mean you'd be a good friend to get me out of trouble...I meant you'd be a good friend because you seem to be the type of person who knows how to be a good friend. Friendship is a two-way street, and sometimes people forget that."

"I know," Mark said nodding his head. "But, I do know how to be a good friend, and I value my friends."

"And that, Chief Mark Mitchell," Kelly said touching his arm lightly, "is exactly what I meant!"

They talked casually as they continued to stroll along the tree-lined Main Street. As promised, Kelly introduced Mark to everyone in sight. Then, Kelly spotted him. He was leaning up against the door of The Cookie Jar, munching a chocolate cookie.

Touching Mark's arm again, she said excitedly, "Mark, now you get to meet one of my favorite Sawyer's Crossing citizens!"

"A.J.!" Kelly yelled excitedly. "Mark, hold my coffee, will you?" Kelly asked, quickly shoving her cup into Mark's hands, just before A.J. flew into her arms, cookie and all.

"Hi, Kelly!" the little blonde-haired boy said excitedly. His blue eyes were gleaming up at her with adoration.

"Hey, A.J., it's great to see you!" Kelly said sincerely, hugging the boy tightly.

As the boy slowly pulled away, Kelly said, in an enthusiastic voice, "I'd like to introduce you to a new friend of mine."

A.J. looked over at Mark, as though he had just noticed that he was there. "Where's Rand?" A.J. said eyeing Mark suspiciously.

"Rand is still around, A.J., but this week I get a special treat." Kelly looked over at Mark, and winked quickly. "This is Chief Mitchell, and he's going to be my partner all week. Isn't that neat?"

"He's the one taking Baily's place?" A.J. asked studying Mark intently.

"Yes, A.J., and you're going to like him very much," Kelly said smiling down at her little buddy.

"Do you like him?" the boy asked her directly.

Kelly smiled, and winked at Mark again. "Yes, A.J., I really do. Chief Mitchell is a good person."

The little boy looked up at Mark, and then quickly back to Kelly. "It's nice to meet you, A.J.!" Mark said in a friendly voice, extending his hand toward the skeptical looking boy.

"Nice to meet you, too, Chief," A.J. said quietly.

"What's wrong?" Kelly asked the boy quietly.

"Is he your boyfriend?" A.J. asked pointedly.

Kelly turned to Mark, and smiled. "A.J., Chief Mitchell is my friend. I've already told you that I don't have a boyfriend."

"I want to be your boyfriend," A.J. said in a grumbling voice.

"A.J.….we've been through this before…," Kelly said shaking her head slowly.

"I know," he said in a disappointed tone. "But isn't Kelly pretty?" the little boy said to Mark, with his eyes glowing.

Mark smiled sweetly at the boy. "She sure is, Son." Then Mark playfully winked at A.J., and the boy rewarded him with a big smile.

As Kelly and Mark continued walking, Kelly filled Mark in on A.J..

"A.J. and I go way back. He was born Archibald Jeddiah, and I quickly nicknamed him A.J. It was hard enough for him to try to fit in with the kids around here having Down's Syndrome…but, having all the kids call him Archibald on top of it…" Kelly sadly shook her head. "He didn't stand a chance."

Mark nodded his head understandingly. "I can see your point, Kel." Mark paused, and then said in a sincere voice, "That kid adores you."

"The feeling is mutual," Kelly said as she quietly nodded her head. "He knows I have a soft spot for him…I always have, and I always will."

Mark smiled tenderly at her. "Do the kids around here accept A.J. pretty well?" Mark asked curiously.

Kelly laughed loudly. "They have no choice! They know that if A.J. complains to me, I'll be after them!" They both laughed. "But, I have to say that because I have become good buddies with A.J., the kids seem to treat him better."

"But you're worried about him?" Mark asked quickly, with his sensitive blue eyes searching her face.

Kelly nodded slowly, trying not to think about his eyes. They unnerved her at times, and made her completely lose her train of thought. "You know," she said forcing herself to look away from his face, "I do worry about him. A.J. has close to no common sense. He's not afraid of anything." Kelly paused and took a sip of her coffee. "Take the river, for instance...A.J. loves to watch the rapids. He sits on the edge of Slater's Bridge, practically hanging over it. One of these days he's going to fall in." Mark's expression darkened, and his face took on the authoritative tone of Chief Mitchell again. "I just hope he doesn't drown before someone pulls him out," Kelly stated in a voice that clearly showed her frustration.

They walked quietly for several minutes, until they came to Grandma's Attic. "Oh, Mark, you've got to come in and meet Gram," Kelly said excitedly.

Gram spotted them as soon as they came in. "Oh, you're the new Chief that Baily has been raving about," Gram said enthusiastically, while extending her hand.

"Thank you, Ma'am. I'm Mark Mitchell." Mark's down-to-earth, honest personality shown bright. Kelly knew by the admiring way her Grandmother looked at Mark, that he had already won her over, without even trying. He was just too easy to like, Kelly thought narrowing her eyes slightly.

Gram's face grew serious as she shook his hand. "I want to thank you for helping Kelly the other day...you know," she waved a hand nervously in the air, "...her asthma."

Mark's face was instantly bathed in compassion. His blue eyes warmed considerably and there was no mistaking the concern or tenderness that Kelly saw in his eyes. She immediately looked away from him, feeling nervous and slightly off balance.

"I'm glad that I was there, Mrs. Wheeler," Mark said in a serious, yet caring voice. "She had quite a serious attack."

"Well, Gram, we have to move on," Kelly said in a light tone, as she rolled her eyes at her Grandmother.

"Kelly hates to talk about her asthma," Gram said in a matter-of-fact voice to Mark.

"Gram!" Kelly said insistently.

"Sorry, Dear," Gram said in an insincere tone, obviously not meaning it. Kelly rolled her eyes and shook her head slightly. Gram was clearly not finished yet, and Kelly nervously watched her, wondering just what she was going to say or do next.

"Mark," Gram said eyeing the good-looking officer warmly, "I'd love to have you come for dinner sometime."

"I would like that," Mark said smiling at the old woman.

"How about next Saturday evening?" Gram persisted.

"I think that should work out fine, Mrs. Wheeler," Mark said in a friendly tone.

As Kelly and Mark took to the sidewalk again, Kelly felt compelled to warn Mark. In a serious tone, she said, "Watch out for Gram, Mark. She is a persistent matchmaker. She has quite a reputation."

Mark laughed loudly. "Is she trying to match us together?" he asked. Kelly's face reddened, and Mark saw it.

"Well," he said in a playful tone, "it's nice to know that I'm not the only one who blushes around here!" Mark laughed again, and Kelly glanced up just long enough to get a glimpse of a very attractive, lopsided smile. She shook her head slightly, willing her normal, level-headedness to immediately return. These feelings of, well, oh, whatever it was that was making her feel tender toward the chief had to stop. He was her boss, after all.

Kelly took a deep breath, and then laughed nervously. "Just watch out for Gram. She appears innocent, but she is really very dangerous."

Mark laughed again, and then said in an amused voice, "Thanks for the warning,

Partner, but I think that I can handle myself around your sweet, little old Grandmother."

Mark took a sip of his coffee, and then said in a tone that sounded entirely too casual, "So...are you seeing anyone?"

"Huh?" Kelly mumbled, choking on some coffee that she'd just swallowed.

"You know," Mark persisted in an easygoing tone, "do you have a boyfriend?"

"No," Kelly said quickly. She didn't like the direction this conversation was going.

"I'm surprised," Mark said in a pondering voice. "I thought that you would have."

"And just what is that supposed to mean?" Kelly asked a bit defensively, studying Mark intently through narrowed eyes.

Mark look over at her, and laughed. "Well, you're a nice girl, and gorgeous as could be...I just thought you'd be spoken for." Mark made his comment in a light, teasing way, but there was an unmistakable serious note to it. The underlying currents of this conversation were almost electrifying.

Kelly looked at Mark for a moment before answering. As she chewed on her lip nervously, she couldn't help but wonder why Mark brought this topic up, and, even more so, where exactly he was going with it. "I have had some serious relationships in the past," Kelly said, carefully weighing her words out, "but my schedule always proved too hectic to give any relationship a fair chance."

"So, you're saying that you're somewhat of a challenge," Mark said arching his eyebrows upward.

"I guess," Kelly said in a quiet, serious voice. She didn't want to be having this conversation with Mark. He was, after all, her boss. She sighed heavily, and then went on. "I was always working. I worked to save money for college...and then worked my way through college...and then the police academy, and well, that brings you up to date pretty much."

"All work and no play," Mark said teasingly, as he flashed her a wide, white, toothy smile.

Kelly laughed. "I know. I've heard that from more then one guy before."

"I'll bet," Mark said agreeing quickly, sounding more serious than Kelly thought he should.

"You know," Kelly said in a thoughtful voice, "I guess I just never met anyone that intrigued me enough to make time for."

"Never met 'Mr. Right,' huh?" Mark said, as his blue eyes twinkled merrily down at her. He looked directly into Kelly's eyes, and held the gaze for a moment.

Kelly turned away first, feeling her palms break into a nervous sweat. "If I didn't know any better," she thought tensely, as she studied a store front across the street, "I'd think that Mark Mitchell wants an application to my Mr. Right Fan Club."

"No," Kelly said laughing nervously, "I guess I've never met Mr. Right. Enough about me, Chief...," Kelly said raising an eyebrow at her boss, "What about you?" It was time for Kelly to do a little "investigating" of her own.

Mark laughed nervously, and then said in a quiet voice, "I was seeing someone back in D.C."

"It didn't work out?" Kelly asked, trying hard not to sound too anxious.

Mark shook his head slowly. "No, after two years, I finally figured out that I wasn't in love with her."

"It took you two years to figure that out?" Kelly asked in an exasperated voice.

Mark laughed at her expression. "Like you, I didn't have a lot of time to commit to a social life. We didn't see each other more than a few times a month."

"I can see how it could be difficult to get to know someone under those circumstances," Kelly said in an understanding voice.

Mark nodded seriously. "The next time I start to date, I plan on giving the relationship priority," Mark said quietly, but firmly.

"That's the only way," Kelly said agreeing quickly. She wanted this conversation to stop now, but she wasn't sure quite how to do that without giving away half the things she was thinking.

"So, are there any eligible ladies you can suggest to me?" Mark said in a joking way, that really wasn't a joke at all.

Kelly laughed nervously. She could not believe this conversation had gotten this far.

He's your boss, she kept warning herself. Watch your step. "I'm not into matchmaking, Mark. That's Gram's department all the way. Talk to her Saturday night, and she'll have you married by Sunday afternoon."

Around noon, Kelly led Mark to the Main Street Deli. They both got grinders and sodas to go, and then Kelly headed toward Stonewall Bridge. As they rounded the corner, the long red and white covered bridge came into sight.

"She sure is a beauty," Mark said admiring the old bridge.

After a quick tour through the bridge, Kelly parked the cruiser, and led Mark down a well-worn dirt path that went directly under the bridge. They sat on the bank, under the bridge, and watched the rapids while they ate lunch.

"So, this is your hiding spot," Mark said smiling teasingly at Kelly.

"One of them," Kelly playfully admitted. "If you're nice, maybe I'll show you the others sometime." They both laughed.

Mark smiled as he noticed the rope hanging under the center of the bridge. "That looks like fun!" he said eyeing the rope excitedly.

"It is!" Kelly said laughing. "It gives a good ride to the center pillar of the bridge."

Mark's eyebrows shot up. "So you've ridden it?"

"Many times!" Kelly said laughing at his surprised expression. "Like I told you before, I'm a pure and simple country girl." Kelly paused, and then said quickly, "You should try it."

"The rope?" Mark asked in a confused voice.

"Yes," Kelly said laughing. "The rope! Unless," she added, in her most challenging voice, "you've been in the city so long you've forgotten how much fun a rope ride is."

"Is that a challenge, Miss Douglas?" Mark asked, narrowing his blue eyes intently at her.

"Yes, Mr. City Slicker,...it is!"

To Kelly's amazement, Mark grabbed the rope. As he swung out to the center pillar, he let out a loud Tarzan yell. The boy in Mark had returned, and he looked like he was having the time of his life.

"I used to do this all the time!" He shouted back to Kelly.

As he swung the rope back to her, Mark said in a challenging voice, "Now it's your turn."

Kelly grabbed the rope, and just smiled at him. "You know, Chief Mark Mitchell...," Kelly said in a mischievous tone, "I've got you exactly where I want you! You're stranded, Boss!" Kelly let out a loud laugh as she watched Mark's face fall.

"You tricked me!" he stated accusingly.

Kelly just laughed harder. "Should I find myself a good lawyer, Mitchell?" Kelly said in a playful tone.

Mark laughed. "Kelly, if you don't swing that rope back here, you're going to need a good undertaker!" Mark said, trying to keep his voice serious.

"Oooh!" Kelly said obnoxiously. "You have such big words for a man who is stranded, Mitchell!" Kelly almost fell over from laughter.

"You can laugh all you want, Darlin'," Mark said putting his hands authoritatively on his hips, "but I promise you that I can cross this river before you can make it up the bank and back to the squad car."

"I'll bet you can," Kelly said smiling to the man stuck out in the center of the river. He had said he was a determined country boy, and

Kelly had to agree with him. His piercing eyes refused to back down just because she held the rope. His entire face appeared cemented in a confident, determined way. Kelly laughed again as she swung the rope back to him, admiring her fearless leader.

Mark quickly swung the rope back in Kelly's direction. "You have to come out here," he said invitingly.

Kelly held the rope in her hands, and pondered his invitation. "Only if you promise not to push me in!"

Mark laughed loudly. "Kel, I don't make promises that I know I can't keep!" They both laughed loudly.

"That's exactly what I thought," Kelly said still full of laughter. "Take your rope, because I'm staying here!"

She swung the rope over to him, only to have him swing it back. "Come on, Kelly. I promise I'll be a gentleman."

Kelly took the rope and swung. To her surprise, Mark caught her by the waist, and helped her land. "Thanks," Kelly said suddenly feeling nervous at how close she was to Mark.

"I didn't want you to fall in," he said looking at her tenderly. Once again, Kelly felt an emotion pass between them. Mark was having an unnerving effect on her heart. She quickly turned her gaze away from his intense, yet tender blue eyes. His interest in her was undeniable. Kelly could see it clearly in his eyes. There was a special tenderness there...

"Be careful...," she warned herself sternly, "he's your boss, and he's ten years older. There's no way that tender-hearted, gorgeous man could really be interested in you."

As she glanced back at Mark, she saw he was watching the rapids. "It's so good to be back in the country. I never enjoyed city life. Every day I was there, I was terribly homesick for the Vermont countryside."

"I can understand," Kelly said quickly. "I love Sawyer's Crossing."

"I already do, too." Mark said smiling at her with genuine warmth.

Kelly felt her heart flutter at his smile–and loud warning bells go off in her head. She quickly turned away, and tightened her grip on the rope. "We should get back," Kelly said looking over at the bank of the river.

"That's true," Mark said in a quiet, regretful voice.

As Kelly swung across the river, she knew she was in deep trouble. She had only spent one day with the charming Mark Mitchell, and she was already losing her heart to him. "How am I ever going to make it through the week!" Kelly thought hopelessly. "It's going to be awkward for us, if he sees my true feelings."

Kelly instantly vowed to herself to get a grip on her heart. She knew it wouldn't be easy, but she also knew that with Mark Mitchell, her boss, the new Chief of Sawyer's Crossing...she had to. Mark Mitchell was nothing less than a Prince Charming, and she knew if she didn't keep her heart in check, she'd make an utter fool of herself over him, and that would be completely humiliating!

"You're a professional!" she scolded herself silently. "Deal with this in a professional manner!" Kelly sighed deeply. She already knew the answer to that. She couldn't deal with this in a professional way because she wasn't a professional in matters of the heart.

"And," she thought shaking her head in a defeated way, "how on earth am I supposed to ignore those captivating, penetrating, tender blue eyes. Eyes," she thought, sighing again, "that seem to miss absolutely nothing." Kelly knew she had hit the nail on the head. The problem was his eyes. It was definitely impossible to ignore the look she saw in his eyes, because, she knew, especially in Mitchell's case, his eyes were only reflecting the feeling that he felt down deep in his heart.

Six

As Kelly helped Gram get dinner ready for Mark on Saturday evening, she reflected on her week with her new boss. Kelly was surprised at how easily and well they worked together. In a short time, they had come to know each other well enough to read each other with remarkable effectiveness. Mark was a very open and direct person, and Kelly knew that was the reason she felt that she had known him much longer.

Kelly had not been surprised at how drawn people were to the new Chief. They responded to his simple, honest country charm as though they were under a spell. More times then she wanted to admit, Kelly could even feel herself drawn to his charming ways. He was fun to be with, and genuine and open. For the hundredth time, she asked herself what she was going to do about Chief Mark Mitchell. And, she thought wearily, Gram inviting him to dinner tonight didn't help either.

A moment later, the doorbell rang and Gram took off excitedly to answer it. "Oh, my," Gram said in a surprised, but pleased voice, "these are simply beautiful. Oh, do come in, Mark. I need to get these in water."

As Gram entered the kitchen, Kelly smiled at the bright bouquet of summer flowers that she held in her hands. Gram glowed like an excited lightening bug at her unexpected gift.

"That was very thoughtful of you," Kelly said to Mark, as he made his way across the kitchen toward her. "You really made Gram's day."

"I'm glad," he said smiling at her warmly. "And now, this is for you." He handed Kelly a single long-stemmed, yellow rose. "After the week that we've spent together, I assume it's safe for me to call us friends. And," he said, smiling that charming smile at her, "since yellow is for friendship, I wanted you to have this."

As Kelly looked down at the rose, she felt speechless. Finally, after a moment, she managed to pull it together enough to mumble out, "Thank you, Mark. It's lovely."

"Well," he said, gently putting a hand on her shoulder, "you were a real sport this week. Not everyone would have put up with me so nicely."

"You're not that hard to put up with," Kelly said softly.

"I'm glad that you think so," Mark said smiling at her confidently, because I was hoping that I could talk you into a walk after dinner."

Kelly nodded slowly. "That sounds like fun."

Kelly couldn't keep her eyes off Mark during dinner. His stories were captivating and humorous, and he had her and Gram in stitches most of the meal. Kelly wished so much that she didn't find Chief Mitchell so appealing. She was certain that she was only in for heartache later on, but her heart refused to listen to her logic.

Kelly's mind inadvertently drifted back to the rose. Why had Mark given her the rose. He certainly didn't have to. Could he possible feel something for her? She seriously doubted it. Angrily she wondered how many young rookies had fallen for this good-looking, sweet talking

Chief. He probably had left a long road of tears behind him.

After dinner, Mark suggested that they all go for a ride out to Jimmy's Way. It was the only covered bridge that he hadn't seen yet. Gram skillfully declined his offer, leaving Kelly and Mark to go alone.

Jimmy's Way covered bridge was located twenty minutes out of town. It crossed the Vermont River, spanning the full half-mile. It was such a long bridge that Kelly always thought that it looked like four covered bridges combined.

As Mark and Kelly rode out to the bridge, they talked easily. "Thanks again for partnering up with me this week, Kelly."

Kelly laughed. "You make it sound as though I were doing you a favor."

"You did," he said quickly. "You introduced me to the whole town, and made me feel quite welcome."

"I did all that!" Kelly said in an exaggerated voice.

Mark laughed. "You're an imp, Kel."

Kelly smirked proudly. "So I've been told!"

When they arrived at Jimmy's Way, Mark pulled his Explorer to the side of the road, and they got out. "This has to be the longest covered bridge that I've ever seen," Mark said in an awed voice.

"It's one of the longest in the country," Kelly said quickly.

"You want to walk it with me?" Mark asked excitedly, like a little kid.

"Sure," Kelly said, as she nodded her head.

"Hey," she said suspiciously, "what's that over there?" Kelly was pointing away from the bridge, and when Mark turned to look, Kelly broke out into a full sprint across the bridge. It was only seconds before she heard the pounding feet on the wooden floor of the bridge behind her. Mark was quick, and before Kelly was a quarter of the way across, he caught her, wrapping an arm around her waist.

"You tricked me, Kel," he said huffing and puffing.

"I needed the head start," she said innocently. "I knew you were fast."

Mark slowly dropped his arm from her waist, and went to look out a nearby square window. "It's beautiful! You should come and see," he said excitedly, as he gazed out at the rocky, winding river. Evergreens lined both sides of the river, and colorful foliage, of red, yellow, and orange decorated the gentle mountains that could be seen in the distance.

Mark slid over so that Kelly could stand next to him. He was so close. So incredibly, distractingly close. Kelly found she couldn't concentrate on the view. Her mind refused to think about anything except the handsome man next to her. Her heart was just too eager to accept his closeness.

Kelly abruptly pushed away from the window, and began heading to the other side of the bridge. Mark silently joined her, looking out each window as they passed it.

His soft, probing voice broke the silence gently. "Kelly, what is it that you want the most from life?"

Kelly looked up into Mark's tender blue eyes, and felt moved by the emotion she saw in them. "Well, a few things, actually," she said looking down at the wide, planked floor. "I want to be the best cop that I can be. I love working with people." Mark nodded. "And, of course, someday...I'd like to meet my Prince Charming, get married, and have a bunch of kids." She paused, reflecting on her statement for a moment before she turned to Mark. Curiously, she asked him, "What about you? What is it that Chief Mark Mitchell wants from life?"

Mark laughed lightly, and then looked over and smiled at Kelly. His smile was so tender, that she felt her heart stop. Mark casually dropped an arm around Kelly's shoulders, and said in a thoughtful voice, "Pretty much the same as you, Kel. I want to make a difference in Sawyer's Crossing as the Chief. I want this community to be a better place from me being here. And," he said, as he dropped his arm from her, "I want to get married and have a house full of kids. But," he said reflectively, "I always want to continue to walk with the Lord. My faith is the most important thing in my life."

"You're a Christian?" Kelly asked in shock, as she abruptly stopped walking.

"Yes," Mark said in a serious voice. "Does that surprise you?"

"Not really," Kelly said thoughtfully. "No, not at all."

As she started walking again, she could feel Mark's eyes on her. "How about you, Kelly? Where do you stand with the Lord?'

Kelly sighed heavily. "Oh, Mark, that's a deep question." This was one area she didn't want to get into with him. Kelly was sure that Mark would never understand her reasons. And besides that, the more she opened up her heart to Mark, the more she fell in love with him. The whole idea of being in love with anyone simply scared Kelly. Mark's soft voice interrupted her thoughts.

"If you want to share...," Mark said invitingly, "I'm a good listener."

His eyes were so full of tenderness and compassion, that Kelly found herself opening up to him. "I asked Jesus into my heart when I was five," Kelly said in a distant voice, looking ahead aimlessly. "And, when I was six, after my parents had both been shot by a mad man, I kicked Jesus out." Her voice had taken on a hard, bitter edge. "I figured that if God was as good and loving as everyone says He is, He would never have allowed my parents to die."

Kelly stopped walking, and looked up at Mark awkwardly. She had been more honest with him than she'd intended to be. "You must think that I'm a pretty terrible person for saying that."

Mark put an arm around Kelly, and pulled her close. "Not at all, Kelly," he said in a gentle, understanding voice. "I just can't imagine what you've been through. It was awful, and I'm so sorry for you."

Mark continued to keep Kelly close to him, almost protectively, as they walked the length of the bridge. "Kelly," Mark said in a sensitive tone, "if you ever want to talk about your parents, or God, or anything...I'm a great listener."

"Most people don't want to listen about what happened to my parents," Kelly blurted out quickly. "I don't think I've talked about the incident more then a couple of times." It suddenly struck Kelly how strange and true that statement was. The people around her whom she trusted most growing up had so much trouble dealing with the death of her parents that they hadn't allowed her to express her anger or her grief. Not until that moment did the reality of the odd situation face her. As a child, and as an adult, she had always kept her feelings to herself.

Kelly's emotions began to overwhelm her as she thought about that awful night. She felt the tears start to rise, and turned to look out a window, to hide her face from Mark. She wasn't quick enough. Mark put a hand on her shoulder, and slowly turned her around. He tenderly pulled her into a large, loving embrace, and held Kelly while she softly wept. He didn't say anything, he just slowly brushed her short blonde hair with a gentle hand.

After a few minutes, Kelly slowly pulled away. "I'm sorry about that, Mark," Kelly said awkwardly. "This is so embarrassing."

Mark slowly put a finger to Kelly's lips to quiet her. "There is no need to be sorry or embarrassed over tears, Kelly. I'm glad I was here for you."

"So am I," Kelly said in a soft, but sincere voice.

Mark offered Kelly a hand, and she easily slid her hand into his, as if it was something that she did all the time. "You want to walk back now? I'm kind of curious to see if there's a rope underneath this bridge," Mark said smiling kindly at her.

His smile brightened her heart. "There is!" Kelly said, slowly feeling her excitement mounting. "And boy, do you get a long ride from it!"

Mark smiled at her. "Let's go!"

Mark continued to hold Kelly's hand, as they walked the half-mile back through the bridge. Kelly was surprised by the strength and courage she drew from his touch. She was also surprised by how much she hoped he would continue to hold her hand. She was enjoying this time with Mark Mitchell more then she wanted to admit.

They slowly climbed down the steep embankment to the river's edge. Mark let a loud holler ring out when he spotted the long rope under the bridge.

"You want to go first?" he asked invitingly.

Kelly laughed at his boyish excitement. "No, you go," she said grinning at him ear to ear.

Mark made a running leap, and grabbed the rope in midair. He swung to the first bridge pillar, and then sent the rope back for Kelly.

As Kelly held the rope in her hands, she smiled at Mark teasingly. "Oh, no!" he said throwing his hands on his hips. "You're not going to strand me again, are you?"

Kelly laughed loudly. "Not this time. You have the keys. I won't be able to get home."

Then Kelly swung out to him, and Mark quickly grabbed her waist, and pulled her to the concrete base. They sat down on the base, resting their shoulders lightly against each other.

"I love these long summer evenings," Mark said lazily. "The nights seem to go on forever."

Kelly slipped her sneakers off, and dropped her feet into the water. A moment later, Mark did the same thing. "Hey, do you think that I can toss my sneakers to the bank?" Mark asked eyeing the distance.

Kelly laughed. "Probably. But, if you miss, you'll be diving for them."

"Good point," Mark said smiling down at her. "Actually," he said turning to look at the water longingly, "I really wouldn't mind going for a swim. This reminds me a little of the swimming hole that I went to as a boy."

"You want to swim?" Kelly asked playfully, giving Mark a small shove toward the water.

A wide grin quickly spread across his face. "Kelly, if you push me in," he said arching his eyebrows up, "I guarantee you'll be coming with me."

Kelly laughed. "I bet you would, wouldn't you!" Mark just smiled confidently at her.

"You know, if it was earlier, I actually wouldn't mind a swim. But," Kelly said looking regretfully at her watch, "it's getting kind of late."

"Maybe another time...," Mark said looking at her seriously.

"That would be fun." Kelly said as she stood up and grabbed the rope.

"What are you doing tomorrow after church?" Mark asked her quickly.

"Oh," Kelly said as though just remembering, "I have a date." Then she swung to the bank, leaving Mark with a puzzled expression on his face.

As she swung the rope back to him, he said in an unsure voice, "I thought you said that you weren't dating anyone."

Kelly laughed. "I'm not."

Mark swung across the river, and backed Kelly playfully against the bank. "Let me get this straight," he said, never taking his probing blue eyes off her. "You're not dating anyone, but tomorrow you're going on a date."

Kelly smiled and nodded. "That about sums it up."

"A girl type thing, or with a guy?" Mark asked, pretending to be interrogating her.

"Oh, definitely a handsome man," Kelly said broadening her smile. "And," she said dramatically, "he's simply crazy about me!"

"Something's going on," Mark said firmly, narrowing his gaze. "I'll tell you right now, Little Lady, if you come clean with me, your penalty will be lessened."

"Would you care to join us?" Kelly asked teasingly.

Mark laughed. "This is the first time that I've been asked to go out on a date with a girl and her date. It sounds awkward," Mark said scrunching up his face a bit.

"Not really," Kelly said casually, "I promised A.J. that I'd bring him to Hop's Pond tomorrow. You're welcome to join us if you want."

"A.J.!" Mark practically shouted in surprise. "As in the little blonde, ten-year-old boy...A.J.?"

Kelly simply nodded and smiled. "That's the one!"

Mark laughed, and then grabbed Kelly's hand. He started dragging her up the bank, toward his Explorer.

"Hey!" Kelly yelled. "What are you doing?"

"You," Mark said turning around, and facing her squarely, "are a dangerous tease. I'm bringing you back to the station to lock you up and throw away the key."

Kelly laughed at his antics. "What! No trial? No community service? What kind of a judge are you?"

"Hum...," Mark said, still holding her hand. He began to walk slowly toward the Explorer. "You might have an idea there!" His face displayed just a hint of a smile, and Kelly found herself totally caught up in his game.

"An idea?" Kelly asked in a confused voice.

"Yeah," Mark said grinning at her flirtatiously, "I like the community service idea. It holds endless possibilities."

Kelly's heart stopped. They had reached the Explorer, and she found herself leaning against the passenger door for support. "What exactly do you mean? "Kelly asked in a soft, but determined voice.

Mark just smiled down at her for a minute before answering her. "How would you like to work off your community service hours starting next Saturday?"

"Saturday?" Kelly asked quickly.

Mark nodded, and continued to smile charmingly at her. "Yes, Saturday," he said looking at her intently, as if he were trying to read her mind. "We could go out for a pizza, and then a movie. What do you think?" Mark's confident expression had faded away, and was replaced by a look of vulnerability. It made Kelly's heart melt and reach out to him.

"Really?" Kelly asked in a surprised voice.

Mark just grinned, and slowly nodded his head. "Does it surprise you, Kelly...that I'm attracted to you, and that I'd like to go out on a date with you?"

Kelly felt like the wind had been knocked out of her. To say that she felt surprised at this moment would be a gross understatement. "You're attracted to me?" Kelly said quietly, still trying to make sense of the situation.

"Yes," Mark said smiling tenderly at her. When he smiled like that, it always made Kelly feel as though she was going into major heart failure. "But," Mark said stepping back from her a little, "I don't want you to go out with me Saturday night, unless you really want to. This is strictly personal."

Kelly had to look away from his heart-searching gaze for a moment. He wanted to go out with her...she could hardly believe it. Mark Mitchell wanted to go out with her! She wanted to jump up and down and scream at the top of her lungs! Instead, she turned back to him calmly, but she couldn't stop the smile that was spreading across her face. "Mark," she said in a voice barely containing her excitement, "I'd really like to go out with you Saturday. I think we'd have a fun time."

"Me, too!" Mark said smiling with obvious relief.

As Mark started to drive back to Gram's house, Kelly couldn't stop smiling. As she glanced over at Mark, she noticed that he was smiling, too.

"What are you smiling at?" Kelly asked curiously.

Mark laughed lightly. "I'm smiling because I have a date with you!" Then he leaned toward Kelly, and asked in an inquisitive tone, "And just what are you smiling at, Miss Douglas?"

Kelly laughed loudly. "I'm smiling, Mark, because you finally asked me out!"

Seven

In the small, simple, New-England-style church the next day, Kelly spotted Mark off to the side and a few rows up from her. She had a good view of his face, and she watched him curiously as he sang and listened to the sermon. She could see his reaction to the pastor's words on his face, and it confirmed to her that Mark was a man close to God.

"Why?" Kelly pondered earnestly. "Why would Mark Mitchell be interested in me? I told him clearly how I feel about God. Why would a man with a heart close to God want to pursue me?" Kelly knew she would have to talk to Mark about it soon. It bothered her, but she didn't exactly know why.

Before the sermon had ended, Mark's pager went off, and he quickly left the sanctuary. He returned five minutes later, as the closing hymn was being sung. He gently touched Kelly on the shoulder, and said in a quiet voice, "Can I see you for a minute?"

Kelly followed Mark, and once they were outside the small church, he spoke in firm, serious tones, sounding very much like Chief Mitchell, and not Mark. "Something has come up, and I'm not going to be able to go to Hop's Pond with you this afternoon."

"Trouble?" Kelly asked instinctively, turning into Officer Douglas.

"Yes," Mark replied in a solemn voice. "There has been a robbery out by the Wooden Covered Bridge."

"The Wooden Bridge?" Kelly asked in a confused voice. "What happened?"

"It seems three masked men pulled the job. When an out-of-state car, probably a tourist, entered the bridge, two trucks, one on either end, blocked the exits of the bridge. Then they robbed an elderly couple at gun point."

Kelly paled, and said in an unbelieving tone, "You've got to be kidding..."

Mark's features had darkened, like a cloud blocking the sun. He slowly shook his head at her. "I'm afraid not."

When he paused, Kelly mumbled, "Just like in the old days. Covered bridges were prime hiding spots for thieves. They often robbed the people who passed through them...sometimes even killing them."

Mark sighed heavily. "Yeah, well, the elderly couple that got hit is out three hundred dollars, plus the wife's jewelry."

"That's awful!" Kelly said angrily. "What can I do to help?"

Mark's expression softened, and he look down at her tenderly. "You've got a date with a smiling, ten-year-old blonde guy...remember?" Mark said laughing softly. "A.J. would be heart-broken if you cancelled. Take him to the pond, and have a great time. I'll try to call you later."

At Hop's Pond with A.J. that afternoon, Kelly had trouble keeping her mind off the robbery at the Wooden Bridge. Sawyer's Crossing was a town of about eight thousand. Crime was so low that many people never locked their cars or their houses, even at night. Whoever had hit the bridge was probably not a local. It was just a gut feeling that Kelly had, but almost all of the trouble that they'd had in the past, had been from outsiders. And, Kelly wondered, narrowing her eyes, would they stop with one robbery, or carry their scheme on to the other bridges in Sawyer. Kelly could think of seven bridges right off the bat that would be prime targets because of their isolated locations.

Later that afternoon, she was still thinking about the crime, when Mark pulled into the driveway. He wearily climbed the porch steps, and sank into the glider beside her. "How was your time at Hop's Pond?" Mark asked in a sincere voice.

"It was OK," Kelly said quickly. "A.J. had a great time."

"How about you?" Mark asked, leaning forward to look directly into her face.

Kelly laughed lightly. "To be honest with you, Mark, I would rather have been down at the station. My mind has been buzzing with the robbery news."

"I didn't mean to ruin your afternoon," Mark said honestly.

"Mark," Kelly said touching his arm quickly, "you didn't ruin my afternoon. Whoever robbed that poor elderly couple did."

Mark nodded, as he sighed, and relaxed against the back of the swing. Suddenly, he sprang forward, and looked intently at Kelly. "You lock your doors at night, don't you?" he asked in an earnest, concerned tone.

Kelly laughed, and shook her head. "For as long as I can remember, Gram has never locked the doors. I doubt she still even has the key for the doors."

Mark looked at her completely appalled. "Kelly!" he said in a voice that was quickly rising, "You should always lock your doors!"

"Mark," Kelly said in a calm voice, "this is Sawyer's Crossing, not D.C. I bet most of the people in town don't lock their doors."

"That has to change," Mark said in a determined voice. As he glanced at his watch, he shook his head disgustedly.

"What's wrong?" Kelly asked in a puzzled voice.

"It's too late to get to the hardware store."

"What did you need?" Kelly asked in a hospitable voice. "Maybe we have it in the basement."

Mark shook his head and laughed loudly. "Yeah," he said smirking at her, "and because you don't lock your doors, I could just waltz in there and see for myself."

Kelly rolled her eyes at him. "What did you need?" she repeated calmly.

"I wanted to put a dead bolt on your front and back doors," Mark said looking at her seriously, as he ran a hand through his straight blonde hair. "You know," he said narrowing his eyes at her, "I just know I'm going to lose sleep over this tonight."

"You really shouldn't worry," Kelly said in a relaxed voice.

"Kelly!" Mark said raising his voice slightly, "This town pays me to worry. That's my job!"

A moment later, Mark took her hand and squeezed it gently. "I'm sorry, Sweetheart. I shouldn't have raised my voice at you. I just don't like the idea of you not being safe at night."

"Mark," Kelly said, as she stared at her hand engulfed in his, "one robbery and you're ready to bolt this town down for the night."

"Kel," he said squeezing her hand urgently, "my gut feeling is that those bridge robbers will strike again...and soon. Their plan is too clever to stop at just one bridge."

"I know," Kelly said in a quiet, thoughtful voice. "I feel the same way."

Mark let go of Kelly's hand, and put his arm around her shoulders. Kelly dropped her head onto his right shoulder, and relaxed against him. She always felt so safe with Mark. He was confident and sure of himself, but he was also tender and gentle. Kelly closed her eyes, feeling her heart fall deeper and deeper for this man. He seemed to be everything that Kelly had ever dreamed of...and more.

Mark and Kelly sat quietly, enjoying each other's company for about half an hour more. When Mark got up to leave, he squeezed Kelly's hands tenderly. "Do you want to have dinner with me tomorrow, Kel?"

Kelly smiled up at him mischievously. "Dinner tomorrow, and a date on Saturday?"

Mark smiled down at her warmly. "Can you handle it, or am I moving too fast?" His eyes showed a definite concern.

"No, Mark, you're not moving too fast. I'd enjoy having dinner with you tomorrow night."

"Good," he said as his eyes exploded into excited twinkles. "I'll pick you up around six."

The next day proved to be crazier then ever. The robbers hit Slater's Bridge around seven in the morning. As the force gathered for an emergency meeting around one in the afternoon, Kelly watched anxiously as Mark thoughtfully paced the room.

"Whoever is doing this is so bold that they've robbed both times in broad daylight," Mark said in a tight, serious voice. "This clearly indicates to me that they think that they are above being caught. Which makes them very dangerous," Mark said sighing heavily. "We need a plan, people, and I'm open to your ideas."

Kelly waited for just a moment before she stood up. "Chief," she said looking at Mark in a focused and pensive way, "I have an idea that might work." Kelly noticed that an expression that was curious, as well as concerned, quickly spread across Mark's serious face.

"Go ahead, Douglas," he said looking at Kelly through anxious eyes.

111

"Well Sir," Kelly said looking directly at him, "what I feel that we need to do is beat the robbers at their own game." Mark took a step closer to her, and Kelly continued. "I think we should hide a sharp-shooting team up in the rafters of the bridge. It's just like an attic up there, and there'd be plenty of room to move around. Place a chase team, in hidden cars, on either side of the bridge, and they can chase, if needed, or serve as back up for the shooters."

"I think targeting a bridge is a good idea," Mark said in a thoughtful, authoritative tone, "but which bridge would you target? Sawyer's has a dozen of them."

"Chief," Kelly said quickly, "I think that we can rule out the three right here in town. They're too exposed. Also, Slater's and Wooden Bridge have just been hit. I would guess that they'd try one of the others."

"Makes sense," Mark said nodding his head thoughtfully, as he ran an apprehensive hand through his hair. "But, that still leaves seven bridges. How would you know which one to target?"

"Well, I've thought about that...," Kelly said methodically. "I would temporarily close Jimmy's Way. It's too far out to target. Place some construction trucks in front of it, to make it seem like it's being repaired."

"OK," Mark said following Kelly closely, "that still leaves six bridges..."

"Henry's, Mill Rd., and Carson are all in heavily populated areas," Kelly went on quickly. "I think we can count those out. I don't think that the robbers want an audience."

"Makes sense," Mark said taking another step closer to her. "But that still leaves three bridges. That's too many for our little force to cover adequately. That leaves Stonewall, Brides, and Tim's Path. All three are in isolated areas, and the tourists seem to make a point to drive out to them."

"Well, I've thought about that too," Kelly said calmly. "What if we get volunteers to hang out around Stonewall and Tim's Path. They could be picnicking, or fishing off the side of the bridge. I bet Baily could arrange that," Kelly pointed out quickly. "Then, all we'd have to do is target Brides Bridge."

The whole room was so quiet that Kelly thought that everyone had stopped breathing. "It might work...," Mark said slowly, as he paced back and forth. "But, we're talking about involving a lot of people."

"Sir," Rand Thompson spoke up, "I bet we could get some officers over at Whitewater to help us. I know that they're concerned about their own bridges being hit."

"They could serve as decoys, Chief," Noah Olin said quickly. "Then we wouldn't have to worry about the thieves recognizing one of us."

Mark turned suddenly to Scott Ables, his second in command. "Scott," he asked, narrowing his eyes at the older man, "who is our best sharp shooter in Sawyer?"

"Besides you, Sir," Scott said in his usual serious tone, "Officer Douglas holds the best record."

Mark's mouth literally dropped open as he stared at Kelly in disbelief.

Scott missed his boss's expression, and continued on. "I would recommend that we put you and Douglas in Brides Bridge's rafters."

"No," Mark said emphatically. "It's too much of a risk."

"Sir," Scott said quickly," Douglas can hold her own. She's the best sharp shooter in the state."

"No," Mark said angrily shaking his head. "We'll think of something else. Everyone take a break."

As the room cleared, Kelly stayed in front of her own chair. As she was about to speak, Mark said firmly, "In my office. Now."

Kelly followed him to his office, growing angrier with each step. "You're not being fair. If it was any other officer but me, you'd be going through with this plan."

"That's true," Mark said in a determined voice. "But the truth of the matter is, it's not any other officer, it's you!"

Kelly was floored that he had actually admitted it. "You're not being fair," she repeated.

"Maybe not," he said in a hard tone, "but, I'm not willingly going to place you in a compromising position."

"Mark!" Kelly protested. "I'm a cop! I'm willing to put my life on the line everyday. Why are you asking me to change that now!"

Mark stared at her in such a way that Kelly knew he had finally gotten the message. "You're right." he said looking away from her. "I have no right to let my personal feelings influence my professional decisions."

He sighed heavily, and ran a hand nervously through his hair. Then, he turned to look at her, with a proud smile growing on his face. "Are you really the best gun in the state?"

Kelly smiled. "Next to your record...yes."

"Man....," Mark said sighing again. "Are you really up for this?"

"Yes, Chief," she said eyeing him confidently. "I want them stopped."

"You're still a rookie," Mark pointed out quickly. "Are you going to have trouble shooting someone if it's necessary?"

Kelly smiled confidently at her boss. "They're bad guys, Chief. I don't have any trouble shooting bad guys."

Mark laughed at her comment, but his expression quickly sobered.

"Well, if we're going to do this, we'd better get the wheels rolling. There's a lot to be done before tomorrow."

"Tomorrow?" Kelly said in a surprised voice.

"I think we should get out there as quick as possible to catch the bad guys, don't you Kel?" Mark said in a teasing tone.

Kelly laughed. "Yeah, I do."

"You go back on patrol with Rand. Come by my office around four, and I should be able to give you a clearer game plan."

"Are we still on for dinner?" Kelly asked curiously.

"Definitely," he said smiling at her. "It will be a good distraction from our plan."

Mark picked Kelly up at 5:45. "I packed a quick picnic. I was wondering if you'd want to head over to Riverside Park. It would be a shame to eat inside on a beautiful summer evening like this."

"That sounds great!" Kelly said enthusiastically. "Just let me grab my sneakers."

When Kelly came back downstairs, Mark took her hand gently, and led her to the

Explorer. "You look great!" Mark said smiling at her sweetly.

Kelly thanked him. "This is the only clean thing in my closet right now besides my uniforms." The blue and white striped tank top along with her khaki shorts looked like they were made for each other, and Kelly felt relieved.

"You look very nice yourself," Kelly said quickly, as Mark helped her into the Explorer. The maroon polo, with the blue shorts, made him look sporty and preppy.

When they got to Riverside Park, they walked along the water's edge, hand in hand, until they came to a grassy section that was surrounded by evergreens. "This is so beautiful," Kelly said excitedly.

Kelly helped Mark lay an old quilt down, and they stretched out on either end, placing the food between them. After Mark said a quick blessing for the food, they dug in.

Kelly began to grow quiet as she thought about why Mark would want to date her. With his heart so on fire for the Lord, why was he interested in her.

"A penny for your thoughts," Mark said suddenly.

Kelly smiled quietly, and looked at him. "Mark," Kelly began hesitantly, "if I ask you something, do you promise to answer honestly?"

Mark sat up straighter, and leaned slightly forward on his knees.

"Kelly, I will always be honest with you. It's the only way I know."

Kelly smiled and nodded. She had guessed as much. "Mark," Kelly said nervously, "I'm trying to understand your interest in me." Kelly paused for a second, and then plunged on, before she lost her nerve. "I mean, I am interested in you, but, I'm just surprised that you are interested in me."

"Why?" Mark asked earnestly. "Why is it such a surprise to you?"

"Mark," Kelly said nervously fiddling with the corner of the old quilt, "your love for the Lord is obvious. I think it's wonderful, but, you know that I don't share the same love."

Mark smiled at Kelly gently. "I think you do," he said softly, but with deep conviction. "I think you've repressed a lot of your love for

God...but it's there, Kelly. I can still see it in your heart."

Kelly shook her head determinedly. "I don't think so."

"Kelly," Mark said kindly, "why do you go to church every Sunday?"

"Because I don't want to hurt Gram's feelings," she said quickly.

Mark shook his head slowly, and smiled at Kelly for a minute. "Sweetheart," Mark said in a loving voice," I don't think the Kelly Douglas that I know would go to church every Sunday, if she really didn't want to be there, just to please someone else. I think that if you really didn't want to be there, you'd just level with Gram about it."

Kelly looked at him in shock. The truth of his statement was just sinking in now. Mark laughed gently at Kelly's surprised expression. "Sometimes we hide the truth even from ourselves," Mark said tenderly, as he took Kelly's hand, and squeezed it.

"Kelly," he said urgently, "when I look at you, I see a beautiful young woman, both inside and out. I see a young woman who was deeply hurt as a child. I see a young woman with walls around her heart, because of all the pain she's been through." Mark paused and squeezed Kelly's hand again, trying to send as much love as he could through his touch. "I believe you're healing, Honey," Mark said looking deeply into her eyes, "but to completely heal, you need to fully face your past. And," he said eyeing her more intently, "something tells me that you haven't done that yet."

Kelly just stared at him for a full minute, before sighing loudly. "Don't tell me," she said in an amused tone, "I bet you minored in Psychology. Am I right?"

Mark laughed loudly, and squeezed her hand again. "You're very funny, too, Darling." Mark grew serious again. "And," he said as he touched the tip of her nose, "I just bet you've used your humor to avoid a lot of questions that you don't want to answer, and cover up a ton of pain from your past."

Kelly felt alarm slam through her body at Mark's perceptive insight.

His accuracy was deeply disturbing to her. "Mark," Kelly said quickly, in a shaky voice, "I'm not ready to talk about the past."

"Kelly," Mark said gently, willing her to understand, "I know that you're not. But," he said pulling her up into a standing position, next to him, "I hope that you will trust me enough to turn to me when you are ready to talk."

By the time they drove back to Gram's, it was almost nine o'clock. As Kelly got out of Mark's Explorer, she was immediately drawn to the sky. "Oh Mark," she said in a breathless voice, "look at all the stars! They're so beautiful!"

"Wait here," Mark said in an excited voice. A moment later, he was spreading the quilt down on the front lawn. "Lie down here, and look up at the stars. The view is awesome."

Kelly sat down on the quilt, and began to tilt her head way back, so much so, in fact, that she fell backwards.

Mark laughed. "You could hurt yourself by doing that. It's just easier to lie flat on your back."

Kelly did, and her eyes excitedly studied the sky. "I used to do this all the time with my Dad.

He knew the names of many of the constellations...we had so much fun."

"OK," Mark challenged, lightly touching her hand, "What's that one called?" he asked pointing upward.

Kelly's eyes followed his hand to the direction he was looking at. Then she laughed quietly. "Oh, that's an easy one, Mark. That's the Big Dipper, and, next to it, is the Little Dipper."

"Very good," Mark said quickly, sounding like an approving professor.

Kelly broke up laughing.

"What's so funny?" he said resting his head in his hand, and leaning slightly toward her.

Kelly just stayed flat on her back, with her eyes focused on the sky. "When I was a little girl, I thought that my father said that the Little Dipper was called the Little Dripper." Kelly paused again, filling the air with laughter. "Not until I asked him where it was dripping did he correct me."

Mark and Kelly laughed together.

"And the Big Dipper...," Mark asked in a teasing tone, "did you think it was called the Big Dripper?"

Kelly laughed. "Of course. If the little one was dripping, I naturally assumed that the big one was dripping, too."

Mark chuckled. "That's funny. Did you confuse any others?"

"The only other one I remember was Orion...you know," Kelly said flipping her hand casually in the air, "the guy with the belt."

"Yep," Mark said as he pointed upward. "There he is."

"Yeah, well, that guy up there...," Kelly said studying Orion. "I asked my Dad what the 'O' stood for. I wanted to know what 'O. Ryan's' first name was."

Mark laughed again. "It's easy to confuse things."

"That's for sure," Kelly agreed.

After twenty more minutes of stargazing, Mark started to get up. "You know, Kelly, I could stay here all night. I love watching the stars, but," he said raising his eyebrows up, "we have an important appointment tomorrow."

"Oh yeah," Kelly said growing silly, "Good Guys and Bad Guys! What are we again?"

Mark laughed. "Kel," he said kneeling down next to her, "we're the Good Guys, and we catch the Bad Guys."

"Oh yeah," Kelly said pushing on Mark just enough to make him lose his balance. As he toppled over, Kelly said playfully, "Thanks for refreshing my memory, Chief!"

Kelly jumped to her feet, and Mark was next to her in a minute. He dropped an arm around her, and with a serious expression, he asked her, "Are you ready for tomorrow, Kel?"

"Yes," Kelly said in a serious voice. "I'm ready."

"Good," Mark said squeezing her shoulders. As he walked her to the door, he said in a matter of fact voice, "I'll pick you up at 5:00."

Kelly nodded. She knew that Mark wanted everyone in place before the rush hour traffic started. "Are you going to be able to sleep?" Kelly asked him curiously.

Mark laughed. "I can never sleep before a showdown. I'm just too wired. How about you?"

"I'll rest, but I don't think that I'll sleep much. I have trouble shutting my mind off."

"I know the feeling," Mark said nodding understandingly at her.

Mark turned and gave Kelly a quick hug. "Rest well, Sweetheart." Then, Mark stood back and smiled at Kelly proudly. "You know, with your blonde hair, sparkling blue eyes, and rosy cheeks, you look far too friendly to be Vermont's number one sharp-shooter."

"It's my disguise," Kelly said smiling up at him.

"It's a great disguise, Kel. You would have completely fooled me. You look more like a Girl Scout, than a sharp-shooter."

"Looks can be deceiving," Kelly said wiggling her eyebrows at Mark.

Mark simply laughed. "That's true, Sweetheart. And in your case, the bad guys won't have a clue as to your abilities. I guarantee they won't even see you coming."

Eight

The next morning, Rand dropped Kelly and Mark off at Brides Bridge, and then disappeared quickly. They didn't want a group congregating outside the bridge, drawing attention to themselves.

As Kelly stood in front of the old red-and-white covered bridge, she laughed softly. "You know, Mark," she said as she walked toward him, "we look more like bad guys, dressed in black outfits, carrying shot guns and pistols...than we do good guys. I hope no one gets confused!"

Mark laughed and nodded. As he walked into the covered bridge, he asked Kelly what the best way was to get up into the attic.

"Now, that I know!" Kelly said walking to the far end of the bridge.

"Brides Bridge used to be one of my favorite forts as a kid. It's the only bridge in Sawyer that has a full attic. Here," Kelly said as she handed Mark her shotguns, radio, and pistol, "hold these while I climb the trusses to get up."

Mark watched in amazement as Kelly skillfully climbed the wall of the bridge, and then swung herself into the narrow attic opening. "I can tell that you've done this before," he said smiling proudly at her.

"Many times," Kelly said in an amused tone. "The covered bridges were a great place for us country kids to play on a rainy day. No kid could have asked for a better fort."

"I'll bet!" Mark said in an envious voice, as he handed up their arsenal to Kelly. Mark followed Kelly's pattern in climbing the sides of the timbers, and Kelly watched him in amusement. It wasn't everyday that she'd get to watch her boss climb the inside of a covered bridge. He looked more like a ten-year-old boy right now, than he did a grown adult.

"Why doesn't Brides have any windows?" Mark asked as he climbed. "This is one dark place!"

Kelly laughed as she watched Mark swing himself up into the attic.

"Good job, Boss," she said smiling at him. Then she answered his question. "Mark, covered bridges were built solely for people to be able to cross rivers. They were expensive to build, and expensive to maintain. Windows would let the rain and snow in, which would rot out the floors quicker. Brides is the oldest covered bridge in Sawyer, and it was built with longevity in mind, not esthetics. If the bridge began to rot out, and the small town didn't have the budget to repair it, they'd be in trouble. People might have to drive miles away, to another town, just to cross the river."

"So, when did you become such a bridge expert?" Mark asked humorously.

Kelly laughed quietly. "Mark, when you grow up in a town that has a dozen covered bridges, you're bound to know a thing or two about them."

Mark smiled. "I guess that's true."

As Mark picked up his radio to check in with the different teams, Kelly took her flashlight, and explored the old attic. It had been years since she was up here. Right away, she noticed how dusty the attic was. She knew that she'd have to stay close to the attic's opening, or she'd risk having an asthma attack.

Just then, something glittered in the beam of her flashlight, and she quickly crawled toward it. A slow smile spread across her face as she picked up an old silver police canteen. She crawled back to Mark, and showed him.

"This used to be my Dad's," Kelly said proudly. "When I was six years old, he gave it to me. I have driven myself nuts for years wondering where I left it."

"How long has it been missing?" Mark asked curiously.

"Since I was a young teen," Kelly said smiling fondly at the old canteen. "I'm glad I found it."

Mark smiled at her. "You must have been quite a tomboy."

"Still am," Kelly said as she fiddled with her canteen.

Mark leaned over the side of the opening, and shined his flashlight to examine the inside of the bridge. "Looks a lot like a barn," he said matter-of-factly.

As he pulled his head back inside the attic, Kelly laughed gently.

"What do you think a covered bridge is, Country Boy?" she asked in a teasing voice. "It's no more than a narrow barn across a river."

Mark laughed. "That's true."

They lay down on the wooden attic floor, and Kelly watched curiously as Mark propped his head up with his hands. "OK, Miss Bridge Expert, tell me the history of Brides Bridge. Why do they call it Brides?"

"Oooh, it's kind of a romantic story, Chief. You sure you want to hear it?" Kelly asked in a teasing voice.

Mark gave Kelly his best charming smile. "I'm a romantic guy, Kelly," he said as he winked at her flirtatiously. "I love a good romance story."

Kelly looked away from his twinkling blue eyes. What in the world had ever possessed her to team up with Mark. How was she going to be around him all day long, and not lose her head. Her heart was already a goner. The only protection she had against Mark Mitchell's charm was her level-headedness. "Keep it together, Kel," she silently warned herself.

Mark cleared his throat loudly, and Kelly's mind popped back to reality. "Where were you just now?" Mark asked, giving her a very curious look.

Kelly laughed nervously. "Mark Mitchell, you don't even want to know. Now about the bridge..."

Mark's hand quickly shot out, and covered hers. "Now, about your thoughts...," he said smiling at her, yet his look was extremely intense. "What's going on in that pretty little head of yours?"

Kelly was completely captivated by Mark's face for a moment. His smile was warm and wide, with beautiful white teeth shining back at her...and his eyes...his eyes got her every time. The deep blue eyes that now studied her were gentle, but fully alert, with just a trace of humor in them.

Kelly slowly pulled her hand away from his, and tucked both her hands firmly beneath her chin. As she slowly turned her eyes away from his emotion-filled face, she smoothly went on with the history of Brides Bridge. "Brides Bridge was originally called Clayton's Bridge,"

Kelly continued ignoring Mark's questions. "In 1935, it was renamed Brides Bridge, because the small church burnt down, and two brides used this bridge as their church, and got married right down there," Kelly said pointing to the area below the attic.

Mark just stared at her for a moment, in a quiet, thoughtful way, and then said in a slow, calm voice. "That's very interesting, Kelly, but I'm more interested in where your mind is at? What were you thinking before?"

Kelly laughed nervously. "You just don't give up, do you?" she said rolling her eyes at him, as she tensely twisted some strands of hair tightly around her fingers.

"No," Mark said quickly, as if the thought of giving up hadn't even occurred to him. "Now, what were you thinking?"

A slow smile spread across Kelly's face, and she said in a quiet voice, "Mark Mitchell, you are not only a seasoned flirt, you are a robber as well."

A wide grin split Mark's face. "A flirt and a robber?" Mark said in an amused voice, as though Kelly had given him a grand award. "I can't argue with you on the flirt charge, Miss

Douglas, but," he said raising his eyebrows at her, "you have to help me understand the robber charge. You kind of lost me there."

Kelly turned, and looked at Mark with a serious expression. "You!" she said throwing an accusing finger in his direction, "are a robber of hearts. You are quite dangerous, Mitchell. You should be locked up, and the key should be thrown away."

Mark laughed, obviously amused. "Oh yeah, Officer...," he said crawling closer to her, "and just whose heart are you charging me with robbing?"

"Attempted robbery!" Kelly pointed out quickly.

"OK," Mark said, looking at her closely, "whose heart do you think that I'm attempting to rob?"

Just then, a car came through the covered bridge. Mark and Kelly instantly rolled back into the shadows. As the car exited, they saw the Massachusetts license plate, and they knew it was a tourist. As the car pulled out of sight, Mark and Kelly crept back toward the opening.

Mark touched Kelly's hand gently, and said in a low voice, "Whose heart am I being accused of robbing?" His expression had grown too somber for Kelly's comfort.

Kelly pulled her hand away from his again, and fiddled nervously with her flashlight. "You know whose heart, Mark Mitchell," Kelly said in such a quiet voice, that she wasn't sure if Mark heard her or not.

Mark put a finger under Kelly's chin, and slowly turned her face toward his. "I would take good care of your heart, Kelly," Mark said in an honest voice, full of sincerity.

Kelly turned her face away from his steady gaze. All the love that Mark held in his heart for her was clearly reflected in his eyes at this moment. She couldn't bear to face the emotions that she saw in his eyes. They simply overwhelmed Kelly, to the point where she felt out of control.

"Kelly," Mark said earnestly, "I don't want you to be afraid of me. I would never, ever hurt you. I promise you that." He turned her face back toward his. "Kelly," he said in a more urgent voice. Mark was feeling almost desper-

ate to get through to her. "I am extremely interested in getting to know you. I want to spend as
much time as we can together." He paused, and
took her hand gently. "I flirt with you,
Sweetheart, because I'm absolutely crazy about
you!"

"How can you be?" Kelly asked quickly. "We
haven't known each other that long."

"No," Mark said tenderly, never taking his
eyes off her, "but we've spent a lot of time
together...and we talk openly with each other. I
feel we've come to know each other well."

"That's true," Kelly said reflectively.

"Kelly," Mark said squeezing her hand, "you
can trust me with your heart."

Kelly slowly shook her head. "Mark, how
can I? I don't even trust God with my heart."

Mark just smiled lovingly at her. "In time,
Honey, I believe that you'll come to trust both
of us with your heart." He paused and looked at
her with pleading eyes. "Let's just take things
slowly, OK, Kel?"

Kelly nodded, but didn't say anything. How
could she trust Mark Mitchell with her heart?
She had never let anyone close enough to her

heart to hurt it. Kelly closed her eyes tightly for a moment as the truth of that situation hit her as hard as a slap in the face. The reality was that Mark Mitchell was not only near her heart, her love for this man was already inside her heart.

In a few weeks time, she had foolishly managed to let herself fall head-over-heels in love with the tender-hearted, gorgeous police chief of Sawyer's Crossing. She knew she was now in unfamiliar territory. Never had she been in love before, and Kelly felt uncertain, and frightened as to what she should expect. A chill ran down Kelly's spine, as she suddenly had an image of herself driving down a lonely mountain road in a car that had no breaks. The idea of being in love with Mark was just as frightening to her. She felt as though she was losing control. Wasn't love supposed to make you feel safe and secure, instead of frightened to death? It was all so overwhelming, but she'd have to think about all this some more.

The rest of the day passed without anything eventful happening. At four-thirty, Mark drove Kelly home, and told her he'd pick her up at five o'clock the next morning.

"How long are we going to stake out the bridge?" Kelly asked Mark curiously.

"I usually go with the three strikes policy," Mark said smiling casually at her. "If our bandits don't show up by Thursday, we'll regroup our plan."

Gram and Kelly had a quiet dinner that evening, and afterwards, Kelly told Gram that she was going to head out for a walk.

"Any place special?" Gram asked her as she cleared the dishes off the table.

"Not really, Gram," Kelly said picking up her plate, and joining the older woman at the sink. "I just need to stretch my legs. Lying up in the attic of the bridge all day made me very stiff. Also," Kelly said affectionately, patting their Golden Retriever, "Copper looks as though he could use a walk. We'll be back before dark."

As Kelly and Copper started up the hill behind Gram's house, Kelly admired the beauty around her. The forest was a peaceful place for her. It was a place that she often took refuge in. Kelly smiled as she saw the sunbeams breaking through the treetops. They made friendly beams of light in front of her, as though they were guiding the way for her.

When she reached the top of the long hill, Kelly could look down and see the small village of Sawyer's Crossing below her. She had a clear view of the four covered bridges, and part of the downtown area that was nestled into the mountainside.

Copper padded over to Kelly, and dropped a stick at her feet. The old dog playfully barked at her, while he danced around impatiently in front of her. Kelly knew the drill well. If she didn't throw the stick soon, Copper would start to growl at her, in a low, grumbly tone. Kelly picked the stick up and waved it teasingly in front of Copper for a moment, before she sent it sailing over the dog's head and half way down the hill. Kelly laughed quietly as she watched Copper race down the hill after his prey. His back end always tried to pass his front end, putting the dog in jeopardy of a major wipe out.

When Copper returned proudly with the stick, Kelly grabbed it from the dog's mouth and threw it toward the other side of the hill. As she started walking down the path on the other side of the hill, she stopped suddenly at the sight of the old house. It was the house that she had grown up in as a girl. Kelly hadn't been inside it for over ten years, and now, despite the painful memories, she unexpectedly felt compelled to go in.

As Kelly walked toward the tiny, blue, four-room Cape, she began to feel flooded with memories. "So many good memories here...," Kelly said in a quiet, but unmistakably sad voice. "And all it took was one crazy person to ruin everything."

As Kelly walked passed the old clothesline post, a vivid memory of her mother came rushing back to her. Her Mom was a tall, blonde-haired woman, and Kelly knew that in appearance, she had grown up to look just like her. Yet, she thought affectionately, she definitely had her father's spirit and heart. He was outgoing, and mischievous, and loved being around people. Her Mother was low key, and quiet. She enjoyed spending her evenings reading and stitching.

As Kelly pushed the old back door open, a musty odor attacked her senses. She left the back door open, and immediately went to open the front door. Airing the house out took no time at all. It was so tiny that you needed only a few good breezes to blow through.

As Kelly leaned against the peeling kitchen counter, she tried, as she had over the years, to remember exactly what had happened. It seemed to her that the more that she wanted to remember the past, the more her mind refused to detail the events of the awful night. It was almost as if her brain were a computer that was refusing to give her access to a certain file. Her brain wanted this file destroyed, but she knew that to survive, and go on with her future, she must not only access it, but process it.

Kelly closed her eyes to concentrate better. She could remember her Dad coming home. She always looked forward to that time of day, and greatly anticipated playing with him. Kelly could remember playing "Hide-and-Go-Seek" that night. She could remember hiding under the old couch. And, she thought as her face grew tight, she could remember hearing the gunshots. She remembered the voice of the gunman, but for the life of her, she couldn't remember his face. She knew she had seen it, but she couldn't ever seem to recall it. Even in her nightmares about the shootings, the man never had a face.

But, she thought as she squeezed her eyes tighter, she did remember the voices. The man had said something about her Dad ruining his life. He had said that Dad had taken away the best years that he had. Then, she remembered him saying, in a steel cold voice, that he was going to take Dad's best years away. Then, right before he shot Dad, her Dad had yelled his name. Kelly knew that the name was the key to finding this faceless man...but she couldn't remember it.

As she dropped to the floor, Copper padded into the kitchen wagging his tail. He came over, and dropped his head in Kelly's lap. The dog seemed to have an uncanny ability to sense Kelly's emotions. As Kelly buried her face in Copper's thick, tan coat, her tears quickly began to soak the dog's fur.

"Oh, dear God," Kelly prayed between sobs, "I know we haven't talked in a long time...but I need to ask You to help me with two things. I need to ask You to help me remember the man's name. I know that I'll never be at peace until Dad and Mom's killer is brought in." Kelly paused, and shuddered at the truth of that statement. "And, dear God, I need help in finding my way back to You. I can't do it alone. Please, God, please help me."

As Kelly made her way back to Gram's, the sun was slowly disappearing behind the mountain. Its afterglow guided Kelly like a bright flashlight. As Kelly finally dropped down on Gram's back steps, a thought struck her so hard that her body actually shook. Why didn't she start going through her father's old case files? She had always felt that the killer had been a criminal that Dad had helped put away. If that was the case, Dad's old files might help I.D. the killer.

"Why didn't I think of that before!" Kelly said quietly, as she thumped the side of her head.

Kelly ran into the house to find Gram, and Copper quickly chased after her. "Gram!" Kelly said excitedly, "I'm heading down to the station.

I have some work that I need to do. I'll probably be there all night...so don't wait up for me."

"You need your sleep, Kelly," Gram said in a protesting voice. "You have to work tomorrow."

"Gram," Kelly said in a matter-of-fact voice, "you know that I never sleep well before a stakeout. I'd rather work. Don't worry...I'll leave Copper with you."

"Oh, take him, Kelly...," Gram said waving a hand at her. "He misses you so much when you're gone. He'd really be happier with you."

"Hey, Boy!" Kelly said clapping her hands together. "Do you want to go for a ride?" Copper jumped around excitedly, and started wagging his tail enthusiastically.

After Kelly hugged Gram good night, she and Copper got into the Celica and headed for the station. Kelly knew that night was a perfect time to conduct her private investigation. Only a skeletal crew would be around, and most importantly, Mark wouldn't be there. Kelly definitely didn't want to explain any of this to him...at least not right now. First she would gather her evidence...then she would approach Mark.

Much to Kelly's dismay, the files that she wanted were not even logged into the station's computers. So Kelly went down to the basement and into the station's archives As she pulled out the boxes with her father's name on them, she anxiously gathered an armload of files. The shooting had taken place in the 1970's, but Kelly needed to start at the beginning of her father's career. He graduated from the Vermont Police Academy in 1966 and immediately started working for Sawyer's Crossing. Kelly smiled to herself as she scanned her father's first year. She felt as if she was finally getting to meet Sgt. Jerry Douglas for the first time. It bothered Gram too much to talk about her daughter and son-in-law, and Baily just about refused to. Kelly felt as though this was the only way she was going to get to know her father.

Kelly laughed quietly at some of the comments that Baily had made on her Dad's evaluations. "You're doing on excellent job, Jerry, but you need to keep your speed down." Kelly laughed again. So, driving fast was a family trait. A wide mischievous grin covered her face as she thought about what Chief Mark Mitchell would say about this.

By four that morning, Kelly had covered the first two years of her Dad's life on the force. Even if these files didn't lead to the killer, they led Kelly to a better understanding of who her father was as a cop. Even Officer Jerry Douglas's first two years were impressive. He had saved five people, been highly decorated as an officer, was on Vermont's Sharp-Shooting Squad, and was very active in the community. Kelly always knew that her Dad had been a special guy, and now she was staring at the proof of that.

As Kelly drove back to Gram's at 4:30 a.m., she felt revived inside. Finally after all these years, she was getting to know the father that she missed terribly.

By the time that Mark showed up at 5:00 a.m., Kelly had showered and eaten and was waiting for him. "You look tried," Mark said immediately as she climbed into his squad car.

"I'm fine," Kelly said smiling at him confidently.

"What did you do last night?" Mark asked in a casual way that Kelly had come to recognize as anything but casual. When he wanted to pump her for information, he always used this laid-back form of questioning. He was doing it right now, and Kelly immediately felt on guard.

"I called you a couple of times...," Mark continued, sounding indifferent, and entirely too carefree, "and Gram said you were out for a walk."

The red flags were flying in Kelly's mind. Could he have known she was down in the basement poking through old files? She immediately decided not to advertise that fact, and just try to act as laid back as Mark was now acting. "That's what I did," Kelly said giving him her best friendly, I'm-not-up-to-anything type of smile. "I was just out walking."

"The whole night?" Mark said in an amused voice. But his interest in her was becoming far too intense. "What?" he asked in a joking voice, "Did you walk to Canada and back?"

Kelly laughed nervously. "No, Mark. I just took a walk with Copper up the hill." Kelly knew that she had to be careful with her answers. By the look on Mark's face, she could tell that Chief Mitchell was on duty. She also knew that he was dangerously close to interrogating her. This thought sent a cold chill down her spine. Being on Mark's bad side was definitely not a positive thing, and, with him being Chief and all, it only made matters two times more complicated.

"So, what did you do?" Kelly said throwing the ball back at him.

His investigative blue eyes searched her face for a moment before responding. "Oh...," he said casually, but still eyeing Kelly with that you're-hiding-something look. It was unnerving. "I caught up on some paper work, and," he said laughing lightly, "caught up on some sleep as well."

Kelly smiled warmly at the sleep reference. Right now she could use some serious Z's. A big yawn forced its way out of her mouth, and Mark instantly frowned.

"You didn't sleep well, did you?" he stated, narrowing his eyes at her.

Kelly turned away from him, as a smile slipped onto her lips. "Didn't sleep well...," she thought to herself. "No Chief Mitchell, I didn't sleep at all."

"Oh look," Kelly suddenly said, in a voice that was full of relief, "there's Rand. I'm heading up to the attic." Kelly jumped out of the car and jogged through the bridge without ever looking back at Mark.

She climbed the wooden trusses and then slid into the attic. As she lay down, waiting for Mark, she rested her weary head on her arm. Within minutes, Kelly was sound asleep.

The sound of a car driving through the bridge awoke Kelly. Her head popped up quickly, and she stared over at Mark with a confused expression on her face.

"Good morning, Sleeping Beauty," he said smiling brightly at her.

"Ugh...," Kelly grumbled as she straightened up. "I can't believe I fell asleep. What time is it?"

"Nine," Mark said in an amused voice.

"It's nine o'clock!" Kelly said in a panicked voice. "You're kidding!"

"It's all right, Kelly," Mark said kindly. "I'm glad you got some sleep. I knew you looked awfully tired when I picked you up this morning."

Kelly rubbed her eyes, trying to push the sleepy feeling away. "I can't believe this!" she said in an upset voice. "I have never fallen asleep on duty before!"

"Don't worry about it," Mark said in an easy, sincere tone.

"By the way...just what did you do last night?" Mark's voice took on a tone of determination, and his eyes were penetrating and piercing. She knew she was officially under an unofficial investigation.

Kelly turned away from his probing eyes. "Not much," she replied evenly. "I just have trouble shutting my mind off sometimes."

"What where you thinking about?" Mark asked casually. But Kelly knew better. She knew his casual voice was just part of his interrogation routine.

"Listen, Mark," Kelly said growing angry, "is this an official inquest, or are you just nosey? You're making me feel like I'm on trial here."

Mark laughed, but studied Kelly intently. "I don't know, Kel. You tell me. Should it be an official inquest?"

"Do you always answer a question with a question?" Kelly asked coolly.

"I don't know, Kel, do I?" Mark asked in an amused tone.

Kelly had to laugh. "Yes, Mark, you often do. And, in case no one's ever told you before, it's rude to do that, and you're extremely nosey."

This brought a loud laugh from Mark. "Is that so?"

"Another question?" Kelly said arching her eyebrows at him.

"You know, Kel," he said crawling over toward her, "there is something evasive about you. I can't quite put my finger on it yet, but I always get the feeling that you're holding back."

"Holding back what?" Kelly asked easily.

"I don't know...," Mark said looking at her too insistently.

"Oh yeah," Kelly said in a mock serious voice, "I guess I forgot to tell you that I used to be involved in the mafia. I used to smuggle guns and drugs along the east coast. Those are probably," she said wiggling her eyebrows at him, "the dark, deep secrets that you see."

Kelly burst out laughing, and Mark had to join her. "I don't think so, Kel."

"Well, Mr. Nosey, you just crawl back over to your own side. I'm tired of feeling interrogated."

Mark moved over a few inches. "I'm sorry, Kelly. I don't mean to make you feel like you're being interrogated. I just worry about you."

"You don't need to worry about me, Mark Mitchell. I'm a big girl, you know."

"Chief!" the radio squawked. "We have spotted two old pick-up trucks heading toward the bridge. They match the description of our suspects."

"OK, Rand," Mark said, instantly turning into Chief Mitchell again. "Let's take it as a go."

"I'm going to the other end of the attic. You cover this exit," Mark commanded.

About three minutes later, Kelly could hear the rumble of the truck on the wooden bridge floor. It drove just past the bridge and pulled off to the side of the road. In the shadows of the attic, where Kelly hid out of sight, she could see two men. They seemed very young, Kelly thought in surprise. They were probably in their late teens.

A chill ran down Kelly's spine as she spotted the guns. "I have two men here, with two shotguns," Kelly said quietly into her radio.

Kelly heard an engine go off at the other end of the bridge, and assumed it was the other truck. "One man with one shotgun on this end," Mark said quickly.

The robbers only had to wait for a few minutes before two plain-clothes officers, one male and one female, arrived in an old Buick. The robbers quickly went into action. They blocked off the ends of the bridge with their trucks, and approached the vehicle with their shotguns pointed at the driver and passenger.

"Well," one of the bandits said in a cold, emotionless tone as he strolled up to the car, "we're tollkeepers, People and it's time you pay the toll."

As the driver quickly handed over his wallet and his "wife's" pocket-book, the robber's took their guard down for a minute. Mark radioed for the entire backup to pull in, and as they did, he signaled for Kelly to jump down.

"Freeze!" Mark yelled at the robbers with such force that Kelly felt frightened herself.

"Slowly, place your guns down, Boys. Don't try anything funny, or you'll end up with two dozen holes in you." Mark's voice was as cold as steel, and Kelly could tell that the robbers were taking him quite seriously.

After they laid their shotguns on the floor of the bridge, Mark ordered them to put their hands in the air. Three cops went forward quickly, and cuffed the robbers. They were taken away in squad cars before they had time to figure out what had happened to them.

As two more officers moved the trucks out of the way, Mark quickly moved over to where Kelly stood. "You were great, Douglas," Mark said, sounding like a very proud chief. "Standing there, with your shotgun aimed at their heads was very effective."

"That's what I was taught to do at the Academy," Kelly replied seriously. "It's important to let the bad guys know that we mean business."

"You did good," he said smiling at her warmly. "Now," Mark said in a firm voice, "I'm going to drop you at home, and I want you to sleep."

"I'm not tried," Kelly protested immediately.

"You're going to bed, Officer Douglas," Chief Mitchell said in a commanding tone. When the Chief used that tone, Kelly didn't even try to argue with him. She had learned that there was just no point to it. He was the Chief, and he was always going to win the battle.

"You're the boss," Kelly said in a voice that clearly let Mark know she was none too happy with his command.

"I'll drop you home in a few minutes," he said eyeing her sternly, waiting for any last-ditch arguments that might surface. When he was confident that Kelly was going to comply, he swiftly turned around and headed back toward a group of officers.

Kelly noticed Rand, and quickly walked toward him. "Well, that went well, don't you think?" Rand asked her in a satisfied tone.

"Yeah, almost too well," Kelly said shaking her head. "Things don't usually go like clockwork."

"It wasn't exactly like clockwork, Kel," Rand said in a matter-of-fact voice. "We had to hang around two whole days waiting for them."

"That's true," Kelly said in a weary voice, dropping into a seat in the cruiser, next to Rand.

"You look tired," Rand said as he studied the dark circles under Kelly's eyes.

"Why does everyone keep saying that!" Kelly said in an exasperated voice.

Rand let a loud, rumbly laugh escape from his lips. "Oh, probably because it's true!"

Kelly stared at her partner through tight narrow eyes, trying to look angry, but Rand only laughed harder. "You never like anyone telling you something that you don't want to hear."

Kelly laughed loudly. "Who does?" They both laughed, and Kelly turned her head just in time to see Mark approaching.

"Rand, you ride back to the station with Lauren. I need to take Officer Douglas home." Mark was still eyeing Kelly in a concerned, parental way, and she found it increasingly annoying.

"Yeah, that's a good idea, Chief. Kelly is wiped...but she won't admit it," Rand said looking at her seriously.

"I know," Mark said as he slid into the driver's seat. Kelly just sighed and shook her head. She hated when Rand and Mark ganged up on her.

As they started for home, Kelly asked Mark who the bandits were.

"You wouldn't believe it," Mark said in a puzzled tone, "they're all from the same family. Three brothers..."

"Brothers?" Kelly said in surprise.

"Yeah," Mark said nodding his blonde head slightly, "the Pitman brothers."

The name Pitman sent a jolt through Kelly like an electrical shock. Mark noticed her reaction and slowed the car. "Kelly, are you OK?"

Kelly didn't respond, and immediately Mark pulled the car to the side of the road. He gently put a hand on hers, and his soft touch brought her mind back to reality. Slowly, she looked over at Mark.

"What's wrong?" Mark asked, in a quiet, concerned voice.

"I...I don't know," Kelly replied nervously, but honestly. As she drew a ragged breath, she suddenly became aware of her trembling.

"Kelly," Mark said squeezing her hand, "as soon as I mentioned the name Pitman, your face went as white as a ghost." He paused, and searched her face intently. "Honey, that name must mean something to you."

"I know," Kelly said, feeling choked up and completely frustrated. "But I honestly don't know what. I don't know why that name bothers me."

Mark could see the look of fear and confusion on Kelly's face, and knew there was a battle going on inside of her. He decided to leave the situation alone for now. "If you ever want to talk about this, Kel, call me," Mark said squeezing her shoulder quickly.

After Mark dropped Kelly off at home, she walked around the empty house in a daze. Kelly was glad that Gram was already at work. She needed some quiet time to think. Every time she said the name Pitman, it was like something just went wild in the back of her mind.

Kelly decided to shower and change, and head to the station's archives. Putting herself to work was the best way she could think of to keep her mind off that haunting name.

Kelly and Copper snuck into the station's basement. Kelly went immediately over to the storage room that held all the old records, and locked the door behind her. She brought the boxes that held her father's files over to the old metal table, and started going through them again.

Kelly was on year three of her Dad's life on the force, and she could tell that this had been a very interesting year for him. He had gone undercover to help catch a man accused of smuggling guns and drugs into the state. Kelly read the file with great interest. The operation had taken six months, and in the end the criminal had been sent away for thirty years. As Kelly continued to read the file, she suddenly saw something that literally knocked the wind right out of her. The name of the man that her father had helped send away, for thirty years, was George A. Pitman.

The file ended, and Kelly mechanically grabbed the next file which had been updated. She forced herself to keep reading, even though she could hear herself wheezing loudly.

The file stated that George Pitman's wife was deceased, but he had three sons.... Kelly turned her eyes away. She couldn't read any more. Besides, she didn't need to. She had already found out more than she had intended to. Pitman killed her father, and his sons were the bridge robbers.

"Oh, dear God...," Kelly mumbled as she began to tremble all over. The night of her parents' death came rushing back to her as though she were being swept away by a tidal wave. She was a six-year-old girl again, and she was hiding under the couch. The shots from the bad man's gun rang out just as loudly as if someone were shooting a gun off in the room she was in right now. With every shot, Kelly's body jumped. Then, in a voice as clear as if her father was right in the room with her, she heard him scream, "No, Pitman!"

By this time, Kelly was trembling so violently that she found herself clinging to the table for support. "Oh, God," Kelly whispered in prayer, "it was Pitman. Pitman killed my parents."

As quickly as Kelly had said those words, other words struck her with such force that she jolted right out of her chair. Baily's haunting words from long ago came back to her. "Don't tell anyone that you've seen him."

Baily had said urgently to her, in a voice filled with panic, "You are the only witness, Kelly, and the bad man will come after you."

Kelly dropped her head to the table and sobbed. It was all too awful, and just too much to bear. Kelly had always known that her father had been killed for revenge...but now, she not only knew why, she knew who did it.

Kelly stood stiffly, and dropped the files back into the box. In a mechanical walk, she placed the box back onto the shelf. She called to Copper, and then quickly exited the police station. She was still shaking so badly that she could hardly shift through the Celica's gears.

One question kept persistently repeating itself loudly in her mind: Now that she knew... what was she going to do about it? What? What? What?

Kelly stumbled into Gram's house, found her way upstairs, and threw her trembling body across her bed. She quickly curled up in a ball and held herself, slowly rocking her body back and forth. Tears streamed down her face like a raging river. After all these years, she finally knew. "Now," she thought, as she squeezed her arms around her legs even tighter, "what am I going to do?"

Nine

Kelly was living through her nightmare again. She was screaming. Screaming loudly. The bad man had just shot her parents to death, and now he was coming after her. He saw her under the couch and fiercely yanked her out. He shot her again and again. Kelly couldn't stop screaming.

The bad man with the gun finally had a face. Kelly saw his face clearly now. She could now remember every detail of his livid face. It was the vengeful face of George A. Pitman.

"Kelly!" Mark said shaking her. "Kelly, wake up! You're having a bad dream!"

Mark's arms were around Kelly, and she fought with him as though she were fighting with Pitman himself. "Kelly!" Mark said, trying to make eye contact with her, "It's Mark."

Kelly immediately stopped struggling, and looked up at Mark with a completely confused expression on her face. Then, in a soft, grateful word, she whispered, "Mark..."

Kelly felt her body drop against Mark's chest. Even though she stopped struggling against him, she couldn't seem to control her trembling. Mark's loving arms engulfed her, pulling her close to him in a protective way.

"It's all right, Kelly. You're going to be all right." Mark kept up a steady flow of soft but reassuring conversation.

Then the tears came. Kelly wept openly in Mark's safe arms. Torrents and torrents of tears rushed out of her. She couldn't have stopped them even if she had tried.

After about fifteen minutes, the tears did subside, but the shaking didn't. Kelly was shaking so hard that she thought she was going to fall apart. "Cold," Kelly said to Mark through her chattering teeth. "I'm so cold."

Gram, who was standing by Kelly's side, quickly slipped Kelly's sneakers off. "Honey," Gram said tenderly, "Mark and I are going to tuck you into bed." Kelly nodded, vaguely aware that she was still wearing her tee shirt and jeans.

Mark sat on the side of her bed, gently stroking her head. "I stopped by on my way home to see how you were doing," he said looking at Kelly tenderly. "I'm glad that I did."

"Thank you," Kelly said softly.

"Kelly," Mark said in a concerned voice, "that was an awful dream. Do you want to talk about it?"

Kelly firmly shook her head, "No."

Gram's worried voice broke through the silence. "Kelly has been having horrible nightmares, several times a week, since her parents died." Gram paused, and then said in an anxious voice, "This was one of her worst."

Kelly closed her eyes tightly at the truth of her Grandmother's words. It had been one of the worst nightmares she had ever had.

"Kelly," Mark said in a pleading voice, "you don't have to carry this burden alone. Let me help you."

"No," Kelly said quietly, but adamantly. Tears began to puddle in her blue eyes again. "I'm sorry, Mark. I just can't talk about it."

Kelly felt so frustrated at that moment. How could she ever make him understand...she had enough trouble understanding everything her-self. She had to sort things out in her own head first, before she went to Mark.

When Kelly turned to look up at Mark, the first thing she noticed was that he had tears in his own eyes. "Kelly," Mark said tenderly, "I wish that you'd trust me enough to let me help you. You can't live your life like an island."

"Oh, Mark," Kelly said in a pained voice, "I don't think anyone can help me. I'm not even sure I can help myself."

"Let me help you!" Mark said in an earnest voice, begging her with all his might.

Kelly simply shook her head.

A look of pure frustration covered Mark's face. Then, in an ultra-calm voice, he said slow-ly, "This conversation between us isn't finished. It's just postponed for a while." When Kelly started to protest, he put a single finger across her lips gently. "Sweetheart," he said lovingly, but firmly, "if our relationship is going to con-tinue to grow, you're going to have to deal straight with me. If we aren't honest with each other, about everything, then what have we got?" Mark paused, and then took a deep breath. "I want things to work out between us Kelly...more than I've wanted anything in my life." He paused again, and than said in an earnest voice, "Give me a chance, Kelly...give *us* a chance."

Ten

Mark continued to pester Kelly relentlessly about the dreams she had been having. He wanted her to discuss them with him, and she soon learned that Chief Mark Mitchell didn't take no for an answer. The next week, she found that Mark shadowed her so much that by the time the Summer Carnival arrived at the end of the week, Kelly was at an all-time-high of impatience with the man.

Rand and Kelly were on patrol duty at the carnival, and they talked freely as they casually strolled the festive area. "What's eating you, Kel?" Rand asked in a low voice. "You seem to be wound up tighter than a knot."

Kelly sighed heavily. Rand had been a good friend for years, and she knew that he was honestly concerned. "Oh, Rand," she said in a frustrated voice, "I had a bad dream the other night," Kelly said arching her eyebrows at him, "and I don't want to talk about it..."

Rand smirked at her, and laughed loudly. "I didn't think you would...." He knew Kelly well.

"Anyway, Mark has been on my case to talk about it."

"And," Rand said in a dramatic voice, "let me guess, you don't want to talk about it. Am I right?'

"Yes, Rand, you're right. It's none of his business," Kelly said angrily. "But you know the Chief, when he wants in on something, he doesn't stop."

"Kel," Rand said kindly, "Mark is concerned about you, and, frankly, so am I."

"Oh, Rand, "Kelly said, becoming defensive, "not you, too. I can't handle both of you ganging up on me at the same time."

Just then, a booming voice broke through their conversation.

"Officer Douglas, come over here and give this your best shot."

Kelly looked over to find Mark yelling at her from his seat at the dunking booth. Kelly's eyes narrowed menacingly.

"Oh, never mind, Douglas," Mark said in a confident tone. "No one's been able to dunk me yet. I'm sure your luck wouldn't be any better." He was almost obnoxious in his challenge. "No one seems to know how to throw a ball around here." He was obviously baiting Kelly.

"I'm sorry, Chief," Kelly replied evenly, "but I'm on duty." She quickly began walking away from him.

"I'll make an exception in your case," he said smiling charmingly at her. "This is for charity, you know."

"This is your chance for revenge, Kelly," Rand said in a quiet voice. "The man is practically begging to be dunked." Then in a low chuckling tone, Rand encouraged Kelly. "Go for it, Partner. You may never get another opportunity like this as long as you live."

"You're right!" Kelly said firmly as she walked up to the dunking booth.

Lauren Curtis, an officer from the department, greeted her. "Kelly," she said in a determined tone, "I hope you sink the Chief good. He's been up there for almost an hour, and no one's been able to dunk him. He can be so obnoxious."

Kelly smiled at Lauren. "Tell me about it…"

Kelly looked up at Mark with a competitive smile confidently planted on her face. "Ready to take a swim, Boss?"

"Yeah, right, Douglas…you'll never be able to dunk me. You probably couldn't hit the broad side of a barn!"

Kelly's response to his taunt was to step up behind the line. She picked up her first softball, and fired it at the target, hitting the bulls-eye dead center. Mark went down with a loud splash, and Kelly smiled victoriously.

"Way to go, Partner!" Rand said patting Kelly encouragingly on the back. "Now, do it two more times," he instructed her intently.

"Lucky shot, Douglas…," Mark yelled at her arrogantly. My…," Before Mark could finish his line, Kelly had him in the water again. This time her smile was a mile wide.

"Hey, Boss," Kelly said between chuckles, "you want me to throw some floaties in there for you?" Kelly thought that revenge never tasted sweeter. After all of Mark's badgering this week, sinking him in the drink was very satisfying.

"No. No floaties, Douglas," Mark said climbing back onto the bench.

"You'll never hit the target three times."

Boom! Kelly had him swimming in the water again. As Kelly watched him bobbing in the tank, she waved at him triumphantly, before she and Rand continued their patrol.

"That was quite satisfying!" Kelly said grinning from ear to ear at her partner. "What an excellent way to relieve stress!" Kelly and Rand both laughed.

As Rand glanced down at his watch, he said in a serious tone, "I'd give it about two minutes."

"What?" Kelly asked looking at him curiously.

"I'd give Mark about two minutes before he starts to chase you down. You know he's going to come after you, don't you?" Rand said laughing.

Kelly laughed, too. "That's OK, Rand. Any retribution he might give me was totally worth what I got to do to him. I savored each dunk!"

"Red Alert!" Rand said quickly. "Enemy approaching at two o'clock."

Kelly turned to see Mark heading her way at a quick, determined pace. He was dry now, dressed in a tee shirt and jean shorts.

"Where did you learn to throw like that?" he asked, smiling at her proudly.

"Well," Kelly said wiggling her eyebrows at him playfully, "I am Vermont's number one sharpshooter." Kelly grinned at him victoriously.

"Yeah, you go ahead and smile," Mark said narrowing his eyes at her. "I'll think of some way to get you back." He quickly winked at her.

"Is that a threat, Boss?" Kelly asked laughing.

"You can laugh all you want, Missy," Mark said crossing his arms tightly. "And no, it's not a threat...it's a promise!"

"Oooh!" Kelly and Rand said in unison.

"Hey, Rand," Mark said lightly, "you mind letting me steal your partner for a few minutes?"

"Sure, Boss," Rand said quickly, and started walking away.

"Oh, I get it," Kelly said in a teasing voice, "you're trying to take away my back-up, so you can take me out easier."

"Sweetheart," Mark said in a flirtatious voice, "trust me when I say that all the back up in the world could not keep me away from you!"

"Ooh...," Kelly said studying Mark wide-eyed, "that sounds interesting."

"It will be. I promise." He winked at her quickly. "Are we still on for tonight?"

"I'm off in fifteen minutes," Kelly said smiling at him.

"I need to head back to the station quickly. How about if I pick you up in forty minutes?"

"Sounds great," Kelly said smiling at him. "I'll be ready."

"Oh yeah," Mark added quickly, "wear your swimsuit."

"Swimsuit?" Kelly said in surprise.

"You promised to take me swimming at Tim's Path Bridge. If we don't do it soon, it will be too cold."

Kelly laughed. "So I did...OK. I'll be in my suit, and waiting for you."

Eleven

Kelly sat on the riverbank, under Tim's Path Bridge, and laughed at Mark's Tarzan impersonations as he swung across the river. "What a big mouth you have!" she said quickly as he swung by.

Mark only laughed, and yodeled louder. Finally, he let go of the rope, making a big splash into the river.

"Mark Mitchell," Kelly said in a teasing tone, "you are such an exhibitionist! You shouldn't have joined the police force, you should have joined the circus!"

Mark laughed, and sent a spray of water flying her way. "Come on in, Kelly! This is a blast!"

Kelly jumped on the rope, and swung quickly past Mark. She stayed on the rope, swinging back and forth in front of Mark for so long, that he finally shouted at her in exasperation. "Kelly, if you swing by me one more time, I'm pulling you off that rope!"

Kelly only laughed loudly. "Don't strain yourself, Boss. You *are* ten years older!"

"That's it!" Mark said determinedly. As he tried to reach up and snag the rope, Kelly quickly let go of it, plunging into the water.

When she popped up, she discovered that she was under a well-planned water attack. "OK, Wise Girl, now you've had it!" Mark said in a growling voice.

Kelly knew that she couldn't out-power Mark in a water fight, so she did the next best thing. She swam underwater, so that he couldn't find her. Their game went on for another ten minutes before Mark caught her foot.

"Oh, look what I have here!" he said triumphantly." Are you ticklish, Kel? Well...let's see."

Kelly broke out into instant giggles, but managed to threaten Mark enough so that he let go of her foot. She swam over to him, and said in a serious voice, "For future reference, I absolutely hate to be tickled. And, if you try to tickle me again, I shall have to resort to nasty tactics."

"Oh yeah, sweet Kelly,...just what could you do?" Mark asked moving toward her in a flirtatious way.

"Any number of things," Kelly replied evenly, with her hands thrown on her hips defensively. "My personal favorite is spiking the food. Do you know that there's stuff that you can put on someone's food that will keep him in the bathroom for days?"

Mark's eyes bugged out. "That's terrible!" he said in an appalled voice.

"Oh yeah," Kelly said narrowing her eyes at him, "and, did I ever mention that I'm an incredible shot with a paint gun? I have a special gun that can shoot from over five hundred feet away. You'll never know where I might be lurking...," she said raising her eyebrows at him.

"That's awful, too!" Mark said heading for his towel. "I don't think that I want to play with you any more, Kelly Douglas."

Kelly roared with laughter. "Just don't tickle me, and you should be fairly safe."

"That doesn't sound very comforting, Kelly. If I get plopped in the back with a blob of paint from your paint gun, you're going to be in big trouble, Young Lady."

Kelly grabbed her towel and stood next to him. "Oh, Mark," she said seriously, as she touched his arm, "I'd never shoot you in the back. I'd shoot you in the front, so you can see my smiling face."

"That's it!" Mark said in an aggravated tone. He quickly scooped Kelly up in his arms, and waded into the river, tossing her in.

Kelly came up laughing.

"You're laughing?" Mark said trying to act angry. "You're not supposed to be laughing. I just dumped you in, you're supposed to be mad."

Kelly could only laugh harder. "You can be so funny, Mark! Besides," she said getting solemn again, "I don't mind being tossed in the river, it's tickling that I despise!"

"And believe you me...I'll remember that!" They both laughed good and hard.

"Hey, are you getting hungry?" Mark asked as he watched her swim about.

"No," Kelly said casually. "I'm fine." She swam back and forth in front of Mark, smiling.

She could tell that he was starving, and she was enjoying teasing him.

"Kelly..,." he said in a low, grumbly, warning voice.

"Yes, Mark?" she asked innocently.

"Do you mind coming out? I'm hungry."

"Oh, you're hungry!" she said in a surprised-sounding tone, as she slowly made her way to her towel.

"You know," Mark said grinning at her, "you're about the worst tease that I know."

"Well," she said smiling at him, "I firmly believe that whatever you do, you should do it to the best of your ability."

Mark laughed, but then quickly grew thoughtful. "Oh...is that right?" he said as he slowly walked toward her. He had a mischievous look in his blue eyes that made Kelly instinctively back up.

"Kelly, does that motto apply to everything that you do...?" Mark said grinning at her flirtatiously. "Because, if it does, it just might make things interesting."

Kelly looked him squarely in the eye, with her hands planted firmly on her hips. "Mark

Mitchell," she said in a scolding tone, "just where is your mind?"

Mark continued his advance, completely undaunted by her. "Well, I'll tell you, Miss Kelly Douglas...right now, my mind is on kissing you!"

Kelly couldn't hide her shock, or the small gasp that had escaped from her lips. "I thought you were hungry," Kelly said nervously, backing up some more.

"Not any more," Mark said smiling down at her. "Right now, food is the furthest thing from my mind."

Kelly panicked. She knew that she was falling hard for Mark, but she was afraid that if he kissed her, she'd be a goner. Quickly, she turned and ran up the bank. "Well, I'm suddenly starved," she said trying to justify her flight.

Mark caught up with her, just as she reached the Explorer. He gently took her hand. "Kelly," he said in a concerned voice, "you're afraid to have me kiss you, aren't you?"

"No," Kelly said a little too quickly.

"Yes," Mark said firmly. "You are." He paused for a moment, and then opened her door for her. As Kelly climbed into the passenger seat, Mark smiled tenderly at her.

"You know, Kelly, there's only one way to deal with that. I'll just wait for you to kiss me."

Kelly gasped loudly. "I couldn't!" she said adamantly protesting.

"Yes," Mark said taking her hand, "you could. And," he said touching the tip of her nose lightly, "that way I know I won't be rushing you. And as for me...," he said winking at her playfully, "you can kiss me anytime you want. I'm more than ready!"

Kelly sighed heavily, and Mark laughed softly. "Kelly, you don't have to ever kiss me if you don't want to. But, if you decide to, I'd feel better letting you make the first move. Then I would know for sure that you're ready."

They headed back to Gram's to change, and then drove into town to grab a pizza. After dinner, they strolled hand in hand around the quaint New England town of Sawyer's Crossing. The shops were lit up for the night, and Kelly always felt that this part of town looked like a child's fairy tale book. The brick walks, old fashioned black iron lamp posts, covered bridges and antique brick buildings only added to the fairy-tale illusion.

As they walked across the town green, Mark led Kelly over to the white gazebo. "The stars are coming out," he said gazing up at the sky. "Hey, isn't that the Big Dripper?"

Kelly slapped his shoulder playfully. "And you think that I'm a tease!"

Mark laughed, and then took both her hands in his. "You, my sweet darlin', are definitely a tease!"

Kelly felt gentleness and tenderness in his touch. As she looked up into his eyes, there was no mistaking the love that she saw there. She let her head drop softly against Mark's chest. His arms lovingly cradled her against himself, and Kelly felt so overwhelmingly loved and cherished at that moment. She had never felt that way before in her life.

"Kelly," Mark said softly, "please sit down for a minute. I want to tell you something."

Kelly sat down on the white wooden bench, and watched as Mark put a hand in his pocket. "Close your eyes for a second, Kel, will ya?" When Kelly did, he put a beautiful gold chain in her hands, that had a small gold heart on the end of it.

Kelly stared at her gift in shock. "It's beautiful!" she said looking up at Mark with a bewildered expression. "What's the occasion."

Mark sat down next to her, and said in a tender voice, "Kelly, I wanted to give you something the first time that I told you that I loved you." Kelly's mouth swung open in shock. "I love you, Kelly Douglas. I have never told another girl that before in my life. I love you so very much, Darling."

As Kelly looked into Mark's eyes, she knew it was true. "Can I put this necklace on you, Kel?"

Kelly slowly nodded, and watched as he carefully put the necklace on her. Then he put an arm around her shoulders, and smiled lovingly down at her. "I love you," he said softly, but earnestly.

Kelly took her eyes away from him for a moment, and quickly scanned the town green. When she confirmed that it was empty, she slowly turned her face back to Mark's. As she looked up into his sparkling eyes, and saw all that love looking back at her, she slowly lifted her lips to his, and kissed him gently.

Mark tenderly returned Kelly's kiss, sending his love from her lips all the way down to her toes. The kiss was tender, and made Kelly feel completely cherished.

When they parted, Mark looked back at her, and smiled lovingly. "I'm glad that you kissed me, Kel. I love you so much."

"Mark," Kelly said shyly, in a quiet voice, "I love you too."

Mark put his hands on her shoulders, and searched her face anxiously. He looked like he was going to explode with excitement. "Really, Kelly? Are you sure?" he asked gazing deeply into her big blue eyes.

Kelly smiled and nodded at him. "Yes, Mark. I have loved you for a long time. I was just too afraid to admit it."

"Oh, Kelly," Mark said pulling her close to him, "never, ever be afraid of me. I cherish you like a rare jewel. I love you, Kelly."

Kelly looked up at him and smiled. "I could get used to hearing that from you, Mark Mitchell."

"I hope so, Kelly Douglas, because you'll be hearing it a lot."

Mark slowly lowered his head, and brushed a quick kiss across Kelly's cheek. When he heard her softly sigh, he lowered his head again, letting his lips softly press against hers. This time he kissed his love more passionately.

When Mark slowly lifted his head from Kelly's, she saw a serious Mark Mitchell looking tenderly at her. "I love you, Kelly. I love you so much."

As Kelly rested her head against Mark's shoulder, she could never remember being happier. Mark's love was the best thing that had ever come into her life, and she cherished it with all her heart.

Twelve

"Oh, come on, Rand," Kelly said in a disgusted voice, "let me drive! You always snag the keys before me!"

Rand laughed loudly. "That's because I want to make sure I'm driving! You drive too fast!"

"Rand," Kelly said firmly," I've slowed down a lot."

"Yeah," Rand said in a sarcastic tone, "you've slowed down to about warp speed. My wife made me promise her that I wouldn't let you drive me around. She doesn't want to be a widow." Then Rand laughed loudly. He knew his statement would ruffle Kelly, but there was a lot of truth to it as well.

Kelly's eyes narrowed, and she put her arms across her chest defensively. "That's not true, Rand, and you know it."

"Kelly," Rand said dropping an arm around her shoulders in a brotherly way, "one word of advice for you, my friend. I can pretty much guarantee that even though you're dating the Chief, he isn't going to fix your speeding tickets for you. You'd better learn to slow down."

Kelly quickly pulled away from him. "Rand," she said angrily, placing her hands on her hips, "I have slowed down. And," she said shaking her blonde head angrily, "I'd never ask Mark to fix a ticket for me."

Rand grinned at Kelly obnoxiously. "That's because," he said as he climbed into the driver's seat, "you wouldn't want him to even know about the ticket, Kelly. I know how you think."

"Rand Thompson," Kelly said in a frustrated tone, "you are such a pain sometimes. I don't know how I put up with you!" Kelly got into the cruiser, and buckled herself into the passenger side.

Rand laughed loudly as he glanced at his partner. A few minutes later, as Rand slowly drove through town, he turned to his partner with a serious expression on his face. "So, Kel," he asked in a concerned tone, "how are you doing?"

When Rand Thompson asked you how you were doing, he didn't mean it in a casual, empty-greeting-type way. He meant, how are you honestly doing? How's your heart? Kelly smiled over at her big bear of a friend and partner kindly. "I'm getting there, Rand." Kelly said slowly. "I feel like, for the first time in nineteen years, I'm starting to come back." Kelly paused, and then sighed heavily. "I feel like I'm starting to come back to life again, and to God."

"That's great!" Rand said sincerely. "Becca and I have been praying for you."

"Thanks, Rand," Kelly said eyeing her partner warmly. "I finally feel like I'm going to be OK."

"You will, Kelly,." Rand said in a confident voice. "And turning back to God is the best place to start."

Kelly nodded in agreement. "You know, for so many years, I ran from God. I blamed my parents' death on Him. Now," Kelly said pausing, as she ran her hand through her straight blonde hair, "I realize that the blame lies on the crazy man that shot my parents, and not on God."

"True," Rand said seriously.

"But," Kelly continued, in a painful, confused voice, "I don't think I'll ever be able to understand why God didn't prevent their deaths. That's a part of it...that I just have to let go. I know it will never make any sense to me."

Rand was quiet for a moment, and then said in a solemn voice, "Life can be awfully cruel at times, Kelly, and just downright confusing. Sometimes it can be very hard to make sense of things. Sometimes," Rand said glancing quickly at Kelly, "it's almost better if we don't try to make sense of it. I don't know why God allowed your parents to die, Kel. But, I do know, from experience, that God is good. That's the part that I choose to concentrate on, Kel. God is good."

"I'm starting to see that, Rand," Kelly said in an honest, understanding voice. "Thanks for being such a great friend."

"Anytime, Kel. You know that Becca and I are both here for you anytime."

As Rand rounded the corner of the red-and-white covered bridge that everyone referred to as the "Candy Cane" Bridge, Kelly spotted him immediately. "Oh no, Rand, would you look at A.J.?" Kelly said in a voice that instantly held great alarm. "I've told him a million times not to sit on the guard rail like that. One of these times he's going to fall in the river."

"Do you want me to pull over when we get to the other side of the bridge?"

"Yeah, Rand, would you?"

Kelly instantly became alarmed when they exited the bridge and A.J. was nowhere in sight. "Where is he?" Kelly asked as she quickly whipped the car door open.

Kelly instinctively looked down toward the fast, raging river, and spotted A.J.'s blonde head bobbing along. "Oh, dear God, help us."

Kelly quickly unbuckled her gun belt, and tossed it into the cruiser. "Rand," she called to him, as she scrambled down the steep bank," call the medics, and meet me at Slater's Crossing. If you see us pass under the bridge, drive down to Henry's Bridge. I've got to get to him before he hits the falls at Brides Bridge."

Kelly threw herself into the cold October waters. The river swept her up immediately, and she fought to maintain control against the strong current. The water was moving so fast that Kelly was being slammed against the river rocks as though a boxer were throwing direct punches at her.

Kelly could already feel her body going numb, so she decided to swim, the best she could, with the current. It would be the fastest way to reach A.J.

Kelly could hear A.J.'s frightened voice calling her name. He had spotted her, and he was waving his arms frantically for help. Every now and then, the small boy would disappear under the water, only to resurface again screaming agonizing, frightful cries.

"A.J.," Kelly shouted to him over the noise of the roaring river, "try to grab onto a rock."

"I can't! I can't get one!" He was so panicked that Kelly didn't think he could do much of anything but be swept away, at the mercy of the river.

Kelly was closing the distance between herself and A.J., but not fast enough. As they passed under Slater's Bridge, Kelly could see Rand and another patrol car take off for Henry's Bridge.

"Oh, God, please protect A.J. Don't let him crack his head open on a rock. Watch over him, Father, and help me reach him."

Kelly aggressively picked up her pace in a quieter part of the river. She got close enough to A.J, so that she was able to lunge toward him. Kelly grabbed his left foot, and hung on. Soon, the current pulled them apart again, and Kelly was left holding A.J.'s sneaker.

"Hey, my shoe!" A.J. said in an upset voice. "My shoe came off."

"Don't worry about your shoe, A.J.," Kelly said trying not to sound too impatient. The kid's life was in danger, and he was worried about his shoe! Kelly prayed for patience, and a level head. She knew A.J. didn't understand the danger he was in, and she really didn't want him to understand now. That would only make the boy more panicked.

"My Mom's going to be mad!" A.J. said immediately protesting.

"No kidding, A.J.," Kelly thought to herself, "your Mom's going to be furious that you fell into the river." Instead, Kelly said in a calm, reassuring voice, "A.J., I'll buy you another pair of sneakers. Don't worry."

"Ouch!" A.J. suddenly screamed. "My arm! I hurt my arm."

Kelly had watched helplessly as the boy was slammed against a river boulder. From watching the force of the accident, Kelly was pretty sure that A.J.'s left arm was broken.

"Please, God, anything but his head," Kelly prayed urgently.

The good thing about A.J. colliding with the rock was that it slowed him down enough for Kelly to grab him. She wrapped her arms tightly around his chest, placing his back against her chest.

"Hang on, Buddy," she shouted at him, "the river is going to give us a ride again."

"My arm!" A.J. yelled. "It hurts!"

"I know, A.J., I'll look at it as soon as we get out of the river."

"I want to get out now, Kelly," A.J. said in an adamant tone that clearly showed Kelly that he didn't have a clue as to the mess they were in.

"I'm trying, Pal," Kelly said keeping her tone confident, "but it's not that easy."

Kelly's heart sank as they passed under Henry's Bridge. She knew that from this point on, the river would only run quicker, with more rapids and more rocks in their path.

Kelly suddenly heard a blood-chilling scream. It took her several moments to realize that the voice was her own. The pain in her left side was so severe, that she couldn't breathe. She and A.J. had been thrown into a large boulder. She had taken the brunt of the crash, and A.J.'s frightened face turned slightly to stare at her.

"Kelly, your face has blood on it," A.J. said in a scared voice.

Before she could comment, the current grabbed them, and took them off again. Kelly shifted A.J.'s weight to her right side. The way that her left side was screaming at her, she was fairly confident that she'd cracked or broken some ribs.

"A.J.," Kelly shouted to him, "we're going through some quick-moving rapids in a minute. Anytime that you get your head above the water, grab all the air that you can. When we're under water, keep your mouth closed."

A.J. nodded slightly, and Kelly prayed that he could follow through. As it turned out, A.J. fared the rapids better than Kelly. As she fought with the water, trying to steer A.J. around the rocks she could see, her own body took a beating as she took direct hit after direct hit from one rock after another.

As Kelly tried to grab onto each passing rock, she failed to maintain a hold on them, and only succeeded in ripping the skin off her hands. She knew that her left side was a mess.

As they rounded a bend in the river, Kelly saw her worst nightmare approaching. Brides Bridge. On the other side of the bridge, was a twenty-foot waterfall. At the bottom of the falls, were a series of sharp, large boulders. Kelly knew that if they went over the falls, the rocks below would probably kill them.

With all the renewed strength of a person staring death in the face, Kelly began to aggressively, almost violently, kick toward the riverbank. Every time that she got a foot closer, the river always succeeded in pulling her back to the center. The grip the water had on her was too controlling and powerful for her.

Then, an idea struck Kelly. As she saw the center of the bridge rapidly approaching, she knew that her only hope would be to aim for the center pillar, and cling to it. Kelly tried to jockey her position, to put her body between the concrete pillar and A.J. A moment later, they slammed into the pillar. The force was so great, that Kelly was afraid that she was going to black out. She let out another loud scream, as pain knifed through her left side.

"Kelly," she heard a voice yell to her from the roof of the bridge. She looked up to see Lauren Curtis lowering a harness with a rope attached to it.

"Get this on A.J. The guys are going to pull him ashore."

Kelly nodded, as she mechanically fastened A.J. into the harness. She was continually fighting waves of nausea and dizziness. Her eyes struggled to focus, and she fought with her mind not to let her body black out. When A.J. was secure, she yelled back to the team, and they began to pull the boy to shore.

Kelly was immensely relieved to be able to release A.J. She climbed up onto the pillar's base, and dropped her hurt, exhausted body onto the six-foot section. She was in so much pain that she couldn't seem to think straight. So many areas of her body were screaming out to her in agony. A moment later, the darkness closed in around her again and she passed out.

"Chief!" Lauren Curtis yelled back to the shore team, "Kelly just passed out!"

Mark grabbed the rope and harness, and scaled the side of the bridge quickly. "Rand," Mark said urgently, as he tossed him the other end of the rope, "tie this around your waist. You guys are going to pull Kelly and me in."

Mark slid into the harness, and slowly climbed down the side of the bridge. As he reached Kelly, he undid the harness, and fastened her into it.

"Pain...," Kelly mumbled.

"I know, Sweetheart," Mark said in a sympathetic voice, "but you've got to hold on for a few more minutes."

Then Mark carefully lifted Kelly, and put both his arms firmly around her waist. As he signaled to the shore team, they slowly began pulling them to shore.

Kelly's ribs screamed at her every time the rope jerked forward. "Hang on, Kelly...," Mark said trying to sound confident. Yet every time she screamed, he felt as though someone had thrust a knife into his heart.

Kelly passed out again, and didn't wake up until she was in the ambulance. As she slowly openly her eyes, the first thing she saw was a very wet Mark Mitchell hovering over her.

"How are you?" he asked her anxiously.

"A.J.?" Kelly mumbled.

"He's on his way to the hospital," Mark said quickly, understanding Kelly's need to know how the small boy was. "Besides being scraped up, and having a broken arm, I think he's going to be OK."

Mark smoothed Kelly's wet hair out of her face, and then asked, as he studied her face closely, "How are you?"

"I think I broke some ribs...," Kelly said wincing in pain. "And my left arm...." Kelly made the mistake of trying to turn slightly to get a better look at her arm. She screamed as pain ripped through her beaten-up body again.

Mark's eyes filled with tears, as he gently said to her, "Yeah, your left side is pretty banged up." Mark squeezed Kelly's hand tenderly, and when she looked up at him, he said in a choked-up voice, "Kel, you saved the boy's life. He never would have survived the ride without you." Mark leaned forward, and gently pressed his lips to Kelly's forehead. "You saved A.J., Kelly. I'm so proud of you. "

Kelly smiled weakly at him. "I love A.J., Mark. He's my buddy."

Mark smiled at Kelly understandingly. The bond between A.J. and Kelly was special. "I know, Kel. I love that boy, too."

When they arrived at the hospital, Gram was waiting for Kelly with a bundle of dry clothes. As she hovered worriedly over her granddaughter, like a mother hen, she said to Mark in a commanding tone, "You'd better get changed too, Mark, or you'll get sick."

"I will," Mark promised, smiling at the firm expression on Gram's face. Right now, it was Chief Gram that was in command, and not Chief Mitchell. "Rand is bringing me a change of clothes," Mark replied compliantly.

By the end of the morning, the verdict on Kelly was in. She had broken three ribs, her left arm in two places, gotten a gash in her forehead that required twenty stitches, and was basically one solid bruise on the left side.

"Man, Kelly," Mark said shaking his head at the sight of her, "you never do anything half-heartedly, do you?"

"No, she never does," Gram answered for her in a slightly heated tone. "Kelly plows her way right through life, leaving me to pick up her broken pieces."

Kelly just laughed quietly at Gram's statement. She knew that Gram was annoyed with her. Gram never got upset at Kelly until the crisis was over and the old woman knew that Kelly was going to be all right.

"Can you give me a ride home, Mark?" Kelly asked, trying to change the subject. "I'm already feeling out of it from the pain pills."

Mark firmly wrapped an arm around Kelly's waist, and held her uninjured arm securely. Then he carefully helped the nurse get her into a wheelchair.

"I'm not going to pass out again, Mark," Kelly said trying to sound sure of it herself.

"I'm not convinced, Sweetheart," he said in a tone that clearly left no room for discussion. "You look as white as a sheet."

"I'm fine," Kelly protested weakly.

"Listen, Kelly," Mark said sounding like the commanding Chief Mitchell again, "the only way I managed to get you released from the hospital early was to promise your doctors that I'd personally take care of you. And," Mark stated firmly, as he turned Kelly's face toward his, "that's exactly what I intend to do. Now, no arguments from you. Understood?"

As Kelly glared back into Mark's burning blue eyes, she wished she were spending the night in the hospital. The nurses here were far less pushy and bossy than Mark. She could tell that Mark was going to be a pain about taking care of her, and she knew she wasn't going to have any choice about it. Gram would be just as bad.

Mark drove Kelly home and helped her get settled on the couch. She watched as he began to spread out a pile of things on the dining room table.

"What are you doing?" Kelly asked him curiously.

Mark laughed. "I'm setting up camp here."

"Mark," Kelly said protesting, "I don't need a baby sitter! And," she said narrowing her groggy eyes at him, "you're needed back at the office."

Mark came over, and knelt beside the couch. "Kelly, I'm not baby-sitting you. I'm keeping you company."

"It's the same thing!" Kelly said in an irritated voice.

Mark quietly laughed. "Besides, I promised Gram, and your doctors, that I'd take care of you. Remember? "

Kelly shut her eyes and groaned. Even to her medicated brain, his words did sound familiar, but they also sounded like it was going to be torture for her. She liked taking care of others, but never made a good patient herself.

"So," Mark said raising his eyebrows at her, "I'm moving my office here for the day. I have three cell phones, my lap top computer, and a ton of paper work that should keep me busy for at least three months!"

"Three months!" Kelly said looking at him in shock. "I'm going to charge you rent!"

Mark laughed loudly. "Even when you're in pain, you're still funny! And, as for the rent situation," he said slowly lowering his head to kiss her gently, "I'll pay anything you ask."

Kelly smiled. "This could be interesting. Now, let's see...there's wood that needs chopping in the back, leaves that need raking, and my car needs an oil change."

"You're a slave driver!" Mark said in mock disgust.

Then, growing quiet, he said compassionately, "You try to get some rest, and I'll try not to let the pitiful sight of you distract me. Then maybe I can get some work done."

"Pitiful sight!" Kelly said slightly alarmed.

"Kelly," Mark said gently, "You haven't been by a mirror lately, have you?" Kelly shook her head no. "Good. Then don't take a look in one for about a week. By that time, the bruises should have faded some."

"That bad, huh?" Kelly asked eyeing Mark intently.

Mark walked over to the couch, and knelt next to her again. "Kelly, you are one lucky girl. God definitely had his hand on you. All you needed to do was hit your head on one of those rocks...," Mark's face turned away from her for a moment. "I was so afraid for you..."

When Mark turned back to look at Kelly, his deep blue eyes were brimming with tears. "I never prayed so hard in all my life." He leaned over and softly kissed Kelly on her forehead, and then slowly went over to his makeshift office.

Kelly watched him for a few minutes before she drifted off to sleep. Soon Kelly began to dream. Her mind brought her back to a time she had been at Riverside Park with her parents. They were such a happy family. Kelly clearly remembered the love that her parents had for each other and for her. Her mind blanketed her in the special warm memories. Then, without warning, her mind shifted gears on her, and she was under the couch again, hiding. For the millionth time, she was watching the bad man shoot her parents. Ever since she had discovered the name Pitman, her dreams always included George Pitman's menacing face.

Her mind shifted gears again, and she was an adult. It was dark, and she was in the forest, and Pitman was chasing her. Kelly could feel the earth pound from his heavy footsteps as he pursued her. As always, she recognized that voice. That steel-cold, hard, angry voice. Kelly had never heard a voice like that in her life. It was so void of everything good. Evil was the only thing that she could hear in it. Simply pure evil.

Just as Pitman's big hands grabbed the back of Kelly's neck, she screamed. Kelly couldn't seem to stop screaming. She knew she was only moments away from death. Kelly was desperately trying to get away, but he held her firmly.

"Kelly!" Mark said urgently, as he shook her gently. "Kelly, wake up. You're having another nightmare."

Kelly opened her eyes to find Mark hovering over her, with a concerned expression covering his face. Kelly closed her eyes as he tenderly held her. Her trembling was so violent that it made her broken ribs and arm hurt. "How long, oh Lord?" Kelly prayed silently. "How long will I continue to have these awful nightmares?"

"Kelly," Mark said gently, as he wiped her tears away, "I wish you'd let me help you."

Kelly firmly shook her head no. She feared Pitman, and continued to hold to Baily's warning about him.

Mark sighed heavily. "This is about your parents' death, isn't it?"

Kelly barely nodded.

"Is Pitman somehow connected to your parents death?" Mark asked in a even voice, as he studied her reaction carefully.

"Why would you say that?" Kelly asked in shock.

"Because," Mark said in a determined voice, "while you were dreaming, you shouted, 'No Pitman!'" Mark said gently, holding her shoulders.

Kelly closed her eyes, and sunk back against the couch. Suddenly, it was all too clear to her. This awful nightmare that she was having wasn't a nightmare at all. It was a terrible reality that Kelly didn't want to deal with. At that moment, Kelly knew there was no more putting off the inevitable. She would have to face Pitman straight on, because if she didn't, the nightmare alone would haunt her for the rest of her life.

As she opened her eyes, Mark was still staring at her intently. Too intently, Kelly thought quickly. She knew Mark was trying to read her mind.

"It's all connected, isn't it?" Mark said in a confident tone, as though he had things all figured out.

"Mark," Kelly said in a strong voice, "stay out of it!"

"Kelly," Mark said leaning closer to her, "I can't."

"It's not your problem," Kelly said insistently.

"Kelly," Mark said in a firm, but loving tone. "You're wrong, Sweetheart. It is my problem," Mark continued, looking at her with such intensity that it almost frightened her. "It is my problem, Kelly, whether I want it to be or not, because I love you."

Thirteen

Several weeks later, Kelly stormed into Chief Mark Mitchell's office waving a newspaper in her hands. "What is all this about?" she said in a tone that clearly indicated she wasn't happy.

"You're being decorated for saving A.J.'s life," Mark said proudly.

"Mark, I don't want the attention drawn to myself," Kelly said angrily.

"Kelly, the town is very grateful that you saved the boy's life. It's normal that they would want to thank you."

"Yeah, but at a ceremony on the town green?" Kelly said sounding completely exasperated.

"Kelly," Mark said studying her carefully, "awards are always presented at some sort of ceremony. No one's trying to make you feel uncomfortable. The town just wants to thank you."

"Yeah, well, I can't go," Kelly said adamantly. "You'll have to think of something else, Mark. Give the medal to Rand. He was involved in the rescue, too."

"You're turning down the award?" Mark gasped in shock.

"Listen, Mark," Kelly said in a frustrated voice, "I can't make it."

"But everything's already scheduled," Mark said narrowing his eyes disapprovingly at Kelly. "It's already been put in the paper."

"Yeah," Kelly said angrily, "and who gave you the right to give the paper my life story?"

"Kelly," Mark said taking a step closer to her, "what exactly is going on here?"

"Mark, I hate publicity. And," Kelly said pointing a finger at him, "why on earth did you have to bring my father up?" Mark just eyed Kelly suspiciously. "I can't go," she insisted.

As Kelly turned to go, Mark quickly reached out and grabbed her wrist. In a lightening quick move, he grabbed his handcuffs out of his back pocket, and handcuffed Kelly to himself.

"Hey!" Kelly yelled angrily. When Mark simply looked at her with an amused expression, Kelly exploded. "Mark Mitchell, you remove these handcuffs immediately. This is not funny!"

"I agree with you Kelly," Mark said, casually lifting his wrist to check the cuffs' locks. "This is definitely not funny. It's more dangerous, I'd say."

"Remove these!" Kelly ordered him in a low, grumbly voice.

"No," he said flatly, with just the hint of amusement in his eye.

As Kelly started trying to wriggle her wrist free, Mark laughed loudly. "You should know better than that, Officer Douglas. The only thing that you'll end up freeing is more skin off your wrist."

Kelly swung around, and stood before Mark angrily. With one arm in a cast, and the other one handcuffed to Mark, she found herself feeling extremely vulnerable. "What is going on here!" Kelly demanded.

"You know," Mark said suddenly growing very serious, "I've been asking myself that question almost from the time we met." Mark paused and looked directly into Kelly's eyes.

"You know, Kel, I'd like to know exactly what is going on."

"What do you mean?" Kelly asked in a confused voice.

"I'll tell you precisely what I mean," Mark said evenly. "Your parents' death...the nightmares...the name Pitman...they're all connected, Kelly."

"I won't talk about it, Mark," Kelly said in a firm tone, and then began to walk away from him. The handcuffs pulled her back instantly.

"Yes," Mark said in a commanding voice, "you will talk about it."

"I can't!" Kelly said feeling trapped. "I promised Bai..." Kelly snapped her mouth shut, but she knew enough damage was already done.

Mark's eyebrows arched up. "Well, now we're beginning to get somewhere, Little Lady. What specifically does Baily have to do with your Code of Silence? Is he in on your big secret too?"

"No!" Kelly replied too quickly. Then, almost as an after thought, she said slowly and carefully. "Listen, Mark, I wouldn't put it that way, exactly."

"Then, Miss Douglas, what way would you put it, exactly?" Mark was glaring at Kelly impatiently, waiting to hear answers from her that she knew she could not give him.

Mark just smiled at Kelly knowingly, and she quickly turned her face away from his penetrating stare. "Kelly," he said in a matter-of-fact voice, "this is no longer Mark Mitchell asking you as a friend. This is Mark Mitchell, asking you as Sawyer's Crossing's Chief of Police. It's not a personal matter anymore, Kelly. It's a professional one."

"And just what do you know about it?" Kelly spat out in an arrogant tone, with a definite challenge in her voice.

"You know something, Kelly. I am going to answer that question...just as soon as Baily gets here," Mark replied in an annoyingly, ultra-calm voice.

Mark started walking toward the phone, but Kelly firmly planted her feet on the ground, jerking his arm back. "Kelly," Mark said with a twinkle in his eye, "it really would be easier if you walked with me, don't you think?"

"I'm not moving!" Kelly said firmly.

Quickly, Mark shot out an arm around Kelly's waist, and hauled her alongside of him. "There's more than one way to make this work, Sweetheart."

Kelly protested loudly, "You put me down this instant!" The ribs that Kelly had broken were complaining loudly at this movement.

"Listen, Kelly," Mark said growing impatient, "I'll make a deal with you. If you cooperate with me..."

"You'll take the cuffs off?" Kelly said quickly, in a hopeful voice.

"No," Mark said in a stern tone, staring directly into Kelly's eyes. "I won't toss you in a cell." The heated, determined intensity which he now leveled on Kelly made her feel so frightened that she could feel her body begin to tremble.

"You wouldn't!" Kelly said in a unbelieving tone.

"Yes, Kelly, I would," Mark said firmly. "That's just where I put all my criminals."

"Criminals!" Kelly yelled indignantly. The fear she had was quickly melting away, and turning into defiant anger.

"Yes, Kelly. You of all people should know that keeping vital information from a police investigation is against the law."

"What are you talking about?" Kelly asked furiously.

"I'll tell you in a minute, Kelly. First I want Baily here."

As Mark phoned Baily, Kelly's mind was scrambling to try to make sense of Mark's accusation. What did he know? And, what could he mean about withholding information. After a few minutes, Kelly felt sure that this was all part of a masterly planned bluff by Chief Mark Mitchell.

As Mark hung up the phone, he said in a casual voice, "Baily will be here in a few minutes. Would you like some coffee?"

"No," Kelly replied angrily.

"You know what?" Mark said in an amused voice, "I would. Walk with me, Kelly."

Reluctantly, Kelly followed Mark across his office to his coffee machine. Kelly watched impatiently as Mark slowly prepared his cup of coffee. Her irritation with him heightened, as he annoyingly clanged his spoon against the side of his cup repeatedly, and then tapped it on the top of his cup three times. Kelly knew he usually went through this routine when he was in deep thought. But, right now, if her free hand wasn't in a cast, she would have taken the spoon from him, and chucked it out the window.

Mark opened a bag from Sawyer's Crossing Bakery, and took out two large peanut butter cookies." I would offer you one of these delicious cookies, Kelly, but I'm afraid I can't. You see, I never offer criminals cookies...only coffee. If I did offer you one of these tasty cookies, I could be accused of partiality, and we both know that we wouldn't want that." His words were dripping with sarcasm, and held absolutely no sincerity in them at all. He was trying to infuriate her, and, to Kelly's regret, he was succeeding mightily.

"I don't want one anyway," Kelly said quietly, through a clenched jaw, narrowing her eyes at him.

"Oh, that's good, Kel. That really eases my conscience," Mark said with just the hint of a smile tugging at his lips.

Mark was enjoying this charade immensely, Kelly thought as she gave him her best scathing glare. If the cuffs were off her right now, she would probably try to kill him. Attempted murder...she thought smiling to herself. Well...then at least he would have a legitimate reason to throw me in jail.

Before Baily finally arrived at Mark's office, Kelly had to sit and watch and listen to Mark consume the two cookies and his coffee.

As Baily walked in casually, Mark stood up, and started going over to greet him. "Kelly, you know that you've got to walk with me here."

Kelly was so angry at Mark right now that she felt like clobbering him. She did walk with him, but only because she knew that if she didn't, Mark would drag her, or worse, scoop her up and carry her. Kelly didn't want to make any more of a scene in front of Baily than they already were making.

"What's with the handcuffs, Mark?" Baily asked eyeing them curiously. "That's no way to treat the recipient of the Medal of Courage Award."

Mark laughed casually. "The funny thing about the medal is," Mark said turning to look directly at Kelly, "that Kelly doesn't want it. Now, can you believe that?"

"She doesn't want it?" Baily said in shock.

"Nope," Mark said in an even-tempered tone," Kelly doesn't want it. Now what do you think of that?"

"I don't understand, Kelly," Baily said looking at her with a confused expression on his face.

Mark continued slowly. "You see, Kelly seems to be a little bit publicity-shy, Baily." He paused to take a loud swallow of his coffee, and then went on. "Uh, did you happen to read this morning's paper?"

"Yes, Mark. As a matter of fact I did. What are you driving at?" Baily said growing impatient with Mark's game.

"Let me tell you two a story," Mark said looking from Baily to Kelly. "And, at the end of the story, you let me know if I'm even close to the mark."

Baily shrugged, looking slightly annoyed, but Kelly glared at Mark angrily.

"Nineteen years ago," Mark began in a professional tone, "a little girl was hiding and saw a man barge into her house and kill her father and mother, and the baby the mother was carrying."

Kelly's eyes grew large, and her face visibly paled. As Baily and Mark watched her reaction, Baily said quietly, "Did you really see him, Kelly?"

When Kelly didn't answer, Mark patted her on the knee, and said quietly, "You don't have to answer that right now, Kelly. Let me finish my story."

"You see," Mark went on seriously, "I believe that Kelly not only saw the entire, awful incident, I'm guessing that her father identified the killer, right before the man shot him. So, I feel that Kelly not only knows what her parents' killer looks like, I believe she also knows his name."

"Is this true?" Baily asked Kelly in horror. "For all these years have you stayed silent?"

As Kelly began to tremble, and the tears started rolling down her face, Mark quickly undid the handcuffs. He put an arm around Kelly tenderly, and said softly, "Kelly, you kept your secret long enough. It's time you let it out."

"Why didn't you say something to me, Kelly?" Baily asked her, groping to understand.

"Baily," Kelly said between sobs, "don't you remember telling a little six-year-old girl to keep a 'Code of Silence'? You told me the night that my parents were murdered that if the killer knew that I saw him, he would come back and murder me."

A loud, painful gasp came out of Baily's mouth, and his eyes grew wide in horror. "Oh, Kelly," Baily said in a tight voice, "those words were the words of a grief-stricken man. I was panicked, and wasn't thinking straight. I never, in all these years, dreamed that you'd actually seen the killer."

Baily slowly walked toward Kelly. "Sweetheart...," Baily said gently, taking Kelly into his arms. "I have let you down in the worst way that I could have. Can you ever forgive me?" He paused, pulled Kelly back to look into her face, and said, "I never thought that you really saw him."

Kelly sobbed in Baily's arms as he held her tenderly. "I'm so sorry, Sweetheart," Baily said lovingly, as he stroked Kelly's blonde hair. "I am so sorry."

After ten minutes, Kelly pulled away from Baily and collapsed in a chair next to Mark. "Have long have you known?" she asked him in a shaky voice.

"All the pieces fell together for me a few days ago," he said quietly. Then, looking at Kelly with a tender, compassionate face, he said, "Do you want to tell us about that night?"

Kelly slowly nodded. "After my Dad came home from work, we were playing Hide-and-Go Seek. It was my turn to hide, so I slide under the couch. I liked that hiding spot because I could see the kitchen well, and watch my parents talking at the kitchen table." Kelly took a deep breath, and then continued. "Not more then five minutes after I hid, a big, angry man came storming through the back door, and into the kitchen. He pointed a pistol right at my father's head. He told my father that since my father had taken away the best years of his life...he was going to take the best years of my father's life away. Right before he shot my father, Dad yelled his name. Then, the man quickly turned to my Mother, and said something about not wanting to leave any witnesses around. Then he shot Mom in the head and in the stomach."

Kelly collapsed against Mark's chest, and sobbed again. He held her trembling body, as she softly said, "Not until several months ago did I remember the man's face or his name. I guess my mind blocked it out all these years."

Mark nodded and hugged her protectively. "Kelly," he said urgently, "what was the name that your father yelled before the man shot him?"

"Pitman," Kelly said trembling again. She was shaking so hard, that she felt as though she might fall to pieces. "He shouted, 'No, Pitman!'" Kelly said in a frightened, but determined voice.

A moment later, Baily said quietly, "Jerry Douglas helped convict George Pitman in a guns and drugs scheme. Jerry knew that Pitman had escaped from prison, but neither of us thought that George would come back to Sawyer."

"Well, he did," Mark said sighing heavily. "Kel, I'm so sorry that I had to drag this out of you. Are you going to be OK?"

Kelly nodded slowly. "You know, it actually feels good not be carrying this alone anymore." She exhaled loudly.

"Then you forgive me, Sweetheart?" Mark said with tears puddling in the corners of his shiny blue eyes.

"Yes, Mark," Kelly said looking him in the eye. "Sometimes it's hard for me to help myself, even when I know the right thing to do. I'm glad that you stepped in." Kelly paused and then sighed loudly. "Now what are we going to do, Boss?"

"It's time that Mr. George Pitman was brought to justice," Mark said in an authoritative tone. "He has haunted you for all these years, Kelly. It's time to bring closure to this case."

Kelly nodded in agreement. "So, where do we start?" she asked anxiously.

Mark smiled at her eagerness. "Well, for starters...I'm shipping you and Gram off to Florida to visit Gram's family. I want you as far away from Vermont as possible."

"I'm not leaving!" Kelly said emphatically.

"Kelly, it's not safe for you here," Mark said in a level tone, begging her with his eyes to understand. "I'm sure Pitman reads the papers, too."

"Mark," Kelly said quickly, "it's not safe for me anywhere. And, since you and I hold the best shooting records in Vermont, I think that it's wise that we stick together."

"I hate to say it...but she's right," Baily said quickly. "She's safer with you, Mark."

It was obvious that this was not part of Mark's plan. "I don't like it," he said quickly, as his face darkened.

"Mark, I don't like any of this," Kelly said angrily. "You can send Gram to visit her family in Florida. That would be a good idea. But I'm not going. I'm staying here with you."

Mark sighed heavily. He knew there would be no convincing Kelly to leave. Running a hand nervously through his hair, he said in a commanding tone, "Kelly, if you're staying with me...then you're staying with me."

As Mark snapped the handcuffs back on their wrists again, he said wearily, as he shook his head at the woman he loved, "Until I figure out exactly what to do with you, I literally mean...that you're staying with me."

Fourteen

"Mark!" Kelly yelled in an exasperated voice, "Stop following me around! You're closer to me than my own shadow!"

Mark just looked at Kelly firmly. "That's exactly what I intend to be Kelly–your shadow! And," Mark said, drilling his heated eyes into her, "until Pitman is caught, you'd better just get used to it."

Kelly rolled her eyes at Mark, and grabbed another peanut butter cookie from the box. "Wasn't it nice," she said waving the cookies slightly toward Mark, "that the Sawyer's Crossing Bakery sent these to me?"

"Very nice," Mark said shuffling some papers around his desk.

"And, you know, Chief," Kelly said in a voice that was obviously void of sincerity, "how much I would truly love to share these with you, but I don't want to be accused of partiality." Kelly

225

smirked mischievously at Mark, as she quoted his own line back to him. "However," she said raising her eyebrows, "I will get you a cup of coffee."

"You're very funny, Kelly," Mark said eyeing her with just a hint of amusement in his blue eyes. "But I'd think that you'd want to treat your bodyguard nicer."

"I don't want a bodyguard!" Kelly said evenly. "I can handle myself just fine."

"You don't have a choice, Kelly," Mark said in his most commanding Chief voice.

As Kelly stared at him, with her hands set impertinently on her hips, she knew that Mark was going to be a pain until this ordeal was over. "Oh well, I guess it wouldn't hurt me to share. Here," Kelly said quickly, "have a cookie." Kelly then broke off half of her cookie, and grudgingly handed it to Mark.

Mark laughed. "Gee, Kelly, you're really too generous."

"You're absolutely right,." Kelly said in a hasty voice, as she grabbed the cookie back from him, and quickly popped it into her mouth.

Mark's mouth swung open in surprise, and Kelly burst out laughing at his reaction. After a moment, she laid the box of cookies on his desk. "Oh, you might as well help yourself."

"Thanks," Mark said eyeing her suspiciously.

Suddenly, Kelly's eyes narrowed. "You know, Mark, I am not going to cooperate with your idea for me to spend the nights in jail."

"It's the safest place for you," Mark said objectively. "This station is more secure than Fort Knox."

"I don't care, Mark! You're completely overreacting about the entire situation."

"I'm not," he said firmly as he crossed his arms.

A moment later, Rand walked in. "Here's another package for the hero," he said sarcastically. "How come no one's sending me gifts?"

Kelly laughed, "Take that one, Rand."

"No," he said as he handed it to her. "It's addressed to Kelly Douglas."

Kelly gave him a pitying smile as she opened the box. As soon as she lifted the cardboard lid, Kelly let out a loud scream. Mark jumped up and grabbed the box from her. As he examined the contents of the box, his face tightened into an angry mask.

"Rand! Get this out of here!" he barked at Kelly's partner.

As Rand took the box from Mark, and looked inside, his face visibly paled. "I'm sorry, Kel," Rand said in a voice that sounded very upset. "I had no idea..." Then, Rand immediately left with the box.

Mark swiftly walked over to where Kelly was standing. "Are you OK, Sweetheart?" he asked, still unable to hide the anger in his voice.

Kelly nodded slightly, but she wasn't OK. At that moment, she felt very far from being OK.

"Sit down, Kelly," Mark said in a gentle, but firm tone.

Kelly nodded, and dropped into a wooden chair.

"I think it's safe to assume that, that nice little gift was from Pitman," Mark said in a tight voice, trying hard to control his anger. He loved Kelly so much, that it infuriated him that anyone would do this to her. The gift box that Kelly had received held three dead rats, with a note that said, "Time to get the one that got away."

"He's really out there," Kelly said, staring out of Mark's large office window.

"Don't be afraid, Kelly. We're going to get him," Mark said in a confident voice, gently taking her hand. As she slowly turned her face to meet his eyes, he said to her in a determined tone, "I promise, Honey. We're going to get him."

"Mark," Kelly said in a strong voice, "I have been running from George Pitman for almost twenty years. I'm sick and tired of running, and I'm sick and tired of being afraid." Kelly paused, and then looked at Mark intently. "I want him brought in, Mark, and I want to help."

Mark took an awkward step away from her. "Kelly," he said in an adamant tone, "you're not going to be in on the team. I refuse to use you as bait for Pitman to be lured in by. It's too dangerous."

"Mark!" Kelly said angrily, "I am the bait, whether I want to be or not. He wants me…," Kelly said throwing a finger back at herself. "No one else, just Jerry Douglas's little daughter. And," Kelly said running a hand through her hair nervously, "he'll wait until I'm in my car alone, or in a dark alley, or corner, or, asleep in my bed…"

Mark grabbed Kelly, and took her into a protective embrace as he saw her tears start to spill out of her fearful eyes. "Kelly," he said looking directly into her frightened face, "that's exactly why I'm shadowing you. I'm not going to let that madman get you. Twenty-four hours a day you'll have protection, and at night you'll sleep in the spare room at the station."

Mark put his hands firmly on Kelly's shoulders. "Kelly, I'm not taking any chances with you. I love you."

Kelly looked up into his strong, determined blue eyes. She knew Mark was right, but, also, she knew it wasn't going to be easy. Kelly dropped her head against Mark's chest, and softly said, "I love you, too, Mark."

The next day, the awards ceremony took place in the local high school gym. As Kelly gazed out over the platform, over a sea of friendly faces, she spotted Gram, Baily, and Mel all sitting together. It made her feel loved, and even cherished. The people of Sawyer's Crossing were like a family to her. So many people loved her and supported her...but, she thought solemnly, it takes only one to ruin your life.

As Kelly scanned the crowd, nervously, she wondered if Pitman was here. Mark had stepped up security for the event, and he felt confident that Pitman wouldn't show. Mark felt sure that Pitman wasn't crazy enough to walk into a room crowded with law enforcement officials. Even so, Kelly found herself trembling slightly.

After Chief Mark Mitchell gave a short speech, he and A.J. presented Kelly with the Medal of Courage Award. As Mark leaned over to pin the award on her uniform, he winked at her quickly. His pride for Kelly was beaming all over his face.

Kelly smiled back at Mark tenderly. Kelly thought Mark looked so handsome and sharp in his formal dress police uniform. His entire presence conveyed bravery, honor, confidence, respect, and pride.

After the ceremony, a light buffet followed in the school cafeteria. As Kelly made her way down the familiar school halls, Gram and A.J. were beside her, and her bodyguards, Mark and Rand, were right behind her.

"I'm going to get something to eat," A.J. said looking up at Kelly excitedly. "Do you want something?"

Kelly shook her head. "No, A.J., you go ahead." As the boy took off for the buffet table, Kelly noticed Mark eyeing her seriously.

"You're not hungry?"

"Mark, my stomach's in knots."

"Do you want to head out?" Mark asked leaning toward her.

"Is it too early for the guest of honor to leave?" Kelly asked uncertainly.

"Let's give it another fifteen minutes," Mark said looking at his watch, "and then we'll head back to the station."

Kelly felt relieved once she was in Mark's squad car, heading back to the station. Yet, to Kelly's surprise, Mark drove right past the station.

"Where are we going?" Kelly asked curiously.

"It's lunch time, and since you didn't eat, I thought I'd take you to lunch," Mark said smiling tenderly at her. "I thought we'd grab some sandwiches, and head over to Stonewall Bridge."

"Oh, Mark," Kelly said perking up, "that would be perfect."

As Mark led Kelly down the path and over to their favorite spot underneath the bridge, he said, as he eyed her carefully, "I hope this nippy November weather isn't going to be too cold for you, Kel."

"Mark!" Kelly said excitedly, "I love this weather. And, bringing me to Stonewall was the best thing you could have done for me today! Thanks!"

Mark smiled, and kissed her quickly. "I love you, Kelly. I'm so sorry that you have to go through all of this. But," he said studying her seriously, "the end is in sight."

"I know, Mark," Kelly said thoughtfully. "That's what gives me the strength to go on."

Mark smiled proudly at Kelly. "You're doing a great job, Honey. You're such a special person. I'm so glad that you're in my life."

Kelly leaned over and kissed his cheek softly. "Thank you, Mark. I'm glad that you're in my life, too."

"Kelly," Mark said with an excitement growing in his voice and eyes, "I wanted to get you a little something to show you how proud I am of you."

As he handed her a small, nicely wrapped box, he said in an emotional voice, "This gift is only a token, Sweetheart. I could never give you a gift that comes close to the gift that you gave A.J."

"Oh, Mark...," Kelly said tearing up, "you didn't have to do this."

"I wanted to, Kel," he said holding her eyes with his own lovingly.

As Kelly opened up the box, she gasped softly when she saw the pearl earrings. "Mark! They're beautiful! Thank you!"

Mark smiled as Kelly wrapped her arms around him. "You are so special to me, Mark Mitchell. Thank you so much!"

"You're welcome, Honey," Mark said lovingly. "I love you so much."

"And I love you," Kelly said looking up into Mark's clouded blue eyes.

Mark leaned down, and gently, yet passionately, kissed the woman that he loved. He loved Kelly so much, he had no doubt that they would spend the rest of their lives together. Never, he thought protectively, as he hugged Kelly, never would he let Pitman harm her. Mark knew, if he had to, that he would sacrifice his own life for hers, without so much as a second thought.

After all, he thought as he smiled at Kelly's rosy cheeks, that's what love is all about. Putting the one that you love before yourself.

As Mark kissed Kelly gently on the cheek, he thought that his heart would explode from all the love that he felt for her. Kelly was a special treasure, and he would risk everything to protect her.

Fifteen

By day, Kelly went on her beat with Rand. And by night, she and Copper slept on a cot in the storage room that Mark had converted into a makeshift bedroom. Kelly drew comfort from having Copper with her. Besides, now that she was living at the station, she didn't want him alone all the time at Gram's farmhouse. The old dog adapted to his new home easily. He provided friendship and added security for Kelly. Mark slept on a cot, right outside Kelly's door. If she exited the room at night, she would have literally had to climb over him. The same would go for anyone entering her room.

As Kelly got ready to turn in one night, she said in a regretful voice, "Mark, I'm so sorry that you have to sleep outside my door on a cot. You're really going above and beyond the call of duty here."

Mark slowly shook his head. "Kelly, I love you too much to have you protected by anyone less then Vermont's number-one sharp-shooter. And," Mark said tossing his eyebrows up playfully, "since that happens to be me, I'm more then happy to assign myself to you."

"Thank you," Kelly said smiling at her protector.

"But," Mark said taking her hand gently, "to be honest with you, it almost drives me crazy knowing the girl I love is sleeping only a few feet away."

"Mark!" Kelly said in a scolding voice.

At the strong tone of Kelly's voice, Copper's tan head swung up and stared at Kelly with a questioning look. Both Mark and Kelly laughed at the dog's curious expression. It was clear that Copper wasn't sure what was going on, and how exactly he should react to the situation.

As Mark patted Copper on his soft head, he said to Kelly tenderly, "I know, Honey, it would be wrong for me to go into your room, unless...we were married." Mark's eyes twinkled merrily at her. "And, there is one way to fix that!"

"Mark!" Kelly said smacking him on the shoulder, "don't even tease about such a thing."

Mark's face grew serious, but his eyes overflowed with love. "Sweetheart, I would never tease about such a thing. But," he said squeezing her hand, "right now is not the time for me to discuss this with you. But," he said playfully tapping the tip of her nose, "once this case is over, you and I are going to have a little talk."

Mark kissed Kelly tenderly, and then said softly, "Good night, Sweetheart. I love you."

Sixteen

Every year, the second week of November, the Sawyer's Crossing Police Department held their "Policeman's Ball." The tickets were sold to the town's people, and all the proceeds went to buy food for those in need.

As Kelly stood in the decorated high school gym listening to the orchestra play, Mark, dressed in his formal Chief's uniform, approached her. "May I have this dance?" he said as he bowed slightly before her.

Kelly smiled at him. "You know, you are the most handsome police chief that I've ever seen."

"Does that mean that you'll dance with me?" he asked wiggling his eyebrows at her.

"No," Kelly said in an amused tone. "I'll dance with you because I love you, Mark Mitchell, not because I think you're dashingly handsome."

"Oh, I'm glad that you're not holding the handsome thing against me," he said teasingly.

Mark took Kelly's hand gently and whirled her onto the dance floor in time with a classical waltz. Kelly felt as though she were Cinderella, living a fairytale dream. Mark's strong arms were around her, and held her protectively and lovingly as he led her around the dance floor. He was a real, live Prince Charming.

"Have I told you tonight how beautiful you look?" Mark asked smiling at her lovingly.

"Not within the last five minutes," Kelly said smiling sweetly up at him.

"You look absolutely beautiful, Darlin'. And, I'm madly in love with you," Mark said in a voice that was straight from his heart.

"Madly in love...," Kelly said repeating his words softly.

"Yes," Mark said in a gentle, but determined voice, "Madly in love, head over heels, totally in love...do you catch my meaning, Sweetheart?"

Kelly laughed softly. "Yes...and I'm nuts about you too!"

After the dance, Kelly and Mark made their way to the refreshment table. Kelly immediately spied A.J., and walked over to him. "Hey, A.J.," she said in a teasing voice, "there you are! You promised me a dance! Don't tell me that you're trying to hide out on me!"

A.J. blushed, and he looked up at Kelly shyly. "I don't know how to dance," he said in a small voice.

"Oh, A.J.," Kelly said putting a loving arm around the boy, "neither do I. Let's just go out there and have some fun!"

A.J. nodded excitedly, then suddenly stopped. "Oh...I forgot. This is for you." A.J. handed Kelly an envelope, which had her name scrawled across it.

"Is this from you?" Kelly asked eyeing the boy curiously.

"No," A.J. said shaking his blonde head. "Some guy gave it to me, and told me to give it to you."

Kelly immediately felt alarmed. "Thanks, Buddy," Kelly said as she instinctively began to scan the room. She had a bad feeling about the envelope, but didn't know if she was being paranoid or not.

As she slowly opened the envelope, she saw that there was a Christmas card inside. The picture was a nice country Christmas scene, but when she opened the card, bold, angry words jumped out at her. "CHRISTMAS IS THE SEASON FOR GIVING, AND I CAN'T WAIT TO GIVE YOU WHAT'S COMING TO YOU! MY APOLOGIES, KELLY, THAT YOU HAD TO WAIT 20 YEARS FOR YOUR GIFT."

Mark, who had been reading the card over Kelly's shoulder, picked up his radio, and called his special unit. "I want this building, inside and outside, checked for Pitman. He was here tonight. Find out if he's still on the premises."

Then Mark turned to Kelly. As he slowly took the card from her hand, he said in a firm voice, "We're going back to the station now."

Kelly nodded, agreeing with Mark completely. As she started walking with Mark towards the door, she suddenly stopped, and spun around.

"Where's A.J.?" she asked in a panicky voice.

Kelly's eyes immediately went back to the refreshment table, but A.J. was nowhere in sight. "Mark, do you see him?" Kelly asked urgently.

Mark shook his head, as he and Kelly quickly walked back to the area. They hastily began asking people around the table if they had seen the boy. Just then, as Kelly thought she was going to burst into tears, Noah Olin, a fellow officer, put a hand on Kelly's shoulder, and then pointed towards the ground. From a curtain covering the sides of the refreshment table, one small blue sneaker could be seen.

Kelly bent down, and instantly pulled the foot out. "A.J.," Kelly said in a voice that held concern and relief, "what are you doing under there?"

"This is my fort, Kelly! Want to come in?" he asked her excitedly.

Kelly grabbed the boy, and held him tightly for a moment. "No, Sweetheart. Not right now. But, I do need to talk to you."

Kelly took A.J. over to the big stage, and sat him down. "A.J.," she said in a serious tone, "do you remember the man who gave you the card for me?"

The small boy nodded his blonde head slowly. It was clear that he didn't understand her concern. "Yes, Kelly," A.J. said, still looking at her oddly. "He was a real big, old man."

"What did his hair look like?"

"It was white," A.J. said quickly.

"His eyes...A.J....what color were his eyes?" Kelly said searching the boy's face for any clues.

"They weren't like yours and mine, Kelly," A.J. said in a slow, thoughtful voice.

"Were they brown, like Rand's?" Kelly asked anxiously.

"No. I know what color brown is," A.J. said looking at her with a scowl on his face, as though she had insulted him. "They weren't brown," He said in a determined, confident tone. A.J. paused for a second, and then focused in on Mark's jacket. "They were kind of the color of Chief Mitchell's buttons," A.J. proclaimed proudly, as if he knew he had won the game.

Kelly quickly studied Mark's silver buttons. "Kind of gray, A.J.?" Kelly said looking at the boy for confirmation.

A.J. nodded seriously. "Yeah. I've never seen anyone with gray eyes before."

"A.J.," Kelly said as she handed him a brownie from the table, "you did great. You stay in your fort for a minute. I need to talk with the Chief. OK?" Kelly kept her eyes on A.J., until he nodded that he understood her request.

As A.J. climbed down from the stage, and went under the table, Kelly turned quickly to Mark. "Mark, A.J. is at risk. Pitman may use him to try to get to me."

Mark nodded solemnly. "He already has." He paused thoughtfully, and then said, "Would you like another roommate, Kelly?"

"Really?" Kelly asked in surprise.

Mark nodded again. "I think it would be a smart idea."

"Let's go talk to his parents," Kelly said quickly, as she grabbed Mark's arm.

An hour later, Kelly was back at her room, in the station, with an ecstatic A.J. Mark had set up a cot in the room for the boy, along with a TV, and about a dozen board games.

"This is going to be so much fun, Kelly!" A.J. said practically jumping out of his skin. He clearly thought he was at the slumber party of his life. "I'm so excited!"

"I can tell!" Kelly said laughing at her new roommate's enthusiasm.

"Just remember," Kelly said in a stern tone, "at night you have to go to sleep. Then in the morning, Rand and I will bring you to school."

"I'm going to get to ride in the squad car!" A.J. practically screamed with excitement.

Kelly quickly realized that she had told him the wrong thing to try to calm him down for the night. "A.J.," she said firmly, "you only get to ride in the squad car, if," she said waving her finger at him, "you go to sleep at night."

A.J. jumped into his sleeping bag that was on his cot, and closed his eyes tightly. "I'm sleeping, Kelly. I'm sleeping," he said in an anxious, yet sincere voice.

As Kelly looked over at her little friend, his eyes were indeed closed, very tightly in fact, but he had the biggest smile on his face that Kelly had ever seen. "Sleep good, A.J.," she said tenderly. "I love you, Little Buddy."

"You sleep good, too, Kelly. And Kelly," A.J. said, as he opened his eyes for a minute, "I love you, too."

A.J. quickly closed his eyes again, right before a small tear slid out of Kelly's. A.J. always seemed to touch her heart in such a precious way. She loved the little boy so much.

"Please, dear God," Kelly prayed silently, "please don't let any harm come to A.J. Protect him, Father, and protect the rest of us, too."

Seventeen

The day after Thanksgiving, which Kelly and Mark had celebrated with Baily and Mel, Sawyer's Crossing officially celebrated the start to the Christmas season. The town had special festivities planned on the green, and most of Sawyer turned out for the occasion.

The small green was jammed with booths and tables, holding everything from homemade quilts, to pies and breads. As Kelly, Mark, and A.J. were swept along in the lively, energetic crowd, the aroma of barbecue, fries, and pizza tempted everyone passing by. It was nothing short of a feast, and it was all waiting to be had.

A.J. squealed when he spotted three teams of draft horses off in the distance. They had been hitched up to large red and green wagons, and were waiting patiently for the hay rides to begin. "Can we go get in line for the rides...please!" he said begging Kelly and Mark.

"Why don't we go find out what time they're planning on starting them?" Mark said in a logical-sounding voice.

Kelly nodded to him. "Why don't you and A.J. go, I want to check out some of these craft booths quickly."

About ten minutes later, a very serious Mark returned, with a frustrated-looking A.J. at his side. "What happened?" Kelly asked in a puzzled, yet slightly curious voice.

"I had a little trouble finding out the schedule," Mark said in an aggravated tone.

"I see Bob Brown over there with his team now," Kelly said eyeing the farmer from a distance. "Do you want to go over and ask him? "

"No, I finally got the schedule. They start in about five minutes," Mark said still sounding irritated.

"Who did you ask?" Kelly questioned him in a confused voice. Everyone in Sawyer was so friendly, she couldn't imagine anyone giving Mark a hard time.

He hesitated in his answer just long enough so that Kelly knew that something was really up.

"He asked the clown," A.J. said in a matter-of-fact tone. "The clown wasn't very friendly."

"Which clown, A.J.?" Kelly persisted.

The boy pointed directly to a person dressed in all black and white, and Kelly couldn't hide the smile that was quickly spreading across her face. "Mark," she said as little bubbles of laughter escaped from her lips, "you asked a Mime when the hay rides were going to start?" Kelly covered her mouth as explosions of laughter shook her body.

"So?" Mark said in a defensive way. "He looked friendly enough, but when we got up to him, he wouldn't say a thing. He just kept waving his arms at me in a real obnoxious way. He was so arrogant, I wanted to belt him one."

Kelly was laughing so hard now, that she could barely talk. "Mark, Mimes don't talk. They act things out, without speaking."

"Kelly, I know what a Mime is, I just didn't know that jerk was a Mime. I thought he was a clown...they all look the same to me." As Mark shook his head slowly, a lopsided smile began to surface. The humor of the situation was finally dawning on him.

"Come on," Kelly said looping her arm through his, "let's go get in line for the hay rides. I'll protect you from the big bad Mime."

Mark laughed loudly this time. "You'd better keep me away from that guy, Kel, I still want to pop him one." Mark paused and then laughed again. "I bet if I hit him in the nose real hard he'd talk."

Kelly and Mark both laughed. "I'd better keep on eye on you, Mark. You know that you could get thrown in jail for harassing the clowns."

"He wasn't a clown, he was a Mime..." Mark said in a determined tone. "Clowns are friendly, and amusing. Mimes are obnoxious and down-right rude. I don't think anyone would throw me in jail for punching a Mime in the nose. They're arrogant, and I bet a lot of people have wanted to smack them."

Kelly was having a lot of trouble trying to contain her laughter.

"Are you going to laugh about this all day?" Mark said quietly in her ear.

Kelly just smiled and laughed harder. "No, Mark, I'll probably be laughing about this one for years. It's just so funny."

Mark dropped an arm around Kelly's shoulders as they waited in line for the hayride. "I haven't been on one of these since high school," he said eyeing the wagons excitedly. "This should be fun!"

"Is that a long time, Mark?" A.J. asked innocently.

Kelly laughed. "Yes, A.J., Mark is very, very old. When he was a boy, they didn't have buses, and he had to ride a horse to school."

Mark laughed as he saw A.J.'s eyes widen in surprise. "Kelly is teasing us, A.J. Don't believe a word she says."

A.J. looked up at Kelly confidently, and then smiled. "I don't believe you!" he said to her.

Kelly laughed. "That's because you're a very smart boy, A.J.!"

As they continued to wait in the line that was growing longer by the second, Kelly began to think about how attached she had become to A.J., especially over the last few weeks. She looked forward to having children of her own one day. The thought made her smile, as she lovingly pictured herself and Mark as parents to a large brood of children.

"That looks like an interesting smile!" Mark said quietly, pulling Kelly closer.

"It is!" Kelly said smiling sweetly at him.

"Want to share?" he asked curiously.

Kelly smiled, and then said in a soft voice. "I was just thinking about children."

Mark's smile was brilliant. "Anyone's in particular?"

When he smiled that way, it always made her heart do little flip-flops. "Yes," she said, smiling shyly back at him, "as a matter of fact."

He smiled at her knowingly. She didn't need to say anything more. He gently leaned down, and brushed her cheek with a kiss. "I love you, Kelly," he whispered tenderly into her ear. "I hope we have a bunch of kids some day."

Kelly looked up at Mark, smiling in agreement. She loved this man so much. She knew someday he would make a wonderful husband and father.

As Kelly, Mark, and A.J. climbed into the wagon, A.J. quickly went across the hay, all the way to the front of the wagon. "He likes to be near the horses," Kelly explained to Mark.

"As long as I'm near you, Kelly," Mark said winking at her playfully, "he can sit anywhere he wants."

As they sat down, and Kelly moved close to Mark's side, she felt his gun. "Do you always carry that thing with you?" she asked intently.

"Yeah, Kel, I pretty much do. I guess it's a habit. And," he said, looking down at her firmly, "you should be carrying yours with you too, until this case is closed."

Kelly nodded. "You're right," she said quietly, but seriously.

"Of course I'm right!" Mark said in a pompous, teasing voice, "I'm the Chief." Then he leaned closer to her, and wiggled his eyebrows at her. "Chiefs are always right, you know!"

Kelly immediately responded by smacking him in the arm.

"Hey, don't make me arrest you for assaulting an officer," Mark said trying hard to look at her sternly.

Kelly laughed. "Don't make me arrest you for impersonating an officer!"

Mark dropped his mouth open, pretending to be shocked, and that only made Kelly laugh harder. "That's it!" he said sounding adamant. "More community service for you, Little Lady."

"Oh good!" Kelly said smiling up at him. "I love your community service program, Chief. What is it this time, a movie, or pizza?"

"I was thinking of going out and chopping down a Christmas tree."

"That's an excellent idea!" Kelly said excitedly. "And would I get to help decorate this tree, too?"

"Naturally," he said, as he squeezed her hand. "I would appoint you Director of Operations."

"Oooh...a title." Kelly said straightening her posture to her queen-type of pose. "I like a title," she said in her best British accent.

Mark pulled Kelly a little closer, and then said in a tender tone, "Yeah, Kelly? That's good, because, I can think of at least one other title that I'd like to offer you. Think you might be interested?"

Kelly beamed at him. "Possibly...it really depends on the job benefits."

Mark smiled widely at her. "They're out of this world, Sweetheart. And," he said arching his eyebrows upward, "I believe you'd be an ideal candidate for the position."

"Are you interviewing others for this position, Chief?" Kelly asked studying him carefully.

"No, Ma'am," Mark replied seriously. "You're the only one I'm offering it to."

"Sounds interesting," Kelly said looking up at him with loving eyes.

"I guarantee it will be," he said winking at her.

As the draft horses began pulling the large, wooden wagons through the center of town, the jingling of the sleigh bells and the steady rhythm made by the horse's feet floated through the air in a cheerful, pleasant way.

At Christmastime, Sawyer's Crossing became a fantasy world that magically came to life. You almost expected to see sugarplum fairies dancing on the white, sparkling snow, as the sun gave it a luminous, enchanting glow, before slowly dipping behind the mountains for the night.

As Kelly's eyes drifted over the quaint shops and restaurants, all dressed up in their festive

Christmas outfits, she couldn't help but smile. Lights were strung in every window, and wreaths with big bows were on every door. Sawyer's narrow, winding brick streets were filled with lively shoppers, arms laden with packages, all hurrying in one direction or another.

As the horses pulled the wagon through Keane's Covered Bridge, a new excitement spread through everyone. The inside of the bridge had been decorated in true holiday style. Colored lights had been strung across the ceiling and side timbers of the bridge, and somewhere, from a hidden source, "Joy To The World," could be heard. Kelly smiled quietly in contentment. No bright lights and big city attractions could compare with the fairy-tale world that Sawyer became every Christmas. It was a special town. A town small enough to call everyone by a first name, but a town large enough to attract half of New England to it. It was her town, and in her heart, she prayed that it would never change.

Later in the evening, the folks of Sawyer began to gather around the fifty-foot Christmas tree. The choir from church performed several sacred favorites, from "Silent Night" to "Hark the Heard Angels Sing." Their voices filled the air in a joyous praise that made Kelly's eyes well up. This was the first time in years that she had actually put Christ back in her Christmas celebration. As Kelly listened to the voices sing of her wonderful Savior, her heart overflowed with love toward her Heavenly Father. Never in all her life had she felt so close to God. He was finally at the center of her life, and the joy and peace that she felt was almost numbing.

Moments later, Mayor Mike threw the switch to the Christmas tree, and it came sparkling to life, receiving instant praise from the admiring crowd around it.

The celebration of Christ's birth always proved to unify the small town in a special way. A joy and peace spread through the community that night that was large enough to overshadow life's daily problems. Tonight, the eyes of the people were taken off themselves, and raised in awe to the One whose birth they celebrated.

Kelly prayed that the feeling in her heart would never leave her. That each day, regardless of the season, she would celebrate Christ's birth in her heart, and in the way she chose to live her life.

As the tired threesome made their way back to the station, the surrounding mountains twinkled merrily, as the lights from distant houses shone down upon them. A.J. loved bunking at the station with Kelly and Copper, and was completely oblivious to the danger they were in. As was their routine, after A.J. got into his P.J.'s, Kelly read to him. A.J.'s favorite book for the month was the story about Jesus's birth. He loved looking at all the brightly illustrated pictures, and always listened intently to the story, as though he were hearing it for the first time. A.J. loved Jesus, and was proud to be a part of God's family. The way he totally trusted his Heavenly Father in everything, in such a pure way, moved Kelly deeply. A.J. was such a witness to her as to what she should be like in her own life.

After Kelly tucked A.J. in, she gave him a quick peck on the cheek. "I love you, Buddy," Kelly said smiling down at her special little friend.

A.J. smiled a glowing smile back at her, and said excitedly, "And A.J. loves you, too, Kelly!"

When Kelly stepped out of the room, Mark was waiting for her, eyeing her tenderly. "You're going to be a great Mom someday, Kel."

"Thanks, Mark," she said dropping her tired body in Mark's open arms. "And you're going to have children calling you Daddy someday, that I know are going to adore you."

He squeezed her hand, and then pulled her into his office next door. Looking at her square-ly in the eye, he asked in a concerned tone how she was doing.

She gave him a quick smile, and then said, "OK. I'm really looking forward to all of this being over. I find myself resenting Pitman for putting this fear back into my life." Kelly sighed, and then Mark gently took her hand. "You know, Mark, I wish I could trust God the way that A.J. does. He really casts all his cares on the Lord, and then doesn't look back."

"He's a special little person, with a tender heart," Mark said affectionately.

Kelly nodded. "He sure is." Then, she paused thoughtfully for a second. "Mark, I always get this strange feeling that Pitman is watching me. I can't exactly say why...but I can't seem to shake the odd feeling that he is."

Mark nodded. "That's understandable, Kelly. But, just remember, we've got this place staked out, and people watching for him all over town. If he were actually hanging around, I'm sure he would have been spotted by now."

"You're probably right," Kelly said sighing loudly. "But, just the same, I'll be glad when this is all over."

"So will I, Honey," Mark said pulling Kelly into a tight, protective embrace. "So will I."

Eighteen

As Kelly, A.J., and Rand made their way down bustling Main Street, Kelly hummed merrily to the tune of "Jingle Bells" being played over a loudspeaker. If the music and decorations weren't enough to put you in the Christmas mood, as if on cue, a light snow had gently started falling.

"Rand," Kelly said turning quickly to her partner, "you're off duty now. You should go home to Becca. A.J. and I will be fine at Pappy's."

"Kelly, Mark would personally kill me if I came back to the station without the two of you. Besides," Rand said smiling excitedly down at his partner, "I love Pappy's General Store. And," Rand said eyeing A.J. eagerly, "Pappy has some great new toys. And," Rand said wiggling his brown eyebrows at A.J., "I've heard from a very reliable source that Santa is there, too!"

"Are you going to sit on Santa's lap, Rand?" A.J. asked, eyeing the policeman curiously.

Rand laughed loudly. "No, A.J. I don't think that Santa would let me. I think that I'm too big."

"I think you're right," A.J. said seriously.

Kelly could barely contain her laughter. "Rand, I would like to see you sit on Santa's lap."

"Kelly," Rand said firmly, but with an unmistakable twinkle in his tender brown eyes, "when you grow to be bigger than Santa, he no longer welcomes you on his lap."

Kelly laughed again. "I guess I can see your point, Rand," she said patting her partner on his broad back. "But, it still would have made for an interesting sight."

As the three of them entered the old General Store, Pappy greeted them personally. "Welcome! Welcome!" the old man said in a jolly voice. "And how is my favorite customer today?" Pappy said eyeing A.J. cheerfully.

"Good, Pappy," A.J. said excitedly. "Do you still have your marbles?"

Pappy laughed loudly. "Do I still have my marbles...," he repeated in an amused tone. "Mrs. Pappy doesn't always think so."

Kelly and Rand laughed, but A.J. just stared at the short, merry man with a confused expression on his face. "Yes, A.J., my boy...," Pappy said confidently, "you can find marbles in the toy department. We are having a special on them."

"I know," A.J. said in a sure voice.

"And, make sure you visit Santa while you're back there. Christmas is getting close, you know."

"Yes, I know," A.J. said seriously.

As Kelly began to walk through the old barn-like country store, she couldn't help but smile. She had so many special memories of things that had happened in this store. As a kid, Baily had always brought her to see Santa here, and then let her pick out a bag of penny candy.

Pappy's was a well-stocked, old-fashioned general store. The red barn had been divided off into sections. When you first entered the store, you would walk into the candy and kitchen section. A long pine counter against the wall held Pappy's antique cash register, along with dozens and dozens of jars filled with penny candy. On the other side of the room, was virtually every type of kitchen utensil that you could ever use, along with a few that you weren't sure what to do with.

"Hey, Kelly," Rand said in a teasing voice, "I bet you don't know what this is?"

Kelly smiled at her partner, and shook her head. Her lack of culinary knowledge and skill was a continual source of amusement to Rand. He was quite sure that Kelly couldn't identify any utensils beyond the basic fork, spoon, and knife. "Rand," Kelly said assuredly, "I believe that's called a watchamahoosit. And," Kelly said folding her arms firmly across her chest, "even though I don't know what it's used for in the kitchen, I bet if I hit you over the head with it, it would make a nice bump!"

Rand laughed. He loved teasing his partner. "You're too violent, Kel. Hey! Does Mark know that your cooking skills don't range beyond heating up frozen pizzas?"

"He likes frozen pizza!" Kelly said quickly.

"I hope so," Rand said as he picked up a peppermint stick, "because I have the feeling that he's going to be eating a lot of them."

Kelly smiled at Rand, and then walked into the hardware section. "OK, Rand," Kelly said raising her eyebrows at him, "let's test your basic hardware knowledge."

"Let's not," Rand said quickly. Rand was about as much of a handyman as Kelly was a cook.

"OK, Rand," Kelly said sounding like a stern teacher, "what's this?"

"Oh, Kelly...," he said waving a hand at her, "this whole section is filled with whatamacallits and thingamabobs.

"That's a very specific answer, Officer Thompson," Kelly said smirking at him.

"Hey, I'll admit I'm no expert in the hardware department," Rand said casually. "But," he said waving a stern finger at Kelly, "at least my family's not going to starve to death."

"That's true," Kelly said in a matter-of-fact tone. "Your house is just going to fall in on you. But you're right," she added quickly, "you won't starve."

The next section they walked through was filled with cloth placemats, tablecloths, plates, bowls, and mugs. Kelly picked up a set of blue mugs, with white snowmen on them. "I believe I could put these to use," she said eyeing them thoughtfully.

"Are you Christmas shopping for you, or someone else?" Rand asked curiously.

"Now, Rand," Kelly said in a mock scolding voice, "you know better than to ask me that. You know I'm never going to give you an answer."

Rand rolled his eyes at her. "You're too secretive, Kelly."

Before she could comment, A.J. squealed with excitement. They had just entered the Christmas section of the barn. Pappy had turned a huge room into a Christmas town. It looked like a Dickens Village. There were small houses that you could actually go into, and find a variety of Christmas gifts. In the center of the town was a green with a twelve-foot Christmas tree on it. It had been decorated with colored lights, and traditional Christmas ornaments and wrapped packages had even been added to the base of the tree. It all made for a very festive scene.

At the far end of the room was a small castle. It had been painted red and white, and had a sign on the front door that simply said "Santa." The kids needed no further invitation. A line of at least a dozen children waited excitedly outside the door, as Santa's elves let in one child at a time.

As A.J. strong-armed Kelly to the end of the line, Kelly peeked inside Santa's brightly lit house. The jolly man himself, decked out in his season's best, was sitting on a large throne, smiling and nodding to a little girl on his lap. He seemed patient and kind to the child, and Kelly instantly wondered which Grandpa from Sawyer had volunteered for the task.

"He's good," Rand stated in an approving voice, as he leaned close to Kelly.

"Yeah," Kelly said quietly, "better than Mr. Slater. He always got grumpy after the first hour."

As Kelly waited in line with A.J., she began to survey the assortment of toys that Pappy had displayed. He always had a great selection.

"Rand," Kelly said turning quickly to her partner, "would you mind saving our place in line? I want to show A.J. some of Pappy's new toys."

"Just don't be long," Rand said appearing a little uncomfortable. "I'm kind of big to be waiting here all alone."

Kelly laughed as she took A.J.'s hand and headed off for a train display. Pappy had set the train up so it was winding around the mountains, crossing bridges and rivers, and passing through quaint, snow-covered towns.

"A.J.!" Kelly said excitedly, "Wouldn't you like a train for Christmas?"

"No," he said firmly, as he watched the train with an unimpressed expression on his face. "I want marbles."

Persistently, Kelly dragged A.J. to the next display. "Look at these computer games, A.J.! Aren't these great!"

"I want marbles!" A.J. said adamantly.

"A.J.," Kelly said as she knelt down on one knee before him, "I know you want marbles. But, you can get marbles, and something else."

"I just want marbles," A.J. said emphatically.

Kelly knew the boy well. Every year he got his heart set on one thing, and that's all he wanted. He was a very focused boy, and for some reason, Kelly always felt the urge to at least show him a few other toys.

"A.J.," Kelly said enthusiastically, "look at these remote control cars! Aren't they so cool?"

He looked up at her carefully. "Is that what you want, Kelly?" A.J. asked her innocently.

Kelly bit her tongue to hide her laughter. "Maybe, A.J. I'm not sure."

"Can we go back to the line now, Kelly? I need to tell Santa that I want some marbles."

"Sure, A.J." Kelly said putting an arm around the boy.

"Hey!" Kelly said suddenly. "Maybe you'd like a backpack to put your marbles in!" She felt sure this was something she could get him.

"No. Just marbles," he said seriously. "The marbles I want come in a big jar. I don't need a backpack."

Kelly decided to give up for now. A.J. had more patience in this matter than she did. He always knew what he wanted, and, basically, that was that. She'd have better luck moving a mountain than changing A.J.'s list.

As they walked back to the line, Kelly could hear Rand sigh loudly. "I'm glad that you're back," he said appearing embarrassed. "Santa's elves kept teasing me, and telling me I'm too big for this."

Kelly smiled at Rand, her eyes lit humorously. "Thanks, Rand. I owe you one."

"No," Rand said firmly. "You owe me a lot more then one. You do this to me every year."

The door to Santa's castle opened, and an elf directed A.J. to come in.

Suddenly, the once determined boy was overcome with shyness. He paled as he stared at the big Santa.

"A.J.," Kelly whispered in his ear, "do you want me to come in with you?"

"It's him!" A.J. said in a panicked tone.

"Sweetheart," Kelly said in a reassuring voice, "It's Santa. Do you want to sit on his lap?"

The elf behind Kelly gave her a slight shove, so she could shut the door to the small castle. A.J. kept his back plastered up against the door. Kelly was surprised at the boy's fear. Normally, she had to pull him off Santa's lap because he talked too much.

"A.J.," Kelly said gently, "do you want to talk to Santa from here? You don't have to sit on his lap."

A.J. shook his head. His eyes were large with fear. "I want to go home," he said in a small, wobbly voice.

"No one's going anywhere," Santa said in a hard voice that sent chills down Kelly's spine.

"That voice," she thought as she slowly looked over at the Santa, "I know that voice." As Kelly stared at the Santa in the jolly red suit, she quickly went beyond the gun pointing at them, and his beard, and his gray glasses. She focused in directly on his eyes. Immediately, she recognized the eyes—those menacing, cold, steel-gray eyes that had haunted many of her dreams.

"It's you!" Kelly said in a voice that was barely audible.

"How nice to see you again, Kelly," Pitman said in an icy tone.

A.J. began to cry. "Let the boy go, Pitman. He has nothing to do with this. This is between you and me."

Pitman let only a low, grumbly laugh escape from his crooked lips. "Now, Kelly, you of all people should know that I don't like to leave any witnesses around."

Kelly was surprised at how unafraid she felt. Pitman had been haunting her life for close to twenty years, and at that moment, all she felt was a mixture of pure rage and determination.

"Tell Officer Thompson to clear the store out," Pitman barked angrily at Kelly. "I want only the three of us in here. And," he said quickly, in a voice containing so much evil that it made Kelly tremble, "don't try anything funny. It don't really matter to me if I shoot you now or later."

Kelly opened the door slightly, and called Rand over. "Rand," Kelly said in an amazingly calm voice, "Pitman is the Santa. He has a gun on A.J. and me. He wants you to clear the room out now."

Rand's face clearly displayed the shock and confusion that he felt inside. He looked at Kelly, unable to move, or comprehend what she was really saying. She might as well have been speaking in French. Rand's brain just refused to register the words coming out of her mouth.

Kelly saw the emotions that were running through Rand, and in frustration, to get him to act, she yelled at him, "Rand! Clear the store!" That seemed to snap him out of his trance, and he instantly sprang into action, ordering people out of the store.

As Kelly turned back to Pitman, he spoke to her in a tight, demanding voice, "Give me your gun!"

As Kelly slowly took her pistol out of its holster, she frantically tried to formulate a plan in her mind. She knew from the quick way that he had shot her parents, that she didn't have much time. As Kelly cautiously handed her pistol to Pitman, she turned slightly. In a quick moment, she took her gun, and clobbered Pitman in the head with it as hard as she could. It set him off balance just enough for her to escape the small building with A.J.

Since the biggest thing in the room was the tree, Kelly quickly darted behind it. Not until she and A.J. were safely behind the tree did Kelly realize that she didn't have her gun. Vaguely, she remembered it flying out of her hand when she hit Pitman.

A.J.'s quiet sobs brought Kelly's attention to the frightened child. She knew that she had to get him out of there, and quickly. Kelly spied a large window behind them, and as she moved toward it, she froze as she heard Pitman begin to mumble and speak.

"That was a stupid move, Douglas! Now, I have two guns to shoot you with." Then he sprayed the room with bullets. They shattered everything they touched, sending debris flying everywhere. Kelly instinctively shoved A.J. onto the floor, and covered him with her body.

"I want to go home," A.J. said in a panicked tone.

"I'm working on it, Buddy," Kelly said trying to remain confident.

"But you must be very quiet," she whispered in his ear.

Something caught Kelly's attention. She listened intently for a moment before she realized what it was. It was silence. Silence so loud that it was downright deafening. The bullets had stopped for now, and she knew, like a hawk hunting for its prey, that Pitman was pursuing them.

Slowly, and as silently as possible, Kelly took A.J. and crept over to the back of one of the town houses that Pappy had for display. The window behind it was what she was interested in. Disappointment flooded through her as she tried to push up the window, and it wouldn't budge. She quickly noticed that the window had been painted shut.

Without a second thought, she took her heavy, military police boots, and kicked in the window. Kelly literally threw A.J. out the first floor window. "Go find Rand or Mark and stay with them," she urgently ordered the boy.

As soon as the glass had been broken, bullets began to fly again. Kelly threw herself on her belly, and quickly crawled behind the display houses. Kelly knew she could have gone out the window, too, and probably escaped unharmed. But if she didn't bring Pitman in now, she knew that she'd never have any peace. For the rest of her life, she'd always be watching her back. She hated living that way as a child, and she refused to live out her adult life in that awful fear.

"You can't escape, Douglas!" Pitman declared in a confident tone. "I will get you. I don't care about the boy. It's you that I want."

As Kelly looked to where the voice was coming from, she felt an instant stab of panic. Pitman's large body was blocking the exit from the Christmas room. He had trapped her in here, and he laughed loudly, filling the air with a wretched, vile sound. The man was filled with pure evil.

"I'll just wait for you to move, and then blow your pretty body to pieces." Then he laughed again. He was sure he had won the game. "But, little Kelly, as I remember, you're good at hiding. You were hiding on me last time." He paused for a moment, and then said in a determined voice, "But I ain't leaving this time until I blow you to pieces."

"Oh, God," Kelly prayed quickly, "please help me." Then, as she turned her head, she saw them. A.J.'s marbles. They were in a glass jar, and there were at least one hundred of them. Kelly knew it was her only option for the moment. She quietly got on her knees behind the house and took the large jar and threw it at Pitman's head with all the force she could. As the jar shattered against the side of his head, Kelly literally dove out of the room. She was barely aware of Pitman's bloodcurdling scream.

"Why you little pig...you've cut my head up now!" He looked around the room widely. "I was going to shoot you quick, like I did your Pa...but now I'm going to make you suffer."

Kelly focused her mind, and quickly formed another plan. She knew that Pappy kept a shotgun under the counter at the front of the store. She knew her only real chance at stopping Pitman would be getting that gun. As Kelly kept crawling on her hands and knees, she entered the hardware section. There were plenty of things in here that she could use as a weapon against Pitman, but everything depended on her being very close to him, and she wanted to avoid that at all costs.

Kelly knew that her best bet was Pappy's shotgun. She could take Pitman out with a single bullet. If...she could get to the gun.

"So...you want to play games, Kelly," Pitman said snickering at her. "I like games, Babe. If you want me to hunt you, it will only make it more interesting for me."

Kelly could hear his footsteps behind her. They were slow and calculating steps, no doubt, thoroughly searching the area around him.

"Sweet child," Pitman went on methodically, "while I'm looking for you, let me tell you a little story. Your Pa ruined my life years ago. You see...I had to kill him. I had no choice. His head literally blew apart by my bullets." He paused, and then laughed loudly and bitterly. "And then there was your Ma..."

Kelly tried to block out his words. She knew he was trying to get her flustered, so she would give her position away. Yet, as much as she tried not to listen, his sinister words went right to her heart.

"Yeah, that Ma of yours was one pretty lady. She was a real looker, she was. I actually felt a little bad about having to knock her off. She had such a beautiful face...and then there was the baby."

Kelly closed her eyes in an angry, determined way. "I am not going to listen to this!" she scolded herself. "He's playing mind games...God, help me get a grip."

Kelly poked her head out of an aisle, and saw Pitman with his back to her. She quickly scooted through the door, towards the front of the store. Unfortunately, she made just enough noise for Pitman to hear her. He spun on his heel, and fired three shots at her. Two missed her, but one connected directly with her shin.

Kelly screamed as she dove for the cash register counter. At first the wound didn't hurt too badly. But she had heard enough stories about gun shot wounds to know what to expect. About fifteen seconds after the shot, she began to feel an intense burning pain. She immediately looked around for something to use as a tourniquet, but could find nothing.

Kelly suddenly became aware that she was at the edge of the counter, and not behind it. As she crept towards it, she saw Mark scrambling from the other end of the counter towards her. He put a finger over his lips to tell her to keep silent. Then he put up four fingers, and pointed to various parts of the room.

Kelly nodded understandingly. There were four other officers in the room with them.

Mark took his hand and made a talking motion with it, and then pointed to Kelly.

Again, Kelly nodded. Mark wanted her to talk and lure Pitman into the room. "Pitman," Kelly said in a pained, vulnerable voice, "you've shot me. Please, can't we just work something out?"

Pitman reacted as planned. He quickly moved in the direction of Kelly's voice. As soon as he had entered the room, Rand, who was across the room from Kelly and Mark, yelled, "FREEZE!"

Pitman's reaction was to swing around and start shooting in Rand's direction. Mark quickly leveled his gun, and dropped Pitman with a single shot.

Kelly shuddered as she heard him drop to the floor. As Mark and Rand cautiously approached Pitman, the old man swung around and shot Rand in the arm.

Mark's next two shots went directly into Pitman's head. This time when he fell, he was down for good.

Mark checked Pitman, and as he took away the old man's guns, he yelled to Kelly, "Kelly, he's dead. It's all over."

Kelly collapsed on the floor behind the counter and wept. Mark quickly came over, and scooped her into his arms. As the medics came in to take care of the wounded officers, Mark held Kelly tenderly, as a bandage was quickly applied to her leg.

"Kelly," Mark said earnestly, "it's all over now." Kelly looked at Mark, and wept again. "Sweetheart," he said tenderly, "it's finally time for you to get on with your life. You have so much life to live, Kelly. It's time you started living again."

Kelly clung to Mark as he carried her to a waiting ambulance. She couldn't seem to stop the sobbing or the shaking. Her sobs violently shook her body. All these years of fear and hiding. All the nightmares and the silence. Now, twenty years later, she was free of Pitman. He no longer could threaten her. Yet, Kelly thought disappointedly, the damage that one man had done to her family could never be repaired. She would never have a mother, or a father, or a brother or a sister. As Kelly continued to weigh the cost, she knew that what Pitman had taken from her could never be repaid. The damage was permanent.

The only thing that she could do, with God's help, would be to go on with her life and make a new start. Kelly knew, in order to survive, she had to deal with her past, and then bury it. If she didn't, she knew her past would ruin any hope she had of a future.

Nineteen

The next few days passed in a blurred whirlwind for Kelly. Gram had just told her that she was going to stay in Florida with her sister. Gram's sister was recovering from heart surgery, and Gram wanted to stay there to help her out until the spring. Kelly missed the elderly woman deeply, and hated the thought of always coming home to an empty house. She found it not only lonely, but depressing as well.

And, to make matters worse, Mark had been strangely detached since the Pitman incident. Kelly tried repeatedly to get Mark to open up. Yet, to her frustration, and great disappointment, he never would. He always brushed off her concerns, and told her they were nothing to worry about.

Yet, as the days went by, Kelly felt Mark pulling further and further away from her. They stopped spending as much time together because Mark was always working late. He was even pulling ridiculous amounts of overtime every weekend. Kelly felt sure she was losing Mark, and she was completely helpless to do anything about it. The space that Mark had created between them was not only painful, but confusing as well. She had never in her wildest dreams expected this from Mark.

Every time she tried to reach out to Mark, she felt as though she were grasping at straws, trying to pull a miracle out of thin air. She tried politely to make conversation with him, yet it sounded empty and hollow even to her own ears. She felt completely abandoned by the only man that she had ever loved.

Finally, just days before Christmas, Kelly went to Mark's office. She had prayed, and thought long and hard about her decision. She knew it would be one of the most difficult things she had ever had to say. Her regret was mixed with anger as she thought about the sudden way Mark had pulled away from her.

As she stood in Mark's office, and spoke her well-rehearsed speech to him, his angry blue eyes bore into her intently. "You're dumping me?" Mark said sounding completely astounded.

"Mark," Kelly said through a tight, emotion-filled voice, "I'm only suggesting that we give each other a little more space." Kelly paused, and bit the inside of her lip, trying to prevent the tears from flowing. "Something has happened to you since this Pitman thing," Kelly said, feeling frustrated and helpless. "You've been pushing me away Mark...and I don't know why."

The tears began to roll out of Kelly's eyes in a steady stream. This hurt so much, she felt as though she couldn't have been in more pain if someone had stabbed her with a knife.

"I'm not pushing you away," Mark said slowly, in an unconvincing tone.

"Mark, you try to think up every excuse in the book so you won't have to spend time with me. I think you've wanted to break up with me for a long time now...but you just didn't know how."

Mark's total silence in response to her to her statement only confirmed Kelly's worst fears. It was true. He did want to break up with her. But why? she thought as she stared at him for answers he wasn't about to volunteer. She felt absolutely left in the dark. She was so sure that Mark was the one. What in the world was going on here?

Tears ran faster down Kelly's face, as she quickly handed a small bag to Mark. When he looked inside, his mouth dropped open in pure shock. "You're giving me back the necklace and the earrings?" His quiet voice was full of disbelief.

"I can't keep them, Mark. The memory is too painful." Then Kelly quickly turned and left his office. The memory of the necklace burned a painful hole in her heart. He had given it to her the first time that he had said he loved her. Now Kelly wondered in a painful, confused fog, did he ever love her? Did he really mean it?

As Kelly went back to Gram's house, she felt so alone. Even Copper seemed depressed. She knew it was hard for the dog to be alone all day, but it was almost as if Copper could sense something more. "Oh, Mark," Kelly said quietly in tears, "what ever happened to us? I just wish I knew."

At work, Kelly went out of her way not to run into Mark. She knew that focusing her mind on her work was an easy out for dealing with her personal problems, but it seemed like the only thing keeping her afloat right now. And the fact that Mark never went out of his way to see her confirmed in her mind, even more, that she had made the right decision in ending their relationship.

Christmas Day arrived in Sawyer, with a gentle falling snow. Kelly tried to keep her spirits bright, by concentrating on the fact that this was Christ's birthday. Christmas hymns blared through the house as she readied herself to go to Baily and Mel's for the noonday meal. Just as she was grabbing her coat and keys, an unexpected knock sounded at the front door. As she swung the door open, she was even more surprised to find Mark Mitchell standing on her front step.

A hopefulness passed through Kelly's heart at the sight of him. More then anything she wanted to be back with him. Yet, her dream was quickly dashed, as a very serious Chief Mitchell spoke to her.

"Baily has had a heart attack. Mel asked me to come over here and tell you."

"Is he alive?" Kelly asked, suddenly feeling panicked.

"Yes," Mark said putting a comforting hand on her shoulder. She quickly drew away from his touch as though he had burned her. Then, in a matter-of-fact voice, Mark said, "He's in intensive care. You should go see him soon."

As Kelly grabbed her keys off a nearby table, Mark said in a concerned voice, "Kelly, I'll drive you to the hospital."

Kelly spun around and stared at Mark for a moment. "I don't think that would be a good idea, Chief." She couldn't bring herself to call him Mark. Probably, Kelly thought as she walked past him to her car, because he was no longer Mark to her. Their new relationship had turned him into Chief Mitchell again.

As Kelly backed out of her driveway, and quickly drove down Tim's Path, she wondered cynically if Mark would pull her over for speeding to the hospital. "Even if he hits the lights and siren," Kelly thought angrily, "I'm not pulling over."

Within ten minutes, Kelly was at the hospital and literally running down the halls towards the

I.C.U. A very bad feeling, that she just couldn't shake, gnawed at the back of her mind.

As she entered Baily's room, she immediately saw Mel sitting next to her husband's bed, holding his hand. "Oh, Kelly," Mel said in an emotional voice, "I'm so glad that you made it. He wants to talk to you."

"Made it?" Kelly thought as alarm slammed through her body. "What did Mel mean by that? Baily's always been fine."

Mel told Kelly to take her chair, and then she quickly left Kelly alone with Baily. The old man slowly opened his eyes. Gently, he reached for Kelly's hand. "Sweetheart, I'm so glad that you're here. I need to say good bye to you."

Kelly's eyes bugged out, and she stared at Baily in shock. "Baily," she said in a breathless voice, as though she had just run a major race, "what are you talking about?"

"Kelly," he said in a weak, but confident voice, "I'm heading on to my heavenly home." He paused, gathered more air into his lungs, and then said in a rush, "I'm so thankful that the Lord allowed me to live long enough to say goodbye to you." He paused again for another breath, and then said lovingly, "I have always thought of you as a daughter. I love you so much, Honey."

"No," Kelly said in a choked up voice. Tears were pouring out of her eyes so quickly that she had trouble focusing in on Baily's face. "Baily," she said in an urgent tone, as she squeezed the old man's hand, "you're going to be fine. You're always fine."

A tender smile spread across his weathered face, and he stared at Kelly a moment before answering. "Not this time, Kiddo. My time left here is short." Tears were streaming out of his own eyes as he looked at Kelly. His eyes roamed her face, as if trying to memorize the details of it, for one last time. "You need to promise me," he continued on in a soft voice, "that you'll take care of Mel. She's going to need a lot of support after I'm gone."

"Baily," Kelly said sounding panicked and desperate, "you can't die. I need you."

Baily squeezed her hand reassuringly. "Kelly," he said in a confident tone, "you're going to be fine. Trust in God, Dear, and you'll be fine."

"Oh, Baily," Kelly said between sobs, "you have been more of a father to me then my own father was. The way you took me in, when I was just six...I can never begin to thank you for all you've done for me." Kelly paused, fighting back the choking emotion that was threatening to overwhelm her. "Thank you so much for making me your daughter. I love you so much."

Baily's face was wet with tears, and in a tight voice he said, "Sweetheart, you are a daughter to Mel and me. But," he said squeezing her hand tightly, "you are also a daughter to your Heavenly Father. He will always be there for you, Kelly. It's one of His great promises to us. He will never, ever leave us." He paused, and then drew a ragged breath. "Kelly, you will never be alone. Ever."

Kelly nodded, and said quietly, "I love you."

"I love you too, Dear," Baily said tenderly. He drew another breath, and then said quietly, "Honey, will you get Mel. I need to see her now."

Kelly nodded, and then quickly went to get Mel. As Kelly walked into the hallway, she was not surprised to see all of Sawyer's Crossing's officers there, plus many close friends from town. She quickly spotted Mel, and told her that Baily wanted to see her.

Then Kelly spotted Rand and threw herself into his big, loving arms, crying uncontrollably. What she had said to Baily was true. He had been more of a father to her than her own father had been. Her Dad hadn't lived long enough. But Baily had stepped in lovingly, and raised Kelly as his own. She was so thankful that she had been able to say goodbye to him.

Kelly stayed in Rand's arms for a long time. Finally, when the waves of weeping ended, she dropped herself into a chair near Rand, and put her head in her hands. She was in so much pain that she was surprised that she was even alive. "Why does goodbye have to hurt so deeply?" Kelly thought shaking her blonde head slightly. "I know I'll see Baily in heaven, so why does it hurt so much now."

A thought popped into her foggy head, as she remembered Baily's last words to her. He had said that her Heavenly Father would never leave her. She knew that was true, and she knew she needed to turn to Him right now. "Oh, Father," Kelly prayed earnestly, "give me strength to get through this, and give me strength to be there for Mel."

Kelly literally jumped out of her seat as she thought about Mel. She had an overwhelming desire to see the old woman. As she slowly walked into Baily's room, Mel was holding her husband's hand, and tears were flowing down her face. When she saw Kelly, she said in a whisper of a voice, "He's home now, Dear."

The two women embraced, and wept in each other's arms. Kelly couldn't believe the heart-wrenching pain she felt from Baily's absence.

At that moment, she didn't think that she could ever hurt more. She was going to miss him more than she could ever say.

Mel asked for a few private moments with Baily, and Kelly quickly exited the room. The eyes of everyone in the hallway were on her, but she ignored them, and went directly over to Mark.

"Can I speak to you for a minute, Chief?" Kelly said in a tight voice.

Mark nodded, and followed Kelly down the hall, and around the corner.

"I'm going to need to take my vacation time immediately," Kelly said in a shaky tone. "I need to spend the next week helping Mel."

"Kelly," Mark said in the compassionate voice that she had learned to love, "take all the time you need. And," he said eyeing her tenderly, "this is not counted as vacation time. It's personal time. You've just lost your father."

Kelly's eyes flooded with the realization of the statement. "Yes, Chief," she said putting a hand over her tearing eyes. "I should go now."

"Kelly," Mark said in an urgent voice, as he put a hand on her arm, "I don't like you calling me Chief. I'm Mark to you."

Tears were running down Kelly's face now. It was too much to try to handle two broken hearts at the same time. "I can't deal with you right now. Everything has changed for us. And," Kelly said in a voice that was so tight she could barely get the words out, "I don't know why. I honestly don't have a clue as to what happened to us."

"Kelly...," Mark said tenderly reaching for her.

"No," Kelly said firmly, backing away from him. "Please. Don't touch me."

"Kelly," Mark said with tears rolling down his face, "let me help you through this."

His words hit Kelly so hard that she stumbled backwards. "Help me through this...," she said in a voice that clearly sounded as if the light had just dawned on her. "That's all I was to you," Kelly said staring at Mark in disbelief. "I was a charity case for you...you felt sorry for me..."

"No, Kelly," Mark said firmly, taking a step closer to her.

"You know, I think I finally understand it now." She turned slowly, and began to mechanically walk away from him. Under her breath, she muttered, "How could I have been such a fool!"

"Kelly," Mark said adamantly, "you have it all wrong."

Kelly swung around to face him directly. "No, Mark. You have it all wrong," Kelly said angrily to him. "My first impression of you was right. I should have listened to myself."

As Kelly angrily walked away from him, she called herself every kind of fool in the book for ever loving Mark Mitchell. Now she could see it clearly. Mark was the type of guy who looked for pity cases. And, Kelly thought narrowing her eyes intently, when he healed their hearts from one disaster, he marched out of their lives, leaving them with another one.

Twenty

Kelly didn't get much sleep during the next few days. She moved temporarily into Mel's. Over and over Kelly wished that Gram had come back from Florida to help with all the funeral arrangements. Baily had requested a simple funeral, and both women tried to honor his request.

Two days later, on a gray winter's day, the entire town of Sawyer, and what seemed like half of New England, turned out for Baily's funeral service. The pastor gave a message that helped Kelly refocus her mind and heart. She had to remember that Baily was in a wonderful place. Yet, the huge void that Baily left in her life, and in Sawyer, would be difficult to come to terms with. Kelly knew that dealing with it was going to take a lot of time. She knew it wasn't going to happen quickly.

The only way that Kelly made it through the day was to pray a lot, and focus her attention on caring for Mel. She and Baily had been married for over fifty years. They married right out of high school, and were still crazy about each other all the way to the end. Kelly couldn't even imagine being fortunate enough to find a guy like that.

At the graveside, people were crowded all over the small, country cemetery. Mel had picked out a plot for her husband on the hill overlooking Sawyer. Kelly had to laugh a little as she looked at the spot. Even in his death, it made it seem as though Baily was still watching over the town. The thought comforted Kelly a little.

When it was time to lower the coffin into the ground, Kelly still couldn't believe he was gone. She stood numbly next to Mel, and watched it being lowered down. The whole thing seemed like an awful nightmare. How could Baily really be gone? How could she be at Baily's funeral? Something seemed so unfair about it all. Baily had only been retired for nine months. Why did he have to go now?

Back at Mel's house, Kelly spent the day serving guests in an automatic numb fog. The small colonial was jammed with an ever-changing sea of faces. Not until she actually bumped headfirst into Rand and Becca, did Kelly actually sit down for a minute.

"You look awful, Kel," Becca said in a worried tone.

"I'm fine," Kelly mumbled.

"No, you're not," Rand said in a low, angry grumble. He hated seeing her look so worn. "You look like you're about to drop over."

"I'm fine," Kelly repeated, as a wave of dizziness struck her.

"Kel, you're still coming to our New Year's Eve get-together, right?" Becca asked eyeing her friend with concern.

"Oh, Becca," Kelly said sighing heavily, "I don't think I'm going to be up for it."

"You're coming," Rand said firmly. "Even if I have to drag you there myself...you're coming."

"I need some air," Kelly said feeling her chest tighten. That awful, but unfortunately too familiar feeling of an asthma attack weighed on her. Kelly grabbed her purse, and headed outside. Since people had gathered on the porch, Kelly headed for her car. By the time she walked down the driveway to it, she was wheezing heavily. With a shaky hand, she grabbed her inhaler out of her pocketbook, and shoved it into her mouth. After four puffs of medicine down into her lungs, the tightness began to ease. She dropped her inhaler into her lap, and let her head lean back in her seat. She closed her eyes, willing herself to relax. And, that is just what her body did. She relaxed so much that she fell asleep. When she awoke, to her surprise, it was dark outside. As she scrambled out of her car, she abruptly stopped at the sight of Mark leaning against a tree, watching her. She wondered for a moment how long he had been there.

Mark looked at her tenderly, and asked in a concerned voice, "How are you doing?"

"I'm doing fine, Chief," Kelly said bitterly. "And I don't need you, or your pity."

"Kelly," Mark said in a hurt voice, "it's not like that."

"It's exactly like that!" Kelly said staring at him with fire in her eyes. "I only wish I'd seen it months ago."

As Kelly heatedly stomped off, she said under her breath, "Any time my world is falling apart, he wants to be the one to put it back together. This time," Kelly said solemnly, "I'm leaving my life in God's hands. Baily was right. He is my Heavenly Father, and I need to start acting like His daughter."

Twenty-One

On New Year's Eve, an exhausted Mel went to bed at 8:00 p.m. By 9:00 p.m., Kelly was so bored that she decided to head off to Rand and Becca's. When Kelly got to their house, she saw that they had invited the entire Young Adults Group from church, plus quite a few friends from the force.

Rand and Becca greeted Kelly warmly, and then Becca grabbed Kelly by the arm, and hauled her into the kitchen. "I'm so glad that you came!" she said giving Kelly a big hug. "I know it will be good for you to be here."

"Thanks, Becca," Kelly said sincerely. "You're a good friend." Kelly paused for a moment, and then said, "Can you believe that Mel is already in bed for the night?

Becca laughed. "I'm glad that she is, because if she wasn't, you never would have come!"

Kelly laughed. "That's true."

As Kelly and Becca joined the guests in the living room, Noah Olin came up and greeted Kelly. "Hey, Kelly, I miss seeing you downtown. When are you coming back to work?"

"Soon, Noah," Kelly said smiling at her long-time friend. "Hey, Bec, did you know that Noah and I graduated from the Academy together?"

"No," Becca said, studying the tall, dark-haired officer, "I didn't realize that you guys went through the Academy at the same time."

"We did more then that," the handsome officer said in a teasing voice. "Kelly and I actually went on two dates."

"You never told me that you dated Noah, Kelly!" Becca said in an indignant tone. "You should have told me that."

"Don't worry, Becca," Noah said in a light tone," she probably didn't even remember."

"Yes, I do, Noah," Kelly said quickly. "We had a good time together."

"Is that an invitation, Kel?" Noah said arching his dark eyebrows upward. "I thought you and the Chief were an item. But, to be honest with you, I wasn't so sure lately."

"It's over between me and the Chief," Kelly said quickly. "And, to be honest with you, I'm not ready to return to the dating scene yet."

"Could we do something as friends?" Noah persisted in a gentle way.

Kelly couldn't help but smile at him. "Isn't that the same line you used on me, to get me to go out with you before?"

Noah smiled broadly, and let a quiet laugh escape. "You're probably right, Kel. But in all fairness...I was planning on pursuing you, after you came on board here at Sawyer. The Chief just beat me to it."

As if on cue, Mark walked in at that moment with Wendy Bennett. Wendy was an attractive redhead from church, and about the same age as Mark. She stuck to Mark's side as though there was some kind of invisible leash linking them together.

Kelly could tell that Wendy was working her hardest to impress Mark, and to her dismay, Mark seemed entirely too happy to be with her. "Why do I even care?" Kelly thought, pulling her eyes off of them.

Just then, Noah's voice broke through Kelly's thoughts. "Hey, Kel, do you want to go grab a chair with me?"

"Sure, Noah," Kelly replied quickly. She was relieved that Noah went to the opposite end of the living room from Mark. She purposely turned her back to Mark, and concentrated on the group of people around her.

Soon, she found herself swept up in Rand's lively conversation. Rand was a great story-teller, and he had the group around him in stitches. When the shrill of the phone filled the air, Rand jumped up to answer it.

As he came back from the kitchen, he was smiling at Kelly. "It's for you Kel...a certain young gentleman."

As Kelly got out of her seat, she said quietly to Rand, "Is it A.J.?"

Rand simply smiled and nodded.

"Hi, A.J.," Kelly said relaxing in the empty kitchen. She dropped to the floor and stretched her long legs out in front of her.

"Happy New Year, Kelly. Are you having a fun time at Rand's party?" A.J. asked her excitedly.

Kelly smiled at the boy's enthusiasm. "Happy New Year to you, too, Buddy. And yes, I'm having fun at the party." After they talked for a few more minutes, A.J. said that he wanted to say hi to Mark.

"I'll get him, A.J. Hang on for a minute." Reluctantly, Kelly sought out Mark.

"Chief, A.J. wants to talk to you. He's on the phone in the kitchen." As Kelly turned to leave, Mark put a solid arm around her waist.

"Come with me," he said firmly, dragging her along. As Kelly began to protest, Mark said emphatically, "We need to talk to A.J. together."

Mark talked causally with A.J for several minutes. Kelly listened as Mark told him about the party, and how he wanted to take him sledding soon. "Wait a minute...," Mark said eyeing Kelly curiously.

"A.J. wants to know if you'll join us for sledding?"

Kelly looked at Mark in disbelief. "Mark," she finally said in a determined tone, "that wouldn't be a good idea."

"That's what I thought you'd say," Mark said in a stubborn voice. "So," he said handing her the phone, "you can explain to A.J. why you won't be coming."

Kelly stuck her hands on her hips angrily, and stared back and forth between Mark and the phone he was holding out to her. "You're not being fair!" she said to him, through a clenched jaw.

"I'm being perfectly fair," Mark said in a determined voice. "I'm inviting you, and you're turning me down."

Kelly knew that this was not going to be worked out in a few minutes. She grabbed the phone from Mark, and spoke quickly to A.J., "Hey, Buddy, I can't come sledding with you and the Chief. But, I promise I'll take you another time." Kelly watched in frustration, as Mark calmly leaned against the counter, casually crossing his arms against his chest, as if he had all the time in the world. By the look on his face, she knew that they would be having a discussion as soon as she hung up.

"What?" Kelly said vaguely aware that A.J. had asked her something.

"No, A.J., when I bring you sledding, the Chief will not be joining us." Kelly sighed heavily as A.J. continued to press her on this issue.

"A.J., hang on for a minute," Kelly said quickly. Then, she turned to look directly at Mark. "You can go now. I may be a while."

"I think I'll stay," Mark said in a firm voice. "I want to listen to you explain this to A.J." Kelly narrowed her eyes at him menacingly, and then turned her back on Mark. "Listen, A.J.," Kelly began slowly, "I need to tell you something. Mark and I are no longer dating. We will still be doing lots of things with you, but just not all together."

"Can you be my girlfriend now, Kelly?" A.J. asked anxiously.

"No, A.J., I can not be your girlfriend now. I've explained all this to you before. We are friends. That's all." Kelly ran a hand nervously through her hair. "Listen, Pal, I'll call you tomorrow. OK?"

As Kelly hung up the phone, she eyed Mark curiously. He had a big, obnoxious-looking smile plastered to his face. "So, A.J. is ready to pick up where I left off," Mark said in a cool voice.

Kelly's eyes narrowed. "You know, Mark, he's going to be a better boyfriend for some girl, someday, than you'll ever be. A.J. always speaks what's on his mind. He doesn't play mind games like you do, and he doesn't use or hurt anyone."

As Kelly swung away from him to leave the room, Mark grabbed her hand quickly, and pulled her back. "You're not being fair, Kelly," he said looking directly into her eyes. "And I'm sure you don't really believe that."

"I am being fair, Mark. And I do believe it, because I've experienced it first hand," Kelly said angrily.

"We need to talk," he said taking a step closer to her.

"There is nothing to talk about," Kelly said furiously. "I should go back to the party now."

"You mean you should get back to Noah," Mark said in an accusing tone.

Kelly spun around, and looked at Mark with a bewildered expression. "And, just what is that supposed to mean?" she said glaring at him, as she threw her hands on her hips.

"Just what I said," he said in a chilly voice. "It looks like the two of you were really hitting it off."

"Noah," Kelly said intently taking a step closer to Mark, "is a friend. We graduated from the Academy together. Besides," Kelly said, working hard to keep her voice level, "it looks like Wendy was keeping you pretty happy."

Mark's mouth fell open. "Wendy...," he said as if he had eaten something awful. "You've got to be kidding." Mark paused, and then said evenly, "You're jealous."

Kelly actually laughed. "No, Mark. I'm really not. I might have been at one time...but not anymore."

As Kelly turned to go, Mark said softly, "I love you, Kelly."

Kelly spun around and stared at him. "Don't play games with me, Mark."

"I'm not, Kelly. I love you," he said sincerely. "I never stopped loving you."

"I don't believe you," Kelly said firmly, with tears welling up in her eyes. "I don't think you ever really loved me."

"Kelly," Mark said in a desperate voice, "can we please talk?"

"Mark," Kelly said in a choked-up voice, "you said that I could trust you...and like a fool, I trusted you with my heart. You promised me that you'd never hurt me...and you crushed me. And now," Kelly said throwing an angry hand in the air, "you have the nerve to tell me that you love me." Kelly paused for a moment to catch her breath. "That's not love, Mark. True love isn't something that you turn on and off." She paused again, and ran a hand through her hair. "So, to answer your question...no, I don't want to talk. From this moment on, I expect our relationship to be strictly professional."

Then Kelly spun on her heel, and left the kitchen. She quickly found Becca and Rand, and thanked them, and then headed back to Mel's. Even though she was exhausted, Kelly knew she wouldn't be able to sleep. Who did Mark Mitchell think he was anyway? Did he think that she was a puppet on a string that he could jerk around at will?

Kelly sighed heavily. She knew that she would have to spend her time avoiding Mark

Mitchell, because whenever she was around him, that's exactly what she felt like...a puppet on a string.

Kelly dropped to her knees in a helpless frustration. Bowing her head, she prayed fervently. "Oh, dear Lord, please help me. I know Mark's gone now...but I can still feel him here. I dream about him every night, and see him everywhere throughout my days. I can feel his eyes looking at me, and feel his touch on me, but when I look up, he's not there. Oh, Lord, I keep looking for someone who's not there. Help me, Father, to stop looking. Help me to let go of Mark, and help me to look only to You."

Twenty-Two

Kelly tried hard to return to normal life. Her "New Year's Resolution" was to prove to herself that there was life after Mark Mitchell. As much as her heart ached for what she once had with Mark, she was determined, with God's help, not to dwell on the past, and allow God to make the future even brighter.

Kelly started regularly attending the Young Adults Group at church. She found the Bible studies not only thought provoking, but truly healing as well. The discussions were always high-energy, and challenging, and Kelly found herself always looking forward to the weekly meetings.

Kelly discovered that the more that she gave her problems up to the Lord, and trusted in Him, the lighter her burden of life became. She could feel herself growing in the Lord, yet through all her growth, she knew she had to completely let go of the past. And she had to forgive. She had to forgive Pitman, and, in another way, she had to forgive Mark. She knew that both issues would not be resolved in her life until she had truly forgiven both men.

Seeing Mark on a daily basis did not make it easier for Kelly to forgive and forget. She knew in her heart that she still loved him, and despite trying to convince herself otherwise, she knew it was all too true. This only infuriated Kelly, and made it harder for her to be around Mark.

As Kelly was trying to make sense of this one morning on the way to work, she suddenly saw the red and blue lights of a squad car behind her. She groaned loudly, and eased her Celica to the side of the road. As Micky Bencher approached her car, Kelly quickly rolled down her window. In an angry voice, she asked, "Micky, what are you doing?"

"Kelly," he said defensively, "you were doing sixty in a twenty-five."

"Really?" Kelly said completely surprised. "Well listen, Mic, I'll slow down. I need to go now, or I'll be late for work."

"Kelly," Micky said as he pulled out his ticket pad, "I need to ticket you. It's the Chief's orders."

"Micky!" Kelly yelled in a panicked tone, "If you ticket me, the Chief is going to kill me. You know that!" she said with pleading eyes. "You can't give me a ticket!"

"Kelly," Micky said putting his hands on his hips, "if I don't give you a ticket, and the Chief finds out about it, he'll have my badge!"

"I swear...I won't breathe a word of this," Kelly said begging him.

"Sorry, Kel, but I have no choice," Micky said in an insincere voice, as he wrote her out a big fat ticket. Micky could be such a rat that Kelly knew he'd ticket his own grandmother for going one mile over the limit.

As Kelly headed into roll call that morning, she wondered just how soon Mark would find out about the ticket. Since Micky's shift was ending just as Kelly's was beginning, she hoped she would get out of the station before Mic spilled the beans.

Immediately after roll call, Kelly grabbed Rand's arm, and began shoving him toward the door. "We have to go now," Kelly said in an urgent voice.

"What's the rush, Kel? I wanted to get a cup of coffee first."

"No, Rand," Kelly said panicking. "We need to leave now. You can drive...," she said tossing the keys to him. "We just need to leave now."

Rand followed Kelly to the squad car and was quiet until they pulled away from the station. "You'd better tell me what's going on, Kel," he said quietly.

"Oh!" Kelly said in a frustrated tone. "That stupid Micky Bencher! I swear that guy hates me!"

"What did he do?" Rand asked in a concerned, but curious voice.

"He ticketed me coming down Tim's Path. Can you believe that?" Kelly said heatedly.

"How fast?" Rand said sounding like an upset parent.

"It doesn't matter, Rand," Kelly replied defensively.

"Yes, Kelly. It does," Rand said firmly. "How fast?"

"I was doing sixty...," Kelly said as if it were no big deal.

"In a twenty-five, Kel...? What are you, nuts? Mark is going to have your head!"

"Maybe he won't find out about it," Kelly said in a hopeful voice.

Just then the radio crackled to life. "Kelly," Trudy, the dispatcher, said in an anxious voice, "the Chief wants to see you back in his office now."

Kelly angrily grabbed the radio mic. "Trudy, Rand and I are doing rounds. Tell the Chief that I'll see him at the end of the day."

"Douglas!" Mark yelled into the radio. "Get yourself back to the station *now*!"

"Yes, Sir," Kelly said quietly.

As Rand turned the cruiser around, he just shook his head at her.

"You're dead, Kel," he said in a worried voice. "I wonder what he's going to do to you this time?"

"I have no idea, Rand," Kelly said running her hand nervously through her hair. "I'm starting to think that maybe I should check out that position down in Whitewater. I'd still get to be a cop, and it's only half an hour from Sawyer."

At that moment, Baily's words came back to Kelly. "Trust in your Heavenly Father. He will take care of you."

Kelly went back to her car, and dropped herself into the seat. She bowed her head, and talked with her Heavenly Father. "Father, I've tried to work this thing out with Mark, but I know I'm not handling it very well. I can't work for him anymore. It's just too painful. Please help me, Father. Help me put my life back together again."

Kelly drove back to her house, crying the whole way. In her heart, she was saying good-bye to Sawyer's Crossing, and it was turning out to be harder than she thought.

As she pulled into her driveway, her mouth dropped open at the sight of a cruiser sitting there. Kelly watched curiously as Rand slowly got out of his car.

"What are you doing here?" she asked him, as she slowly walked toward him.

"The Chief put out an APB on you...," Rand said quietly, "and I wanted to be the one to bring you in."

"Mark put out an 'All Points Bulletin' on me!" Kelly shouted. "What in the world for?"

"I'm not exactly sure," Rand said as he opened the passenger door for her. "Maybe it has something to do with your resignation."

As Rand drove Kelly to the station, she couldn't remember dreading anything more. Why didn't Mark just let her go quietly? And why did he have to humiliate her with an APB?

As Kelly slowly walked through the station, she could feel every eye glued to her. She approached Trudy's desk cautiously. In a whisper, she said, "Trud...if the Chief is busy, I can come back later."

At the sound of her voice, Mark came flying around the corner. He looked like a guard dog, ready to attack. "In my office. Now!" he said in a low voice that held all the fury of a tornado.

Kelly was actually so nervous that she began shaking. What was she going to say to Mark? How was she going to tell him the real reason for her resignation? Kelly desperately tried to think of an answer as far away from the truth as possible. She knew she'd fall apart if she ever got close to the truth.

"Sit," Mark ordered her, as she followed him into his office. He shut the door, and then took a seat behind his large oak desk. "I believe we have a few things to discuss," he said in an even voice that seemed barely controlled. His eyes narrowed intently, and Kelly could see the fire burning within him.

When Kelly didn't say anything, Mark sighed loudly. "OK...I'll begin." He reached down on his desk, and held up her badge and gun. "Do you mind telling me the meaning of this?"

His look was so disapproving, that Kelly had to turn away. "I'm resigning," she said in a quiet voice, that held just a hint of trembling.

As she turned back towards Mark, he was eyeing her hard. "I understand that," he said watching her with the same penetrating expression, "but what I don't understand is the reason why."

Again Kelly looked away from him. She didn't answer. She just didn't trust her wobbly voice to speak.

"Kelly," Mark said in a gentler tone, "I think you owe me some sort of explanation here."

"I decided to accept a position down in Whitewater. Chief Maynard has been offering me a spot on his force for months now...and I've decided to accept his offer."

"That wasn't my question, Kelly," Mark said in a firm voice. She could see Mark's anger building, and felt herself becoming increasingly nervous. "What I asked you is why you want to leave."

Once again, Kelly turned away from Mark's heated, probing eyes. A man like Mark Mitchell demanded the truth, and Kelly knew he would stop at nothing until he got it. This was a good quality for a cop to have, but having this quality turned on you could make you wish that you were dead. Kelly cleared her throat, and then said in as sure a voice as she could, "The reasons I'm choosing to leave are personal. I'd rather not discuss them."

"I'd rather we did, Kelly," Mark said quickly. "I feel you owe me the truth."

"Mark," Kelly said looking angrily at him, "I can't work with you anymore!"

Mark nodded and sighed heavily. "I had thought as much." He ran a hand through his thin blonde hair. "But I thought you could maintain a professional relationship with me. Isn't that what you said?"

"Mark," Kelly said in an exasperated tone, "I can't do it anymore. I'm sorry."

"So am I," Mark said eyeing her tenderly. "I really wanted to discuss our personal relationship." Mark said earnestly.

"Mark, I can't drag myself through that again," Kelly said in a desperate voice.

"Kelly," Mark said leaning forward on his desk, "I am requesting one hour of your personal time." He paused and took a deep breath. "What we had was special. Don't you think it deserves an hour?"

Kelly bit her lip and looked away. She had to admit, she was curious about Mark's sudden emotional departure from their relationship. And, she thought sighing deeply, if she never took the time to find out what had happened between them, she knew she'd always wonder. "When?" Kelly asked looking cautiously at Mark.

"Are you available tonight?" Mark asked, seeming suddenly very vulnerable. "I can stop by around seven."

Kelly felt a lump growing in her throat, and she begged the tears not to come. She hated the way this man melted her armor and simply had a way of turning her into mush. She felt Mark's probing eyes on her, and answered quickly. "That should be fine," she said in a shaky voice.

"Good," Mark said smiling in relief. He sighed loudly, and then said in a hesitant tone, "And now, we need to talk about this." He held Kelly's speeding ticket up in the air.

"Micky was out of line!" Kelly said instantly exploding in anger."

"You were speeding!" Mark said in a hard, authoritative voice. There was no mistaking the anger in his tone. "And...by a lot. It says here that you were doing sixty in a twenty-five!" Mark's volume was rising steadily. He had actually shouted the last sentence at her. Kelly had to turn away from the fury she saw blazing in his heated blue eyes.

"I was planning on paying the ticket, Mark," Kelly said in a defensive tone. "I wasn't planning on leaving Sawyer before I took care of it." Kelly said looking at him with a fire burning in her, that matched his own. "Why are you being such a pain about this!"

"Why?" Mark jumped up from his seat so quickly that Kelly could hardly blink. He swiftly moved around the desk and stood so close to her that his hot, angry breath beat down on her face. "Why?" he said again, his voice growing steadily in volume. "I'll tell you why, Kelly. Speed is the number one killer on Vermont's roads. Not drinking and driving, not drugs, but speeding." He paused and began to pace angrily. "And you," he said tossing an accusing finger at her, "are going to wind up killing yourself, or someone else, one of these days by your speeding."

Kelly just stared at him for a full minute. She was so steamed that she didn't trust what might come out of her mouth. Finally, in a cold voice, she said evenly, "You can't tell me what to do, Chief Mitchell. I don't work for you anymore."

Mark's grin spread slowly across his face. "Ah...," he said in an ultra-calm voice, "now that's where you're wrong, Officer Douglas. Until your ticket is worked off...I can tell you what to do...because I'm still your boss."

Kelly just stared at the huge, victorious smile that was solidly planted across Mark's face. Her first inclination was to smack it off. He just looked so smug, standing there with his arms folded neatly across his chest. In his mind, it was clear that he had won the battle. In Kelly's mind, the war had just begun. "Exactly what are you talking about?"

"Obviously," Mark said sounding quite pleased with himself, "you never read the memo that I sent you on speeding." Mark's eyebrow's rose, challenging her to deny it.

Kelly hadn't. She was angry when she saw the subject content, and chucked the memo in the trash. Now, a small wave of anxiety began to creep up on her, as she wondered exactly what the blasted thing had said. She had a feeling it was Mark's hole-in-one.

"Well, let me review the policy for you, Officer Douglas," Mark said smirking at her confidently. "A first time speeding offense, gets me as your partner for a week. And," Mark said turning his head slightly, as he arched his eyebrows at her obnoxiously, "we did that one...remember?"

Kelly only scowled at him, and Mark actually had the nerve to laugh at her. "I'll take that as a 'yes,' that you remember. And," Mark said casually, as he dropped back into his seat, "a second speeding offense requires two things." He paused a moment, and waited for Kelly to look at him. "Would you be interested in hearing them?"

He was acting so obnoxiously that Kelly sat on her hands so she wouldn't punch him. "Go on," she replied in a low voice.

"A second time speeding offender has to watch *Signal 31* with me and teach Driver's Ed. at the high school."

"No way!" Kelly shouted angrily, jumping up from her chair. "You can't impose your stupid rules on me anymore, Mark! I quit!"

In a quick, firm voice, Mark replied confidently, "That is your choice, Officer Douglas, however, if you leave here without this situation resolved, you'll never get a job as a cop anywhere in Vermont again."

"You'd blackball me?" Kelly asked in an appalled voice.

"No, Kelly," Mark said narrowing his eyes at her, "your own speeding record would do that for you."

"I can't believe I ever dated you!" Kelly said bitterly to Mark. He just stared at her evenly, and gave her a tight smile.

"I'm going to see a lawyer." Kelly said walking toward the door. "This stinks, and you know it!"

"You brought it on yourself," Mark said calmly, without a trace remorse. "I'm not the only one who's cracking down on speeding. Vermont is doing a statewide movement. If you leave here without resolving this...you're finished."

Kelly spun around and faced him squarely. "You can't enforce this," she said in a challenging tone.

"Yes, Kelly...," Mark said standing up and slowly walking towards her, "I can. Not only does the state of Vermont give me the power to enforce this, the town of Sawyer does as well."

Kelly instinctively knew he was right, and that only made her madder. "I will agree to teaching the stupid driving class, but," she said boldly taking a step closer to Mark, "I'm not watching *Signal 31*."

"You've already seen it once when you took your Driver's Ed. class," Mark said matter-of-factly.

Kelly interrupted him, "No, Mark, I never saw that horrible film. Baily was able to get me out of it."

"He didn't do you any favors, Kelly," Mark said drilling angry blue eyes into her. "Maybe if you had seen it, you wouldn't be the rocket driver you are today."

Kelly stood her ground determinedly. "Mark...I've had enough nightmares in my life. I don't need to watch *Signal 31* to give me any more."

"Kelly," Mark said in a gentler voice, "I'm not doing this to be mean. I'm trying to save your life."

Kelly spun around almost violently. "Don't do me any favors, Mark! I'm not watching *Signal 31*."

"This is not a negotiable deal, Kelly," Mark said in a low voice. He was so mad that he was turning red in the face. "It's Driver's Ed., and *Signal 31*."

She turned to him fuming mad. "I...," she quickly snapped her mouth shut.

Mark went and stood right in front of her, with his arms crossed firmly across his chest. "You were going to say that you hate me...weren't you?" Mark said in a very serious tone. "Well, Kelly Douglas, you can go ahead and hate me. You can hate me all you want if it means saving your life."

Kelly was so angry that she bit her lip so she wouldn't say anything more. Mark Mitchell was not saving her life, he was slowly, and methodically destroying it. First their relationship had gone sour, then feeling forced to leave Sawyer, and now...these stupid regulations. The Driver's Ed. class she could swallow, but not *Signal 31*.

Signal 31 was a film made by the Vermont State Troopers. They were so tried of seeing young people killed on the highways that they began taking camcorders with them to real accident scenes and videotaping the deadly results of drinking and driving, and speeding. The outcome of their effort was the famous, yet incredibly gruesome, *Signal 31*. Vividly and up close you saw the accident scenes, and the film spared no detail. The finished film showed accident after accident with bloodied bodies scattered across the highways. Oftentimes, they were dismembered, and the film showed you that up close too.

Signal 31 so strongly affected its audiences that young people often threw up, passed out, or cried openly. Kelly knew if she saw the horrible film, it would be the type of thing that she could never get out of her mind.

"Mark," Kelly said close to tears, "I'm not watching *Signal 31*."

"Kelly," he said soberly, "you'll be watching it twice. Once with me, right now, and again when you show it to your Driver's Ed. class."

"Please don't do this to me," Kelly begged him.

"I have to, Kelly," Mark said in a quiet, serious voice.

"Why are you such a stickler for speeding?" Kelly demanded. "Millions of people speed every day."

"I guess I never mentioned Michael to you," Mark said in a whisper of a voice.

"Michael?" Kelly asked in a confused voice." Michael who?"

"Michael Mitchell," Mark replied in a solemn tone. "It's time you meet my brother, Kelly. He's one of the stars of *Signal 31*."

Kelly's mouth dropped open. "I didn't know you had a brother."

"I did," Mark said looking away from her. "He was a year older than me. He died in a highway accident when he was sixteen." Mark paused, and then cleared his throat. "Come on, it's time you meet him."

Kelly mechanically followed Mark out of his office, and into the conference room. "Have a seat," he said in a monotonous voice.

"Mark, you don't have to do this to yourself," Kelly said in a concerned voice.

"Kelly," Mark said sitting in a chair next to hers, "I need to do this for you. I am convinced that you will end up just like Michael. If I can do something to prevent that, I will." He paused, and then looked directly into her eyes. "Even if you hate me for the rest of your life...I feel like I've got to try to help you."

"I don't hate you, Mark," Kelly said quickly, in a quiet voice.

Mark held her eyes with his own. "I hope you still feel that way after you've seen the film, Kel. It's the worst thing that I've ever seen in my life."

His voice was completely void of any emotion, and it sent a cold chill down Kelly's spine.

As the film began, a picture of Michael Mitchell was put on the screen. Kelly was shocked at how much Michael and Mark resembled each other. "He looks just like you," Kelly whispered in a unbelieving voice.

"I know," Mark said in a voice filled with pain. "He was my best friend. Not a day goes by that I don't miss him." He cleared his throat, and then said quietly, "Michael was a good kid Kel, you would have liked him. He just had one bad habit...speeding."

Kelly closed her eyes as the next scene cut to Michael's accident. His truck had gone off a mountain road, and struck a large pine tree.

"Open your eyes," Mark commanded her.

"I can't!" Kelly said in a shaking voice." I can't watch this!"

"Kelly," Mark said urgently, "if you watch Michael's accident, I won't make you watch the rest of the film."

Kelly slowly opened her eyes, and forced herself to look at the screen. Michael hadn't been wearing a seatbelt, and went through the windshield. The next scene showed Michael's body that had literally been sliced in half from a farmer's wire fence. As the camera zoomed in on the body, Kelly flew out of her seat. Grabbing a near by trashcan, she emptied the contents of her stomach into it.

Mark came over and handed her a box of tissues. As she took them, she saw the tears streaming down his face as well. Kelly dragged herself to the door. "I need to go to the ladies' room."

After Kelly cleaned herself up, she went back to Mark's office. He was behind his desk looking at her seriously as she came in. "Shut the door, please," he said softly. Kelly did, and then went and took a seat in front of Mark's desk.

They sat in a thoughtful silence for several minutes, until Kelly said in a sincere voice, "Mark, I'm so sorry about your brother."

Marked nodded. "He was a good guy, Kel. Everyone loved him."

Kelly nodded compassionately at him.

Mark's face grew very serious, and he studied her a minute. "I'm very concerned about you, Kelly. I've had nightmares about you ending up like Michael." Mark looked at her directly, never taking his eyes off of her. "If you don't slow down, it's only going to be a matter of time."

Kelly sighed deeply. "You're probably right." She paused, and then said in a whisper, "I know you're right. It's just so hard for me to drive slowly. It almost makes me crazy."

"You're going to have to work on that, Kelly. In your case...," he said narrowing his eyes at her, "it's a matter of life and death."

Kelly didn't say anything, but she nodded at Mark. What could she say? She knew she drove like a rocket. And *Signal 31* was a vivid reminder of what happens to rocket drivers. Eventually you stop speeding, or you're stopped.

"So, what do I do now?" Kelly asked Mark in a small, helpless-sounding voice.

"Tomorrow afternoon, you show up at the high school at 2:30. You'll start teaching your Driver's Ed. class. The course lasts six weeks, and," Mark said in a regretful-sounding voice, "at the end of six weeks, you're free to leave Sawyer and seek employment elsewhere."

As Kelly got up to go, Mark called her back. "Officer Douglas," he said as he held up Kelly's badge and gun to her, "you'll need these."

"Thanks, Chief," Kelly said taking the items from him.

"And," Mark continued in an earnest voice, "don't forget that I'll be stopping by your place around seven."

Kelly sighed loudly. "I won't forget," she said looking into Mark's serious face. "I'll be there."

Twenty-Four

As Kelly let Mark in that evening, she thought that he looked worn-out, and older than his thirty-five years. She quietly led him over to the kitchen table, where they sat across from each other.

Kelly watched anxiously as Mark fiddled nervously with his keys. Finally, in a weak voice, he quickly said, "This is real tough for me Kel, so...cut me some slack, would ya?"

"Mark," Kelly said in a soft voice, gently touching his arm, "take your time. I'm not judging you. I'm just very confused by the way you acted. I really want to understand."

Mark looked relieved, and nodded gratefully at Kelly. "It's probably going to be better if I just spit it out." He sighed loudly, and then began.

"During the Pitman incident, when we were at Pappy's General Store, I felt so responsible for you. It was my fault that you were in there with

Pitman in the first place. Because I wasn't careful in doing my job, Pitman almost killed you."

"Mark!" Kelly said in a breathless voice, that was full of disbelief, "None of it was your fault. No one could have predicted or prevented Pitman's crazy actions."

"I disagree," Mark said emphatically. "I'm the Chief, and it was my job to make sure that you stayed safe. I blew it, and it almost cost the woman I love her life."

"Mark...," Kelly said, totally taken off-guard by his statement, "no one saw this coming. Rand was there, too."

"But I was personally responsible for your safety, Kelly," Mark said in an urgent voice, willing her to understand. "And I failed..."

"Mark!" Kelly said touching his hand. She waited until his eyes met hers. "You did save my life. You pulled me behind the counter, and you and Rand took Pitman out. If you weren't there, I would be dead right now."

"Kelly," Mark said angrily, "I never should have allowed you to be in that position in the first place."

"Mark Mitchell!" Kelly said in an exasperated tone. "Do you think that you have the power and control of God Himself? You can't predict life's moves with a hundred percent accuracy. You do the best you can...with the information that you have." Kelly paused, and then said in a sincere voice, "It never once entered my mind to blame you for anything. Mark...," Kelly said squeezing his hand hard, "you saved me. Do you understand that? You saved my life!"

"It was too close of a call, Kel," Mark said in a choked-up voice.

"You're not looking at me like an officer, Mark. You're looking at me like your girlfriend."

"At that time, Kelly, you were my girlfriend," Mark replied angrily.

"Mark, whenever I'm on duty, I'm an officer, and you've got to see me that way."

"I don't think I can separate the two, Kel," Mark said honestly. "I know you're a cop, but you're also the woman that I love. Seeing you so close to death...I felt my world falling apart." He paused, and then said softly, "If you had died that day, I never could have gone on." He paused again, and with great effort pushed on. "After that incident, I tried to convince myself that I could go on living without you. I began to pull away from you..." Mark stopped and wiped his teary eyes. "I thought that if I pushed you away before I lost you to a nut like Pitman, or before you ended up like Michael, that I'd be OK. But," he said looking deeply into Kelly's eyes, "I wasn't OK. Things were even worse without you. I've never been in such pain."

Kelly was crying hard by this time. She could relate to Mark's response. "It doesn't work, Mark. After my parents died, I was afraid to love or trust anyone else for a long time. I began to push everyone around me away, and the only thing that I did was cause a whole lot of pain. It caused pain to those that I loved, and it caused pain to me." Kelly wiped her eyes with her shirtsleeve, and then went on.

"Not until recently did I realize that I needed to trust God not only with my life, but also with those around me. It's the only way that we can truly live, Mark. We need to trust God in all areas of our lives."

Mark looked at Kelly intently, and she continued. "You see, Mark, trusting God is easy when we can see the outcome. It doesn't take much faith or trust at all when life is routine and sailing along smoothly. But," Kelly said, holding Mark's hand gently, "faith and trust take on a whole new level when our lives become uncertain. When we can't figure things out, or see the light at the end of the tunnel, when our circumstances in life make no sense at all...that's when the rubber meets the road. That's when you have to ask God to help you and, through faith, you have to trust in Him." Kelly paused and wiped her eyes again.

"Don't you see, Mark...God wants us to trust in Him, and when we do, life's burdens are lifted off our shoulders, as we allow God to direct our lives."

Mark dropped his head down into his hands and cried. Kelly went over to him, and tenderly placed her arms around him. He allowed her to comfort him, and Kelly felt grateful. After a time, she let go of him, and sat down next to him.

"Oh, Kel," Mark said wiping his eyes with his hands, "I wish I had your faith."

"Mark," Kelly said honestly, "I don't have a great deal of faith. My faith is actually pretty small...but with God's help, it's growing. That's the wonderful thing, Mark, God always accepts us where we're at. We don't have to be at any certain level to come to Him. He wants us to come to Him right where we're at."

"Kelly," Mark said in a voice filled with pain, "I am the Chief here at Sawyer. I'm responsible for so much. I have to justify my actions to the town."

"Mark," Kelly said earnestly, "you have to justify your actions to God. You're forgetting that He's the real boss of this town. In effect, Chief Mark Mitchell, you work for Him."

Mark's mouth dropped open, and Kelly couldn't help but laugh at the surprised expression on his face. "I guess you never thought of that before, did you, Chief?" Kelly smiled at Mark lovingly.

"No, I didn't," Mark said thoughtfully. A smile began to creep across his face. "I guess that changes my job description some, doesn't it?"

Kelly nodded. "I'd say so, Mark. You're a servant of the Lord. You work for Him. And," Kelly said as she folded her arms across her chest, "the sooner you realize that, the better off you'll be. You don't need to carry the burden of this town on your shoulders, Mark Mitchell. Give it over to the Lord."

"Will you pray with me, Kel?" Mark asked in such a vulnerable voice that it broke Kelly's heart.

"Of course, Mark," she said slipping her hand in his."

"Father," Mark began in a heartfelt voice, "I'm so sorry that I've been taking Your job away from You. Please help me to put my job, and my entire life back into Your hands." Mark choked up for a minute, and Kelly squeezed his hand reassuringly. After a moment, he continued, "Father, this burden is too heavy, and there's too much to worry about. Please, dear God, every day, help me to place my life, and my job in Your hands. And, Father," Mark said as he squeezed Kelly's hand hard, "please help Kelly to be able to forgive me for pushing her away. I'm so sorry that I ever did. I love her more then anything. Help her to know how sorry I am, and how much I truly love her."

Kelly felt so choked up, that it was hard to get the words out. "Heavenly Father, keep us both in Your hands. Guide us and direct our lives, and help us to trust in You. And Father," Kelly said in a soft voice, "help Mark to know that I never stopped loving him. Help him to know how special he is to me, and, that he's the best thing that You ever brought into my life."

After Kelly said amen, Mark put a hand to her face, and gently turned her cheek until her eyes met his. He searched her eyes for a moment before he spoke. "Really?" he said, bewildered. "You really still love me?"

"Mark, I never stopped loving you," Kelly said, looking lovingly into his questioning eyes.

"Then why did you break up with me?"

"Mark," Kelly said in a frustrated voice, "I couldn't take the silence between us. You wouldn't open up to me. You looked miserable, and you were definitely pushing me away. That's a painful thing to have happen to you, especially when you love the person who's shoving you aside."

Mark drew Kelly into his arms and held her tightly. "Honey, I'm so sorry. I promise you, I'll never do that again. Can you ever forgive me?"

Kelly smiled at Mark tenderly. "Mark, I forgave you a long time ago."

"Then why do you want to leave Sawyer?" he asked in a confused tone.

"Mark, when you love someone who isn't loving you in return, it's painful to be around them."

Mark closed his eyes, and drew her near again. "I'm so sorry, Kel. I love you so much. I never meant to hurt you."

"I know," Kelly said in an understanding voice.

"So, what are we going to do, Kel?" Mark said turning her face toward his. "I know that you don't really want to leave Sawyer."

"You're right. I don't."

"Can we work this out?" Mark asked in a hopeful voice. "Is there anything that I can say or do, that will convince you to stay?"

A big smile spread across Kelly's face, as she looked over at him lovingly. "I can think of one thing that would make me stay."

"What?" Mark asked, completely clueless as to the direction Kelly was heading.

Kelly took both of Mark's hands in hers, and slowly pulled him up so that he was standing next to her. "Mark Mitchell," Kelly said in a tender voice, "I love you more then I have ever loved anyone in my life. Will you marry me?"

"What?" Mark said in surprise. "You want to marry me?"

Kelly slowly nodded, her face beaming. "Yes Mark, I'm proposing to you."

"You are?" Mark asked, his eyes growing bigger then saucers.

"Yes," Kelly said stepping closer to him.

"Isn't that my job?" Mark asked, as a smile quickly covered his face. "I thought I was supposed to ask you?"

"I was afraid that you might not get around to it," Kelly said in a teasing voice. "So, I decided that I'd better ask you."

"You are serious!" Mark said studying her carefully.

"Yes, Mark, I am," Kelly said, growing solemn. "This is the point in the proposal when you're supposed to answer the question. You either accept the proposal, or you send me packing."

Mark's smile spread ear to ear, and his face was literally glowing with all the love he felt for Kelly. As he looked down into her face, he said softy, but confidently, "Kelly Douglas, I love you with all my heart, and have wanted to marry you since the first day that I met you. Yes, Kelly," Mark said taking her into his arms, "I will marry you. I will marry you very soon. I love you, Sweetheart."

Twenty-Five

The very next evening, Mark invited Kelly over for dinner. As soon as he opened the door, Kelly was immediately drawn to his big, friendly, easy smile. It was the smile of the old Mark. It was the smile that let the world know that everything was well with his soul. And, Kelly thought as she smiled up at her handsome future groom, it was the smile that made her heart do flip flops...the smile that she fell forever-in-love with.

"You look like you're doing good," Kelly said as she took the hand that Mark offered to her.

"I'm doing better than good," Mark said quickly, as he leaned down and kissed her. "I'm doing great! My heart is back on track with the Lord again, and," he said wiggling his eyebrows at her, "the woman I love is going to marry me!"

Kelly couldn't stop smiling. With the Lord back at the center of their relationship, she wasn't surprised at how quickly everything was falling into place.

As Kelly followed Mark into the kitchen, she eyed her dinner with delight. "You cooked me lobster!" she said excitedly.

Mark leaned down and kissed her firmly on her lips. "I wanted to make you something special."

"It's my favorite!" Kelly said as she observed the way that Mark had them arranged with small potatoes and corn on the cob.

"I know, Kel," he said looping his arms around her. "That's why I cooked them."

"Thanks," she said appreciatively, looking up into his glowing face. "I love you."

Mark's gentle smile split his face. "And I love you, too, Sweetheart."

As they settled down to the scrumptious meal, Mark kept smiling at Kelly unbashfully. "What?" she finally asked him.

"I can't believe that we're finally going to be married."

"Well, believe it, Buddy!" Kelly replied in a teasing voice. "Remember, I did ask you!"

"I recall that," Mark said laughing lightly. "And, I'm glad you did. So," he looked over at her flirtatiously, "when do you want to get married?"

"Well," Kelly said smiling back at her blue-eyed man, "when do you want to get married?"

Mark's smile was simply charming. "Right now," he said in a serious voice.

"Mark...," Kelly said firmly.

"I know. I know. We need a little time. How about early spring?"

"Sounds good," Kelly said nodding thoughtfully. "Any time in particular?"

"Well," he said casting her another charming smile, "this is mid-February...how about next week?"

"I can see you're not going to be much help here, Mr. Mitchell," Kelly said crossing her arms across her chest.

Mark laughed. "Can I help it if I'm anxious? I love you, and want to marry you now."

"I'm glad," Kelly said smiling back at him. "Now let's see...I have that six-week Driver's Ed. class to teach....unless you want to get me out of it?" Kelly said looking at him hopefully. Mark gave her an instant hard frown. "I didn't think so," Kelly said shrugging her shoulders sheepishly. "But I thought it was worth checking. Anyways, six weeks puts us to the end of March. How about March 20th?"

"That seems so far away." He obviously was not happy with the wait.

"Well, Chief, if you want to write me an excuse note, to get out of teaching Driver's Ed., I'll marry you this weekend!"

"That's not fair, Kelly, and you know it!" he said eyeing her seriously.

"Well, Mark," she continued in a light, breezy tone, "I couldn't possibly go on a honeymoon if I have to teach that class. And," Kelly said giving him a flirtatious smile, "I suspect you do want to go on a honeymoon."

"Yes, I do. And, I see your point about the class," he said thoughtfully. "But, I really feel that you need to teach it. Especially," Mark said lacing his fingers through hers, "since you are going to be my wife, and one day driving our kids around."

"Oh," Kelly said dreamily, "I like the sound of that...wife."

"How does Mrs. Mark Mitchell sound to you? Or Kelly Mitchell?"

"It sounds great!" Kelly said smiling lovingly at him. Suddenly, she broke into laughter.

"And just what is so funny?" Mark demanded in an amused voice.

"I bet no officer here in Sawyer would give Mrs. Mark Mitchell a speeding ticket!" Kelly said roaring with laughter. "They wouldn't dare! Not the Chief of Police's wife!"

Mark's face instantly darkened. "Oh, yes, they would," he said firmly.

"I will personally make sure, Blue Eyes," he said reaching across the table and touching the tip of her nose, that all my officers help me monitor your speeding. It has to stop, Kelly. It's not a joke." Mark looked so worried that Kelly immediately grew serious.

"Mark, it is stopping," Kelly said looking at his worried, wrinkled brow. "I promise. I'm really trying." Then a smile touched the corners of her lips. "Why, I'm driving so slowly now, that the elderly pedestrians are actually passing me!"

Mark laughed. "That's all I can ask for, Kel," he said squeezing her hand hard. "But it's important that you remember that I will never be a 'Get Out Of Jail Card' for you or the kids. And," he said squeezing her hand again, "it's not because I don't love you. It's because I do. It's important for everyone to take responsibility for his own actions. If you do the crime, it's important to know that you'll have to do the time. If there were no consequences to people's actions, everything would spin out of control."

After dinner, Mark made a fire in the old stone fireplace, and the two of them snuggled on the couch. "I have some things that belong to you, Sweetheart," Mark said slowly standing up, and putting his hand in his jean pocket. "First, this heart necklace. I gave this to you the first time that I told you I loved you. I'd like very much for you to have this back."

Kelly smiled and leaned forward for Mark to put the necklace around her neck. "Thank you," she said as she watched him closely.

"And, these...," he said, holding out a pair of pearl earrings in his hand.

He had given Kelly the earrings after she had saved A.J.'s life. "Would you take these back, please..." Mark looked at her so longingly, that her heart wanted to burst from all the love she saw in his eyes.

Kelly took the small earrings, and put them back into her ears. "Thank you," she said in a choked-up voice.

"And, one more thing," he said digging into his pocket. He pulled out a sparkling diamond ring, and as he gently lifted her left hand, he slid it onto her ring finger. "I love you, Kelly, with all my heart. You have made me the happiest man in the world by agreeing to be my wife."

Mark gently pulled Kelly off the couch, and drew her tightly into his arms. He kissed her tenderly, and passionately, making her feel like the most cherished woman on the face on the earth. He was so in love with her that his head spun. He knew that with the Lord and with Kelly in his life, he was about to start the best part of his life. The joy that he would have being Kelly's husband would by far be the brightest thing in his life, next to his commitment to the Lord.

Twenty-Six

When Kelly started teaching Driver's Education at the high school, she quickly discovered what a frustrating task she had been given. Fifteen minutes into the class, she adamantly decided that none of these immature sixteen-years-olds should be driving. They all seemed too young and too foolish to be trusted behind the wheel.

At the end of the day, as she discussed the class with Mark, he could not help but smile at her. "Mark," Kelly said, clearly frustrated, "this isn't funny! These kids are going to be reckless behind the wheel. I think I'm going to fail the entire class. They're going to kill themselves."

"Kelly," Mark said laughing out loud, "I'm smiling because I'm starting to think that there might be hope for you. You're acting like I did when I confronted you with your speeding. This is a good sign."

"Mark," Kelly said in an exasperated tone, "I'm going to have to spend the next six weeks trying to instill fear in these kids...and I'm not sure that I can do a good enough job."

"That's why we have *Signal 31* Kel. That film will hopefully scare the pants off them," Mark said soberly.

"Yeah, well it scares the pants off me, too!" Kelly said running a hand nervously through her hair.

"Tell me when you're planning on showing it, and I'll be there, "Mark said seriously.

"Really?" Kelly asked grabbing at his words as though they were a lifeline.

Mark nodded. "Yes," he said quickly. "When did you plan on showing it?"

"I think on Friday," Kelly said sighing loudly. "I want them to see that film before any of them go on the road with me."

"OK," Mark said nodding his head again. "That sounds like a good idea. I'll plan to be at the high school on Friday." He paused briefly, and then said, "Would you like me to give an introductory talk?"

"You mean about Michael?" Kelly asked in a surprised voice.

Mark simply nodded.

"Are you sure that's not going to be too hard for you?" Kelly asked, eyeing him with great concern.

"Kelly, if I can help save one other life by talking about Michael's death...then I'll do it in a minute."

Kelly nodded understandingly. "Oh, Mark, that would be great. Take as much time as you want with the kids. Nothing affects people more than personal-experience-type stories."

On Friday, Mark gave a touching heart-to-heart talk to the sixteen year olds who were taking the Driver's Ed. class. He brought a couple of snap shots of Michael with him, and passed them around. The kids immediately commented on Mark's likeness to Michael.

Mark went on to describe Michael to the group. "He was a well-rounded kid, and loved by all. Michael was the captain of his basketball and baseball teams," Mark said proudly. "He was an extremely outgoing type of guy that people just naturally wanted to be around. He was never without a date on Saturday night." Mark paused, and then grew very serious. "Michael was never into drinking or drugs. He only had one problem, and that was driving too fast. Michael Mitchell is a prime example of how speed kills. It is not an exclusive club. It kills popular kids, shy kids, athletic kids, and academic kids. It kills your heroes, your neighbors, and your friends. This club is open to anyone driving fast. And, if you're speeding, you will eventually join this club, whether you want to or not. The bottom line is: speed kills."

As Kelly rolled the film, the room was so quiet that you could hear a pin drop. After the thirty-minute film was over, half the class had thrown up, and everyone was crying. Mark confidently took control of the group again.

"You have a choice," he said firmly, taking the time to look each student directly in the face. "When you get behind the wheel of your car, you will automatically make the choice to speed or not. If you choose to speed, remember my brother Michael. He chose to speed, and now he's dead. It's that simple. Speed kills."

For the next half hour, Mark and Kelly patiently answered all of the student's questions. Kelly could see that *Signal 31*, along with Mark's testimony, had made a great impact on the young people's lives. Silently, Kelly prayed that the impact would last a lifetime.

That Monday, Kelly took her first student on the road. Bobby Steele was a popular baseball player, and Kelly knew that he was going to be her greatest challenge. He was far too confident and cocky, and he had the attitude that he knew everything.

"Before you even turn the car on, I want to go over some things with you," Kelly said eyeing him firmly. "If I find you speeding during your Driver's Training, you'll automatically be bumped from the class until next year. If you pass this class, and get your license, and then are caught speeding, you will lose your license for a year."

"You're kidding!" Bobby said in pure shock. "That doesn't seem fair!"

"Yeah," Kelly said leaning slightly toward Bobby, "well, it doesn't seem fair that Michael Mitchell is dead, either. Does it?"

Bobby slowly shook his head. "Good point."

To Kelly's amazement, Bobby didn't speed at all. A few times, she even had to tell him to go a little faster. As they were heading back to the high school, Bobby suddenly grew very rigid in his seat." Officer Douglas, there's a green pick-up truck that's riding my tail. What do I do?"

As Kelly turned around in her seat, to look back at the truck, she instructed Bobby to pull over to the side of the road, and let the tailgater pass. Yet, instead of passing them, the truck pulled in behind them.

Angrily, Kelly jumped out of the car. "What do you think..." She stopped as soon as she saw the three men in the pickup truck. They were Pitman's sons.

The three of them got out of the truck, and aggressively walked up to her in a threatening manner. As Kelly grabbed her radio and requested immediate back-up, her mind quickly registered the fact that all the boys were taller than her and bigger than her, and the oldest one held a pistol in his right hand that was pointed directly at her.

"Oh, Officer Douglas...if we wanted to do you in now...your back-up would never get here in time," the oldest brother said in an icy voice that sent chills down her spine. "Thing is...we've decided that we're going to ruin your life for a while before we finish you off. We will be in every shadow and in every dark alley. And, Kelly, when you go to bed at night, I wouldn't close my eyes if I were you, because you never know if we might be there, too."

Then the middle son confidently went up to her as if he owned her, and gently brushed her cheek with his fingers. "You sure are pretty, Kelly," he said letting his eyes roam over her body intently, as if he were memorizing every inch of it. His eyes met hers for a moment, and he licked his lips slowly. He turned to his brothers for a second, as a low, evil laugh came out of his mouth. "Man, Bros, revenge has never been sweeter. I love it when they look like models. But," he said, turning back to Kelly, and drilling his dark, sinister eyes into her, "we're going to have some real fun with you first, Babe." His face lit up in eager anticipation of it, and he blew Kelly a quick kiss before he turned around.

As the sirens could be heard in the distance, the Pitman brothers got into their truck and roared off. A minute later, when Noah Olin and Lauren Curtis arrived, Kelly was shaking so badly that she could hardly stand. She leaned against the squad car so she wouldn't collapse.

After Kelly told Noah and Lauren what had happened, Lauren put an arm around Kelly's shoulders. "Kel, I'll take Bobby Steel back to the high school. Noah will bring you back to the station. The Chief is going to want to hear about this immediately."

As Noah drove Kelly back to the station, she couldn't seem to control her shaking. The nightmare was returning, but this time in the force of three. They could make things three times worse for her. And, Kelly thought fearfully, the Pitman brothers were crazy enough and sick enough to do just that.

Twenty-Seven

$\mathcal{A}$s Kelly sat in Mark's office recounting the details of the incident, she felt cold all over. She couldn't seem to stop shaking, or erase the panic that had swept over her. As she replayed the exact account for Mark, she watched as he clamped his fists tightly together and his face turned bright red in anger.

When she had finished her story, she watched Mark pace back and forth in front of her. She could see the wheels turning in his head and knew he was in the process of formulating a plan.

Suddenly, Mark knelt down in front of Kelly's chair. He looked at her squarely in the eye for a moment, and then spoke to her in a gentle, concerned voice, "Kelly, how are you doing?"

"I'm frightened, Mark," Kelly said honestly. "The two older brothers scare me the most. They're really sick," Kelly said sighing loudly, "and they're just crazy enough to go through with their threats."

Mark told the other officers to leave the room, and once the door was shut, Mark pulled Kelly securely into his arms. "Kelly, it's going to be all right," Mark said in a comforting and confident voice. "I'm working on a plan, Sweetheart, and between trusting in the Lord and the officers here, you have got to believe that you'll be all right."

Kelly could feel her nerves begin to calm down as she focused her mind on what Mark was saying. Mark just held her tenderly until her shaking subsided.

"Kelly," Mark said gently, "I've got something that I want to read to you." He paused for a minute to make sure she was listening. "Ever since we got back to together, I've been focusing my personal devotions on trusting in the Lord and not being afraid." He paused again, and kissed her softly on her forehead.

"My gut instinct is to go out and hunt those rotten boys down. I'd personally like to blow them to pieces..." Mark laughed lightly. "But that's Mark's way, and not God's way. And,"

Mark said laughing again, "it's a good thing because I'd end up in jail and I wouldn't be able to marry you."

This brought a smile to Kelly's face, and she felt herself calm down even more. "We definitely don't want you in jail, Mark. That would be very inconvenient."

"True," Mark said laughing again.

Mark got up and went to his desk. He opened a drawer and grabbed his Bible. "Kel, I'd like to read to you a few verses that are helping me." Kelly nodded, and Mark opened up his Bible. "You know how God tells us not to fear..." Kelly nodded. "Well, I just want to read you a few verses along those lines." Kelly smiled, and nodded again.

"OK," Mark said flipping through his Bible, "one of the more commonly known verses in in Psalm 23. Verse 4 says, 'I will fear no evil, for You are with me.' I think those boys certainly fall into the evil category," Mark said smiling confidently at Kelly. Kelly couldn't help but smile right back.

"OK, the next one I have in mind is in Psalm 91. Verses 4, 5, and 6 say, 'He will cover you with His feathers, and under His wings you will find refuge; His faithfulness will be your shield and rampart. You will not fear the terror of night, nor the arrow that flies by day, nor the pestilence that stalks in the darkness, nor the plague that destroys at midday.'"

"Those are a lot of things that we don't have to be afraid of," Mark said looking intently at Kelly. She smiled and nodded thoughtfully.

"OK, I've got one more for you. Isaiah 43:1b, says, 'Fear not, for I have redeemed you; I have called you by name; you are mine.'"

Mark put his Bible down and went and knelt before Kelly. He took both her hands in his, and held them reassuringly. "Honey, I don't understand why you're having to go through this...but we need to remember that God is bigger, and more powerful than all of this. We both need to trust in Him and not be afraid. At a time like this, we need to pray that God will help us keep a level head. We need to take our focus away from the fear that threatens to drown us, and place our focus on God and how we're going to go about hunting down the Pitman brothers."

Kelly nodded again, and Mark could see a new determination growing in her eyes. After that, Mark prayed. He prayed for wisdom and courage, for peace and a sure focus. He prayed for safety, and guidance, and a shield to be around them to protect them from the enemy.

As he ended his prayer, Kelly smiled at the peace and confidence that God was putting in her heart. "Mark, thank you so much for doing that. I must always keep my focus on God, and not the enemy. Sometimes I forget that He is bigger than all my problems. Thanks for reminding me."

Mark hugged her one more time. "I want to bring the team back in here, Kel. Are you ready to get moving on this?" Kelly nodded confidently, but Mark still studied her with concern.

"I love you, Kelly Douglas," Mark said squeezing her hands tightly. "With God's help, I will protect you. And we will get those guys. I have no doubt about it." Mark said intently.

A moment later, Mark called his team back in. "OK, Rand," Mark said getting right down to business, "do you have the portfolios on the brothers?"

"Yes, Chief," Rand said in a serious tone. "The two older ones have a record a mile long. The oldest is Dennis, and he's twenty-two. He's been involved in all kinds of petty theft. The biggest thing that worries me about Dennis is that he's a very accomplished marksman. He holds all kinds of records up at the shooting range. He would be a worthy rival for Kelly's record."

Mark nodded thoughtfully. "OK, what about the second brother?"

"Del is eighteen," Rand said studying the paper in his hand. He doesn't know much about guns. His specialty runs along another line. He's very skillful with a knife. He uses his expert abilities to threaten women and girls he's raped."

Raped?" Mark said in shock. "Has he ever been convicted?"

"He's a repeat offender," Rand said disgustedly. "He's been in court several times, but only convicted in one case. And," Rand said looking at the sheet again, "he never served much time. The kid probably had a good lawyer."

"OK," Mark said nodding methodically, "What about the youngest one?"

"Trey doesn't have any kind of record, except for those bridge robberies last year, "Rand said in a surprised tone. "He's fourteen, but doesn't seem to be nearly as bad as the older two. I believe Dennis and Del are the masterminds."

"So, now we know a little about the enemy," Mark said studying his crew of officers. "I always believe it's smart to learn as much as you can about the criminals, before you go after them.

"Micky," Mark said in a questioning voice, "did you or Callet see any signs of the Pitman brothers at their house?"

"No, Chief," Micky said quickly. "They're hiding out somewhere else.

"Sawyer, and all the surrounding towns are on red alert for the green pickup truck."

"OK," Mark said pacing again. "Kelly," he said smiling down at her, "You're about to be granted your wish to get out of Driver's Education. As of this moment, you're released from that duty."

"Why am I not relieved?" Kelly said wearily.

"And," Mark said in a serious tone, "you'll be using the guest room at the station until this is over." Mark waited for Kelly to protest but she simply nodded. So he continued.

"And," Mark said, as he folded his arms across his chest, "you will never go anywhere unaccompanied." Mark narrowed his eyes at her. "Is that clear?"

Again, Kelly nodded. She hated having her freedom taken away, but she also knew there wasn't much of an alternative.

"And one more thing," Mark said quickly, "wear your ankle pistol at all times. It just might be the backup that saves your life."

"That's a good idea," Kelly said in an impressed voice.

Mark smiled. "I'm glad you think so," he said in an amused tone.

Then he grew serious again. "According to your story, Kelly, I don't believe that the Pitmans are planning on shooting you soon. I feel the most immediate threat may come from them stalking you, or something along Del's line of work."

Everyone nodded in agreement. "I agree, Chief," Rand said quickly. "I think they want to scare Kelly. I think they plan to harass her first, and then they'll plan to finalize things."

Kelly shuddered, and Mark put a firm hand on her shoulder. "So," Mark said solemnly to his crew, "our job is to catch them at their small pranks. I don't want this even coming close to their finalizing plan," he added in a tight voice.

"I would guess that they're going to pull most of their stuff at night," Micky said thoughtfully. "They won't want their truck spotted in the daytime."

"Micky, I think you're giving them a lot of credit," Kelly said quickly. "I don't think they're smart enough or patient enough to work just at night."

"I think that's true," Mark said nodding his head slightly. "The first time they approached Kelly it was midday, and with plenty of witnesses around." His jaw was set in a tight, determined way, and Kelly knew that he was ready for war. She also knew, by the hard expression on his face, that he was already fighting the battle in his mind.

"Another thing," Mark said, addressing the group, "the Pitman boys are going to play by at least one of our rules. And that is that they will have to come to us. Never, under any circumstances, is Kelly to be more than one mile from the station. I don't want them finding her on an isolated, winding country road somewhere." He paused, and looked at the group commandingly. "We make the boys come to us. If there is a war to be fought, I want it done on our turf. I want us holding as many cards in this game as we can."

Everyone agreed, and after the meeting broke up, Kelly looked over at Mark curiously. "What should I do now?" she asked feeling like a fish out of water.

"Go down to the basement and practice your shooting. Targets, moving targets...all different positions and angles...both rifles and pistols. We need you to keep your shooting skills at your highest level."

Kelly agreed, and headed to her locker to get her shooting equipment.

As she surveyed her locker, she realized that she had left her rifles in her car trunk. She exited the station through the basement door and jogged casually to her car. As she grabbed her rifle cases, and ammo from her trunk, she heard the shot and instinctively hit the ground.

Kelly dragged her equipment as she crawled toward the front of the car. "Trudy!" Kelly yelled into the radio on her shoulder, "This is Kelly! I'm in the parking lot, and I'm being fired on!"

Kelly automatically put her sighted rifle together. As she loaded the rifle, two more shots were fired from the hill. Both tires on the other side of her car went flat.

Kelly had Dennis in her scope, and she fired, in rapid succession, knocking his rifle from his arms. Then she shot him in both shoulders. "That should make it a little harder for you to shoot at me, Dennis."

As Kelly was in the process of shooting out all four truck tires, a posse came to the rescue, with Mark at the lead. "They're on the hill near the cemetery," Kelly yelled at the group. "Go after them! I've knocked off their shooter, so you should be pretty safe."

Mark stayed on the ground beside Kelly, and picked up one of her sighted rifles. "OK, Dennis...," he said firmly, "you're not running anywhere, Pal." With one bullet, Mark hit Dennis dead center in his right knee. He went down like a falling tree.

"OK," Mark said, still looking through his sighted rifle, "Dennis is ours, but Del and Trey are long gone."

"Well," Kelly said in a determined voice, "one down, and two to go. And," she said looking at Mark intently, "Dennis is the one we wanted first anyway. According to Rand, the other two can't shoot. Now," Kelly said shrugging her shoulder slightly, "I won't have to worry about Dennis putting a bullet through my head."

"Good point," Mark said getting up. "Let's get inside."

They walked quickly to the station, and once they were inside, Kelly said to Mark resolutely, "I want to speak with Dennis."

"No way," he said, both quickly, and adamantly.

"Mark...I'm the one he wants. I may set him off...you know, get him angry, and make him say something he didn't intend to."

Mark swung around, and studied Kelly through probing eyes. "I see your point, and I'll think about it. By the way," he said taking a step closer to her, "what were you doing outside anyway?"

"I had my rifles in the car," Kelly said matter-of-factly.

"From now on," Mark said placing his hands on her shoulders, "you aren't to leave this building unescorted. And," he said narrowing his eyes at her, "if someone else is accompanying you, you'd better make sure I know about it."

"OK," Kelly said seriously. "Can we go to County Hospital now? I want to speak with Dennis."

"You want to speak with him while he's still in a lot of pain," Mark smiled at her knowingly.

"It's amazing how a little pain can bring out the truth in a person," Kelly said seriously. "It usually is a very effective communication tool."

"Honesty and pain usually do go hand in hand," Mark said dropping an arm around her shoulder. "You're right," he said giving the top of her head a quick kiss, "let's go visit Dennis."

Twenty-Eight

As Kelly walked confidently toward the E.R., Mark eyed her curiously. "Are you really OK with this, Kelly? You're not nervous or anything?"

Kelly laughed. "No, Mark, I'm not nervous. A little ticked-off maybe, and a little angry, but definitely not nervous." Kelly laughed again. "You see, Mark, I guess I'm just not a very good sport, because when someone takes shots at me, it tends to make me angry."

Mark laughed, and then smiled at her. "I can see your point, Kel. I'm sure I would feel the same way."

As they approached the heavily guarded area of the E.R., Kelly boldly went up to Dennis's bedside. "You shot me!" he said in a shocked, but bratty voice. "I could have taken you down...and all I did was shoot your tires out. But you shot me three times."

Kelly stared at him hard for a second. "Actually, I only shot you two times. The Chief hit you once as well. And," Kelly said leaning over the bed to stare directly into Dennis's face, "just remember that I was aiming for your shoulders. If I had been aiming for your head, like I will do next time, it would have been blown off the face of the earth. I never miss my intended target."

Dennis's face had paled, and his eyes had grown large. He looked more like a five-year-old boy who got caught stealing cookies from the cookie jar than a young man of twenty-two. "Hey! Are you going to let her talk to me that way?" he asked looking to Mark for help.

Mark's intense, penetrating gaze burned a hole through any confidence that Dennis might have had left. "Actually," Mark said in a cold, hard tone, "since Officer Douglas is my fiancée, and you were intentionally shooting at her, I'd probably be fighting with her over who gets to blow your head off." Mark paused and glared at Dennis intimidatingly. Kelly knew, from experience, that what Mark said in his cold, penetrating stares, could be worse then what he actually said verbally. Whatever message he hadn't gotten through to you in words, was not only backed up, but made crystal clear for you for through his silence. Kelly definitely felt that his icy, intimidating, commanding stare was one of his most effective communicating tools. He never left you with any doubt as to exactly where *he* stood, and, more frighteningly, he never left you with any doubt, whatsoever, as to exactly where *you* stood.

Mark continued in a low, but confident voice. "You're lucky that I didn't aim for your head, Dennis, because like Officer Douglas, I never miss my intended target."

"You guys are just stinking pigs," Dennis said bitterly. "My Dad was right."

"If I were you, I'd watch what I said," Kelly said through a clenched jaw. "Since your Dad shot my Dad and my pregnant Mother to death, and then tried to kill me...a part of me is screaming for revenge," Kelly said in a wild voice. "And, you should know something...," she said thrusting her finger in his face. "Right now, revenge seems like a pretty good idea. I think I'd actually be willing to lay my badge down for it." Kelly eyed him so hard and intensely that Dennis paled. "You know," she said in a voice that was still very tight, "the funny thing about revenge is that it can make you do crazy things. I just bet that any court in the State of Vermont would let me off with an insanity plea if I plugged you right now."

Kelly's hand automatically went to her gun side. "I think I'd better go, Chief. I'm not sure that I have enough self-control to do the badge proud right now."

As Kelly then spun on her heel and marched out, Mark gave a few orders to the cops guarding Dennis. "Two officers with him at all times. He is never, under any circumstances, to be left alone."

"Don't worry," Rand said eyeing Dennis heatedly, "I'll be with Dennis all night. Oh, by the way," Rand said leaning toward Dennis, "I'm Officer Thompson. Officer Douglas, whom you were shooting at, is one of my best friends and happens to be my partner, too." Rand narrowed his eyes at Dennis angrily. "You and I, Dennis, are going to have a nice, long talk tonight. We're going to play Twenty

Questions. And I can guarantee that by the end of the night, you'll answer all twenty questions, along with a few bonus questions as well."

Twenty-Nine

As the officers assembled for the morning roll call, Rand briefed them on his conversation with Dennis the previous night. "The kid was very cooperative," Rand said with a tight smile. Kelly could only imagine what intimidating tactics Rand had used on Dennis to make him very cooperative.

"The Pitman boys have been staying at their father's hunting cabin in the mountains. Dennis feels pretty confident that Del and Trey aren't there now. He thinks that his brothers are probably on foot, and hiding in the woods." Rand paused for a moment to study the paper in his hand.

"Dennis feels it will be difficult to find his brothers, since they are always on the move. I agree with him. We've got to let them come to us, which," Rand said sighing loudly, "shouldn't be too hard, because they're basically tracking

Kelly. Oh, another important thing...as we suspected, Del is the dangerous one. Even Dennis feels his middle brother is crazy. He's unstable and unpredictable. Also, remember that he is sneaky, and an expert with knives. Dennis says that Del practices throwing knives at archery targets for hours every day." Rand paused, and then said in a concerned tone, "Watch your backs, People, and watch your partner's back. This guy is lethal."

After roll, Kelly and Rand began their daily beat. As they drove around the small downtown, Kelly spoke to Rand in an apologetic voice. "Rand, I'm sorry that you're stuck with me as a partner. Becca must be going crazy."

"What do you mean?" Rand asked in a puzzled voice.

"Rand, because you're my partner, you get stuck riding around with a bull's-eye. You must be tried of watching out for my back."

"Kelly," Rand said softly, pulling the cruiser to the side of the road, "I love you like a sister. When Mark isn't with you, I'd insist on it being me. You're the best partner that I ever had. And as for Becca, she's never slept better at night since we've been teamed up together. She knows that we watch out for each other, Kelly. Right now, the heat is on you. But, I know that if it was on me, you'd be beside me all the way."

"Absolutely, Rand. Without a doubt," Kelly said quickly.

"And that trust, Kelly," Rand said eyeing the younger woman tenderly, "is what makes us such great partners."

Kelly nodded. "That's true, Rand. You know that I'd do anything for you."

"Same here, Partner," Rand said seriously.

They sat quietly for a minute, and then Kelly spoke in an emotional voice. "Uh, Rand, I have a favor to ask you, but please, be honest if you aren't comfortable with it."

Rand relaxed in his seat, and turned to Kelly with a curious expression on his face. "You know that I'm always honest with you, Kel. Go ahead and ask."

"You know that Mark and I are getting married in about a month..."

"Seems to me I've heard something about that," Rand said smiling affectionately at his partner.

"Well, since my Dad had died, I always figured that Baily would give me away at my wedding someday. But," Kelly said in a quiet voice, shaking her head slowly, "since Baily's gone, too, I was kind of hoping that you'd be able to escort me down the aisle. I can't think of anyone else that I'd want with me."

Rand smiled at Kelly tenderly. "Kelly, I would be honored to walk you down the aisle. You're like family to Becca and me...nothing would please me more."

"Oh, thank you, Rand," Kelly said touching her partner on his broad shoulder. "It will be so good to have you there."

Rand put his large hand over Kelly's and squeezed it gently. "It will be my pleasure, Kel," Rand said in an husky sounding voice. "Thanks for asking." Rand cleared his throat loudly, and then said in a curious voice, "By the way, is Gram coming back for the wedding?"

Kelly laughed. "Are you kidding? Gram wouldn't miss it! She tried to get Mark and me together from the very beginning." Kelly paused, and then laughed again. "Oh, she'll be there... trust me, she wouldn't miss it for the world."

As they continued on their beat, Kelly asked Rand to pull into Sawyer's Crossing's Market. "Living at the police station is a pain. I'm always running out of things. I'll just be a minute."

"Don't forget the dog food," Rand said with a smile on his face.

"Rand, Copper has put on so much weight since he's been living at the station, I may never have to buy dog food for him again." Kelly paused, and let a loud breath escape from her mouth. "I've got to get the other officers to stop feeding him. Cookies and potato chips aren't exactly a balanced diet for a dog."

Rand opened his door quickly, and followed Kelly into the store. "Rand," Kelly said protesting, "you don't need to follow me down every aisle."

"Maybe I don't, Kelly, but I'm going to," Rand said in an adamant tone. "So you'd just better get used to it."

As Kelly headed to the back of the store, with Rand in tow, she rounded a corner quickly, and bumped smack into Trey Pitman. "I'm not going to hurt you!" he said quickly, putting his hands up. "I just need to talk to you."

Kelly watched Trey closely. "What are you doing here?" she asked in a confused, but demanding voice.

"I came to warn you," Trey said in an urgent tone. "Del is nuts, and he's obsessed with getting you. He is small, and sneaky, and he can get into places easy."

"I know that," Kelly said firmly.

"But you don't know this...," Trey said leaning closer to her. "Tonight he plans to sneak into the station. He plans to finish you off tonight."

"He can never sneak into the station," Kelly said adamantly.

"Kelly," Trey said in a panicked tone, "he already did! He knows that you sleep in the storage room next to the Chief's office. He even knows that you have a picture of your Mom and Dad right next to your bed." He touched Kelly's shoulder. "He's been in there, Kelly..."

This got Kelly's attention quickly, and she felt as though someone had knocked the air out of her. "How?" Kelly asked, fighting to stay calm.

"The window in the ladies' bathroom," Trey said glancing around nervously. "The window is almost always open."

"But that's on the second floor!" Kelly gasped in shock.

"Del is real good at climbing walls. Don't leave any windows open, because he can climb the outside walls and get in.

"I have to go," Trey said quickly.

"Trey...," Kelly said, grabbing the boys arm, "why are you telling me all this?" She studied him hard. "Why are you helping me?"

"My family has hurt you so much, Kelly," Trey replied quietly, but honestly. "I'm not like my father or my brothers. If I can keep them from hurting you, I will."

"Trey," Kelly said softly, still holding the boy's arm, "come in with Rand and me. We can help you."

Trey only smiled at her gently. "Kelly, right now I don't need your help, but you do need mine. With Del out there...well, I may be the only one that can stop him. I know I couldn't live with myself if I didn't try."

As Trey quickly slipped out of the back door, Kelly turned around to see Rand's gun following the boy. "Did you have your gun on him the whole time, Rand?"

"Aimed right at his head," Rand said slowly, as he put his pistol away.

"What do you think about what he said?"

"I think he's telling the truth." Rand said thoughtfully. "I think that boy is carrying the burden of his family on his shoulders. I think he wants to make things right. And, I also think...," Rand said narrowing his eyes, "that Trey Pitman may be our best back-up against Del."

Kelly nodded. "Let's go talk to Mark, and," she said rolling her eyes at him, "let's make sure all the windows in the station are locked tight."

Kelly sighed heavily. "Rand, Del was in my room. Trey was right. No one would know about the picture of my parents, unless he was in my room."

"We're going to get him, Kelly," Rand said in a determined, relentless voice. "You just hang in there, Partner, because I know we're going to get him."

Thirty

Kelly tried to live as normal a life as possible, but found she was constantly reminded of how normal life wasn't. Mark had Kelly's room changed to another storage area, and ordered the entire station locked down. The doors would stay locked at all times and the officers had to use keys to enter the building.

"This is like a fortress," Kelly said rolling her eyes in disgust at Mark. "It's such a pain for everyone."

"Kelly," Mark said in a reasonable voice, "it has to be like a fortress to protect you. And, even if it is a little inconvenient at times, everyone is handling it just fine. I think you'll find that the crew is more upset that Del got into the station than at having to tolerate the lock down."

"That's true," Kelly said quickly. "Del is a little weasel. I've never met anyone, besides his father, who makes my skin crawl like he does."

Mark pulled Kelly into his arms. "Don't concentrate on the weasel, Honey. Think good thoughts. And," he said, arching his eyebrows at her flirtatiously," I've got a great thought for you to think about. In one month's time, we'll be husband and wife."

Kelly smiled up at Mark's beaming face. "That really is a good thought. I can't wait."

"Neither can I, Sweetheart," he said as he stole a quick kiss from her. "I think about you all the time, Honey. You make it very difficult for me to think about anything else. I love you so much."

Kelly leaned up and kissed Mark quickly on the cheek. "I love you, too, Mark."

Just then Copper came padding down the hall. Orange-colored popcorn was stuck to the fur around his nose. Kelly shook her head disgustedly, and as she knelt down to pull it off Copper's muzzle, the chubby dog looked incredibly guilty. "Copper...," Kelly scolded, "you've got to stop eating anything that's not nailed down." Then Kelly swung her head up towards Mark. "Mark," she said in an annoyed tone, "feeding Copper snacks has got to stop.

It's going to kill him." Kelly paused a minute and laughed. "Not to mention, his stomach doesn't handle junk food well and he's throwing up all over the station. It's disgusting."

Mark laughed, and then shook his head. "Getting the other officers to stop feeding Copper will be difficult. He's a cute, friendly, mutt...with a bottomless pit for a stomach. But I will try," Mark stated in an unconvincing tone.

As they walked towards Mark's office, he suddenly stopped. "Oh, I almost forgot to ask you. Fredricks, up at the Academy, called to find out if you were still coming to give your firearms demonstration."

"Is it OK with you if I go?" Kelly asked in an uncertain tone.

"If you want to go, it's fine with me," Mark said draping an arm around her shoulder. "Especially, since I'd planned on escorting you."

"You'd be coming?" Kelly asked in a surprised tone.

"You'd better believe it, Kel," Mark said quickly. "And, don't be surprised if Rand wants to come, too. He's pretty protective of his partner."

"You don't mind?" Kelly asked honestly.

"About Rand?" Mark said in surprise. Kelly nodded, and Mark let out a loud laugh. "Kel, Rand is the only one that I trust to take care of you, besides me. The man thinks of you as a sister, and without a doubt, I know he'd lay his life down for you. You can't have a better partner than that, Kel."

Kelly nodded. "That's true." She paused, and then said in a concerned voice, "Mark, you don't think that Del will try to follow us over to the Police Academy, do you?"

"I don't think so, Kelly. But you never know..." Mark grew thoughtful, and then said in a serious tone, "If I were a criminal, I wouldn't try to take out a cop at the State Police Academy. Common sense should tell him that he is outnumbered by cops. But," Mark said, as his hand squeezed the back of his neck, "we're dealing with Del Pitman here. And since he has no common sense...I really wouldn't put anything past him."

Kelly nodded understandingly.

"But you, Miss Number-One-Sharpshooter in all of the great state of Vermont, are not to worry about this tomorrow. You just dazzle everyone with your firearm abilities, and Rand and I will blend in and stand guard."

The next day Kelly, Mark, and Rand set off to the State Police Academy in Brattleboro. After they parked in the visitors' lot, Fredricks met them with a jeep, and drove them out to the shooting range.

"Kelly," Fredricks said, sounding like a proud parent, "I can't tell you how good it is to have you back at the Academy. Do you know that no one's been able to beat your record?"

"I'm sure someone will soon," Kelly said modestly.

"Well, I don't share your confidence, Kelly," Fredrick said looking at her with a broad smile across his face. "Your record is quite impressive."

"You always were my number one fan, Fred," she said warmly to her old riflery instructor.

Fred laughed kindly. "I suspect Chief Mitchell holds the number one fan spot now."

Kelly looked back at Mark, and he winked proudly at her. "I would agree with that statement, Fred. I'm very proud of my girl."

They drove several minutes in silence before Fredricks said in a serious voice, "Kelly, Mark has informed me of the trouble that you've been having with the Pitmans. The Academy is on full alert for Del. I almost hope he does show up," Fred said, glancing at Kelly, "so we can have the pleasure of shooting his hide full of lead."

Kelly nodded grimly. "I don't think he'll show, Fred. But if he does, I feel confident that we'll be ready for him."

Kelly went on to give a firearms demonstration in front of one hundred officers. Her pistol and rifle skills amazed even Mark and Rand, who had thought that they'd seen it all. Kelly repeatedly nailed her targets dead center.

As they drove back to the parking lot, Mark touched Kelly on her shoulder. "Man, Kelly, that was very impressive. I've never seen anyone hit so many bull's-eyes consecutively. I'm glad that you're one of the 'Good- Guys.'"

Kelly laughed. "Thanks, Mark. It was a lot of fun to be back here."

After a quick lunch with Fredricks; Kelly, Mark, and Rand got back into Mark's cruiser and headed back to Sawyer's Crossing. About ten minutes into the ride, Rand, who was sitting in the back, spoke in a puzzled voice. "Is it just me, or does anyone else smell gas?"

Kelly laughed. "Rand, I told you not to have that second helping of baked beans."

"Very funny, Kel," Rand said dryly, "but I'm sure I smell gas."

Mark looked at his gas gauge, and then glanced in his rearview mirror. "We're leaking," he said, suddenly fully alert. Mark pulled a U-turn in the road and headed back toward the Academy. "We don't have enough gas to get back to Sawyer. Someone must have cut my fuel line."

The silence in the car was deafening, as the three officers became on guard. Mark picked up his phone and called Fredricks. "Fred, this is Mark Mitchell. Someone's messed with our fuel line. I don't think we're even going to have enough fuel to get us back to the Academy. Could you bring a team down here and pick us up? I'm pulling off the road by Beaver Pond."

"We'll be there in five minutes, Mark," Fred said firmly.

"OK, People," Mark said popping open his truck, "we're putting on bulletproof vests and getting our gear ready. I think we need to assume that Pitman is nearby. Grab all the guns in the trunk and let's head for the woods for cover."

Mark had an impressive arsenal in his trunk. The three of them carried two shotguns and two pistols apiece into the woods. "Rand," Mark said quietly, "you cover the top post, Kelly and I will cover the back door."

As they lay down on the ground, their bodies were pumping with adrenaline. Every inch of them was on full alert. Soon they heard Fredricks arrive with two Jeep-loads of officers. Mark let out a low whistle, and Fred immediately approached them.

"You want in on this?" Mark asked him quickly.

"I've already arrived with my army," Fred replied firmly.

"Good," Mark said eyeing the group of eight men. "Hide the Jeeps. All I want Del to see on the road is my cruiser."

"So, you're pretty confident he's here?" Fred asked intently.

"Yes," Mark said in a grave voice. "I know he is. Hide the Jeeps."

When Mark returned to Kelly, he leaned over and whispered to her. "How are you doing? Are you ready for this?"

"Yes," Kelly said in a determined voice. "I want it over with. And," she said smiling up at Mark, "thanks to this morning's demonstration, I'm all warmed up."

"Good girl, Kel. We're going to nail him," Mark said confidently.

About five minutes later, the roar of a motor cycle could be heard coming down the mountain road. It pulled off to the side of the road next to Mark's cruiser. Kelly could clearly see both Del and Trey get off the bike. They walked around Mark's car, examining it carefully.

"Kelly!" Del yelled loudly, "I know that you're here, Honey. Why don't you make it easy on everyone, and just come out. Your big boyfriend can't hide you from me forever."

Kelly and Mark never took their eyes from their scoped rifles. They watched intently as Del and Trey began to trudge into the woods. Kelly's heart went out to Trey, and she hoped she would get the chance to help him later.

Kelly and Mark kept waiting for a clean shot at Del. With the road behind Del, they both felt reluctant to shoot. They didn't want to take the chance of hitting a passing motorist.

As soon as Del moved into the tree line, Mark opened fire on him. Del moved behind a large maple tree just in time to avoid the spray of bullets.

"So, Kelly," Del said in an angry voice, "you brought some friends with you. That's OK, Sweetheart. It only makes the game a little more interesting for me."

A moment later, a can landed near Kelly and Mark. They instinctively rolled away from it, as the army-issued smoke bomb exploded between them. Immediately, Kelly could hear other cans hitting the ground. As she rolled away from them, she felt her lungs tighten up. The smoke was triggering her asthma and she instantly knew that she was in big trouble.

As she stumbled through the woods trying to get away from the cloud of smoke, she suddenly realized that she had lost Mark. Her first thought was to scream for him, but the realization that she'd be giving her location away to Del as well made her keep her mouth shut.

As Kelly tried to escape the gas, she found herself shuffling deeper into the woods to get some air. "One breath of air," she thought nearly panicking. "All I need is one breath of air." Her wheezing was getting louder with each step. Feeling the dizziness overwhelm her, she sank to the ground by a large pine tree and grabbed her inhaler. The medicine opened her lungs up momentarily, only to have the smoke suffocate her again.

Kelly worked hard not to panic, but she felt not only trapped, but helpless as well. With the thick smoke all around her, she felt confused and disoriented. "Have to keep moving," she coached herself. "I have to get away from this smoke."

With great effort and determination, she pulled herself up and dragged her body through the pine forest. A moment later, Kelly stumbled against something. As she fell to the ground, she found that Del was on top of her in an instant. His dark hair had been greased back, and his pale white skin looked clammy. But what sent waves of fear through Kelly was the evil that she saw lurking in Del's narrow, beady eyes. It was as though she had come face to face with the devil himself.

Then in a chilling, high-pitched, giddy voice, Del yelled, "I've got her! I've got her, Chief, and if you don't call your men back, I'll slit her pretty little throat."

Instantly, Mark called the men off, but took advantage of the remaining smoke screen to keep moving quietly in the direction of Del's voice. He knew he was close, but because of the smoke he couldn't see anyone or anything.

"Pretty, pretty Kelly," Del said in a shaky voice, as he ran a damp hand through her blonde hair, "I have waited so long for you, and now you're finally mine!"

"I'll never be yours, Del!" Kelly spat out angrily at him.

Del blinked in surprise at her response. Then, hardening his face, he said in a cool tone, "Oh, yes you will, Sweet Darling. One way or another, you will be mine."

"Leave her alone, Del!" Trey shouted at his brother commandingly.

Del turned slightly to face his younger brother. "Trey, you're not worried that I'll keep Kelly all for myself, are you. I'd plan on sharing with you, Man. You're my brother."

Mark felt pure rage wash over him at Del's filthy comment. He immediately prayed and asked God to protect Kelly, and keep him calm.

"Del," Trey said stepping closer, "let Kelly go."

Del turned, and stared in shock at the pistol that Trey was holding to his head. He let out a loud, ugly laugh that didn't sound human. "Trey," he said in an eerie tone, "you don't expect me to believe that you'd really shoot me, do you? Stop fooling around, and put the gun away."

"I'm not fooling around, Del," Trey said in a low voice. "If you don't release Kelly, I'm going to drop you here."

Del turned a hard, cold look on Trey. "You would kill your own flesh and blood over a lousy pig?" he asked completely appalled.

"She's a person, Del. And she has just as much right to live as you or me."

"I'm sorry to hear that you feel that way." Del stared at his brother with a scathing look.

"If you take one step closer to me, I'll cut Kelly up like a steak."

Trey simply leveled the pistol at Del's head. "Last chance, Del. Let her go."

"No," Del said challengingly, as he pressed the knife further into Kelly's neck.

As soon as the shot rang out throughout the quiet woods, Kelly could feel Del's arms release her. At the same time, she could hear Del's voice cursing his brother. Del slowly rolled off Kelly, and lay on the ground in a lifeless heap. As Kelly turned away from Del's bloody body, she stared openly at Trey. He had knelt on the ground near his brother and was crying.

"I'm sorry, Del," he said sounding like a frightened child. "I just couldn't let you kill her. Our family has hurt her so much."

Kelly looked up to see Mark, Rand, Fredricks, and the other men around her now. "Come on, Son," Rand said quietly." I need to bring you downtown." Trey cooperated numbly as Rand cuffed him and led him over to one of the hidden Jeeps.

"He saved my life," Kelly said in an emotional voice to Mark. "Del would have cut my throat if Trey hadn't shot him."

"I know Kelly...," Mark said solemnly. "We're going to get Trey help, don't worry."

"Is Del dead?" Kelly asked nervously.

"Yes," Fredricks said from behind her. "He's dead. It's finally all over."

Kelly put her hand to her throat, and rubbed it gently. "Did he hurt you?" Mark asked taking her hand away from her throat, so that he could examine it.

"No," Kelly said in a trembling voice.

"Kelly," Mark said engulfing her in a safe, protective embrace, "it's over. The nightmare is finally over."

Kelly collapsed in Mark's arms and sobbed. For so many years, she had felt hunted by the Pitman family, and now the awful ordeal was finally over. There would be no more fear, no more hiding, no more feeling like she always had to watch her back. Kelly knew, as she cried in Mark's arms, that after all these years, she could truly start living again. She felt as though she had been released from prison. No longer would the Pitmans' chains hold onto her. She was free. She was finally free.

Thirty-One

As soon as Mark had driven Kelly back to Sawyer, she went directly to the room where they were holding Trey. Mark followed her in and stood by the door as Kelly went straight over to Trey.

"Trey," she said in a choked-up voice, "you saved my life. Thank you."

Trey was affected by the emotion he saw in Kelly, and turned his eyes away from her as his own began to fill up. "You're a good person, Kelly. You didn't deserve all the trouble my family made for you. No one did."

"Trey," Kelly said in a sincere voice, "you're a good person, too. You can't blame yourself for the actions of your father and brothers. Every man answers for himself."

Trey shook his sandy blonde head slightly. "No, Kelly," he said adamantly. "My slate will never be clean. My brothers forced me into all kinds of crimes. If I hadn't joined them, they would have killed me."

"Trey," Kelly said compassionately, as she took a step closer to the tall, lanky boy, "we know about the bridge robberies, and the car thefts...was there anything else?"

Trey shook his head. "No, Kelly, but that was enough. I'll never forget the faces of the elderly couple we robbed at the Wooden Bridge. I thought the old guy was going to drop dead right in front of us from fright."

"But you were forced into pulling those jobs, Trey," Kelly said emphatically. "Let the past die behind you, and start a new life."

"I'm long as I'm a Pitman, nobody in Sawyer will ever see me as anything but a lousy criminal."

"You could change that, Trey. Once people get to know you, they can't help but see the difference. I did," Kelly said confidently, reaching out to touch the boy's arm. "Right away I saw the difference."

"I don't think anyone would give me a chance," Trey said honestly, as he shrugged his shoulders. "Too many bad things have happened. Every time people see me, I'm going to be a constant reminder of all those awful things."

"No," Kelly said shaking her head. "You are going to be known as the boy who saved Kelly Douglas's life. You're different, Trey, and people will notice it."

Trey dropped down into a chair, and wept into his hands. "We have a lot in common, Kelly. I saw my Pa kill my Ma when I was six. She was the only good thing in my life. She was the only one who ever believed in me."

"Trey," Kelly said in a choked up voice, as she a put a hand on his shoulder, "I believe in you, the Chief believes in you, and God believes in you."

"God!" Trey said in a tone full of disbelief. "Why would He ever want anything to do with me?"

"Trey," Kelly said warmly, "God loves you. He loves you so much that He sent Jesus to die for your sins."

"I'm familiar with that story, Kelly," Trey said as he wiped away some stray tears. "Only Jesus didn't die for people like me, He died for people like you. He died for good people, not the scum of the earth."

"Well, I hate to argue with you, Trey, but that's not what the Bible says. It says that Jesus died for all mankind. It says that when we were still sinners, Christ died for us. It doesn't say that He died for us when we were good people, but sinners." Kelly paused, and looked at Trey intently, hoping her words were getting through to him. "Everyone's a sinner, Trey. There are no categories here...we're all sinners, and Jesus Christ died for each and every one of us." She looked determinedly at the broken boy. "God offers His forgiveness to everyone, Trey. He's not exclusive with it. And, all you need to do is take the gift that He's holding out to you."

"Really?" Trey asked in an astonished tone.

"Yes," Kelly said excitedly. She felt as though Trey was so very close to opening his heart up to God. "If I got you a Bible, you could read about it yourself."

"You'd do that for me?" Trey said in shock.

Kelly laughed lovingly. "Trey, you saved my life. Now, let God save your soul."

He looked at Kelly thoughtfully. "Why do you care about it so much? After my mother died, no one's ever cared what happened to me."

Kelly smiled broadly at the boy. "Like you said, Trey, we have a lot in common. And God's love changed my life." Kelly touched his hand lovingly. "I know it can change your life, too."

Kelly went and got her Bible out of her locker, and gave it to Trey.

She opened it to the book of John, and told Trey to start reading there.

"What's going to happen to me now?" Trey asked anxiously, looking from Mark to Kelly.

"We're going to talk to the judge now, Trey," Mark said eyeing the boy tenderly. "We'll probably be a couple of hours. Officer Thompson here is going to stay with you. We'll get back to you as soon as we can."

"Mark," Kelly said urgently as soon as they had left Trey's room, "can I talk to you in your office before we see Judge Henley?"

"Sure, Kel, I have something that I want to talk to you about, too," Mark said, dropping an arm around Kelly's shoulders and pulling her tight to him.

After they had entered Mark's office, he shut the door. "You want to go first, Kel?" he asked, smiling at her.

Kelly nodded. "Mark, what's going to happened to Trey? He's only fourteen. He's a good kid who was forced into things by his brothers. I believe on his own, he'd be a good citizen for Sawyer."

"I agree," Mark said quietly. "Did you know that Trey is a straight 'A' student, and is president of his school's chapter of 'Students Against Drunk Driving'?"

Kelly smiled at Mark. "Yes, I did know that, Mark. I've done a little research on him. But," she said eyeing him curiously, "how did you find out?"

Mark smiled broadly. "Well, I am the Chief after all. Besides," he said winking at her, "like I told you before, I make it a point to learn all I can about the enemy. The thing is," Mark said running a hand through his hair, "the more I investigated Trey Pitman, the less he looked like an enemy to me. He looked a lot like an innocent bystander who got sucked into the crime by threatening older brothers."

"You make it sound as if you like Trey," Kelly said studying him closely.

Mark laughed. "I do, Kelly. My heart really goes out to the boy."

"Well, that's good," Kelly said, wrapping her arms around Mark's waist, "because, it will make my next request easier to ask."

"You have a request?" Mark said raising his eyebrows teasingly at her.

"Something I want us to pray about for a while...," Kelly said thoughtfully.

"OK," Mark said seriously.

"What would you think about starting our family early? I know we're not even married yet, but we will be soon."

"In three weeks...," Mark said smiling flirtatiously at her. "And, by starting our family early," he said growing more sober, "do you mean adopting Trey?"

"I think that we should pray about it," Kelly nodded seriously. "God has touched my heart for that boy. The first time I met him...," she paused, too choked up to continue, but then willed herself to push on. "I don't know...," she said in a tight voice, "there's just something so vulnerable and heroic about him, all at the same time. I know he's only fourteen, but he stands up for his convictions like the bravest person I could possibly imagine."

Mark's eyes were filled with tears of his own. "Kelly, that's exactly how I feel. I was instantly drawn to Trey also. Let's pray hard about this for a week. Then at the end of the week, we'll talk again."

"That sounds great, Mark. Thanks."

"Don't thank me, Kel," Mark said laughing lightly. "That's what I wanted to talk to you about. We need to seek the Lord in this and see what His plan is."

As Mark and Kelly went before Judge Henley, their hearts were singing. God was giving them an overwhelming peace concerning Trey. It was as though they had instant confirmation. Even so, they determined not to act on anything for a week."

"So, Judge," Mark said anxiously, "in light of Trey saving Kelly's life, don't you think his time could be done in community service avenues, rather than jail?"

"I think that's a good suggestion, Mark. But Trey Pitman is only fourteen. He's going to need to get into foster care. It's hard enough to place teenagers now-a-days, not to mention one with Trey's family background."

"I would like to take temporary custody of Trey," Mark said seriously, "until a suitable family is found."

" It could take years to find a family willing at take Trey Pitman," the Judge said honestly. "We could be talking about quite a long-term commitment here."

"I'm aware of that, Judge," Mark replied thoughtfully. "Kelly and I need some time to think about this, but years are just the tip of the iceberg, as to what we think we're willing to offer Trey. Kelly and I are praying about the possibility of offering Trey a second chance. We'd like to offer Trey love, a home, and a real family."

"I'd advise you both to take your time with the decision," the Judge said in a strict tone. It's a big one."

"We'd like to think and pray on this for a week. Please don't say anything to anybody until we get back to you," Mark said to the judge, as he squeezed Kelly's hand.

"I won't," the old Judge said, as he smiled at both of them. "And," he said eyeing Mark admirably, "your temporary custody of Trey Pitman is granted immediately."

Thirty-Two

After speaking with the Judge, Kelly and Mark went back to Mark's office to pray. They prayed for Trey, and asked the Lord for guidance concerning the boy. They also prayed for God's blessing in the temporary custody of Trey. They prayed that Trey would accept the idea, and that the transition would go smoothly.

As Kelly and Mark walked back into the room where Rand and Trey were, they saw Rand sitting quietly, watching Trey read the gospel of John.

"He hasn't put the book down since you two left," Rand said quietly, as he smiled toward them.

Trey looked up from the Bible when he heard Kelly and Mark's voices. "This book is incredible!" Trey said with the awe of one who is sincerely seeking truth from the heart. "I never knew any of this stuff."

"Take the Bible with you, Trey," Kelly said smiling warmly at the boy. "Keep reading it. If you have any questions, feel free to ask Mark or me, or even Rand."

"Really?" he said eyeing the group with surprise. "That would be great."

"Well, Trey," Mark said sitting in a chair opposite the boy, "I've got some things to discuss with you."

Trey looked at Mark intently. "OK," he said closing the Bible." Go ahead."

"First of all, the judge has agreed to give you community service over jail time."

"Really?" Trey said as relief flooded his face. "That's excellent. Oh, I'm so glad," he said as he ran a hand through his sandy blonde hair.

"Do you have any specific areas in the community where you would like to serve?" Mark asked him casually.

"Well, I'm open to advice on that, Chief," Trey said thoughtfully. "I'm working at the homeless shelter on Tuesday evenings, and every Saturday I'm the cook at the town soup kitchen."

Mark turned around and smiled broadly at Kelly and Rand. "Well, Trey, it sounds as if you're already serving more than most people. Why don't you just keep doing what you're already doing. I'll talk to the Judge, and see if it's necessary for you to put in more hours."

"I don't mind," Trey said quickly. "I really love working in the community."

"That's good, Trey." Mark said smiling warmly at him. "I find it very rewarding myself."

Mark paused, and then said seriously, "Now...about the custody issue..."

"Custody issue?" Trey said in a worried voice, with his eyes bugging out. "What do you mean?"

"Trey," Mark went on smoothly, "you're only fourteen. The state won't allow you to live on your own."

"You mean that you've got to find someone willing to take in a teenage Pitman?" Trey said in a choked-up voice. "No one would ever take in a Pitman, Chief, and in all honesty, I couldn't blame them."

"Trey," Mark said firmly, touching the boy's shoulder, "I've already found someone to take temporary custody of you, until a permanent home can be found."

"Really?" Trey shouted in shock. "You've got to be kidding."

"No, Trey, I'm not," Mark said sincerely. "If you'd like, you're welcome to come stay with me, until I find you a permanent family."

Trey's mouth fell open, and he just stared at Mark for a solid minute. "Really?" he said studying Mark. "I'd stay with you in your house? You'd actually let me do that?"

Mark couldn't contain his laughter. "Yes, Trey. It was my idea."

"Why?" Trey said in a disbelieving voice. "My family has been awful to your fiancée," he said eyeing Mark hard. "Why would you do this for me?"

"Trey," Mark said confidently, "you've hit on a very important point here. Your father and brothers have been awful to Kelly, not you."

"Yeah, but they're my family," Trey said in tears.

"Trey," Mark said in a loving voice, "it's time we found you a new family. The Pitman's don't deserve a great kid like you."

Trey's mouth swung open again, as his eyes filled with tears. "Chief," Trey replied in a weak voice, "that dream seems too much to hope for. But," he said, as he wiped his eyes with the back of his hand, "if you're willing to put up with me temporarily, I swear to you, that I won't be any trouble."

"I'm not worried about it, Trey. You being trouble never crossed my mind." Mark paused, and then smiled warmly at him, "I think you and I are going to have a good time."

"Thank you, Sir," Trey said in a genuine voice. "I appreciate everything you're doing, more then you could possible know."

Mark and Kelly helped Trey move into Mark's Cape, and get all his things settled. "You don't have much, Trey," Kelly said looking at his duffle bag.

"I'm fine, Kelly," Trey said smiling at her.

"What's so funny?" Kelly asked curiously.

Trey laughed. "I'm just not used to people caring about me." He smiled shyly at his shoes. "Like I said before, the last person to really care about me was my Ma."

"You remember much about your Mom?" Kelly asked him quietly.

421

"Not as much as I'd like," Trey said shrugging. "I was only six when she died." Trey sighed, and then said slowly, "But everything I remember about her was good. She was kind and loving, and liked helping people."

"You sound a lot like her," Mark said in a warm voice.

Trey blushed bright red. "No one's ever said that to me before, Chief."

"Now, that's something that we're going to have to fix right now," Mark said to Trey in a serious tone. Trey's eye's got big, as Mark continued.

"I would like to know why you always call her Kelly, and you always call me Chief?"

Trey smiled in relief. "Well," he said stuffing his hands into his jean pockets, "that's because she's Kelly, and you're the Chief."

Everyone laughed, but suddenly Trey grew serious. "Should I be calling you Officer Douglas?" Trey asked Kelly in a concerned voice. "I didn't mean to sound disrespectful."

Kelly laughed. "If you call me Officer Douglas, I'll clobber you Trey! We're way beyond formalities." Kelly laughed again, and

Trey's expression looked confused as he eyed Mark seriously.

"Trey," Mark said lightly, "no one who stays as a guest in my house ever calls me Chief. My name is Mark," he said casually. "Do you think that you can handle that?"

"Really?" Trey asked looking at Mark, to make sure he had heard him correctly. Mark simply nodded, and smiled at the boy. "OK, then...," Trey said sounding off-balance, "I'll try to call you that."

After a relaxing supper of pizza, Mark made a fire, and the three of them talked easily. Kelly was amazed at how quickly they were bonding. They talked openly and honestly with each other, and it was apparent to all that a special relationship was forming.

The next few days only brought them all closer. "Kelly," Trey said seriously, "I'm really a pretty good cook. I wish you'd let me help out."

Kelly eyed Trey with an embarrassed expression. "Trey," she said in a regretful voice, "you would have found out sooner or later, but, I can't cook to save my life. If you're patient enough to show me, I'd appreciate any help."

"OK," Trey said smiling at her, "the first thing that we need to do is go to the store. Do you know that Mark literally doesn't have any food in the house?"

Kelly laughed as she herded Trey out the door, and toward the market. Forty minutes later, they were home with all the fixing for a country-style, roast beef dinner.

When Mark came into the house three hours later, his face dropped at the sights and smells from the kitchen. "I must be in the wrong house," he said eyeing the roast like a hungry wolf.

"Trey cooked," Kelly said proudly. "And I helped!"

Mark laughed, and dropped an arm around both of them. "Trey, I'm impressed. At fourteen, you can cook better than both Kelly and I combined. You're going to spoil us, and I'm already looking forward to it."

Mark dropped his arm from Trey and then pulled Kelly closer, planting a quick kiss on her. "How's my girl doing?" he asked her lovingly.

"Great!" she said smiling up at him. "One more week and Gram will be back. And," Kelly said wiggling her eyebrows at him, "two more weeks and we'll be married."

"I can't wait!" Mark said quickly kissing her again.

They spied Trey shyly watching them. "I can't believe that I'm finally going to get to marry the girl of my dreams," Mark said to Trey excitedly.

"She's a great lady, Mark. I'm really happy for you both," Trey said smiling at them.

As they sat down and started polishing off the roast beef dinner, Trey seemed quieter then usual. "What's up, Trey?" Mark asked studying Trey curiously.

"Well," Trey said sighing, "I feel as though I should be moving on soon. I mean," he said nervously, "it's not as though I don't appreciate everything you've done...I really do."

"What is it, Trey?" Kelly asked, laying down her folk.

"You guys are getting married in a few weeks. You're not going to want me hanging around when you get back from your honeymoon."

Kelly and Mark smiled at each other. A week had gone by since Trey had been living with Mark, and they both knew that God had given them their first child. As Mark looked over at Kelly, her huge smile was all the confirmation he needed.

"I was going to wait until after dinner to discuss this with you Trey. But, I guess now is as good a time as any." Mark paused and looked at Trey excitedly. "I found a family that is really excited and anxious to adopt you."

Trey's face fell in complete shock. "You're kidding?" He paused thoughtfully, and then said skeptically. "They know about my family, right?"

"Yes, Trey," Mark said confidently. "They know everything, and they're still very excited about you joining their family."

"Really?" Trey said blinking his eyes at Mark. "I just can't believe it," he said breathlessly.

"Would you like to meet them?" Mark said seriously.

Trey's whole body looked nervous. He was twisting his fingers, his hands, and his feet.

"Yes," his voice cracked, "I would. I'm just a little nervous."

"No need to be nervous, Trey. They're already nuts about you," Mark said smiling at the boy.

"You mean it's someone I know?" Trey said almost sounding appalled.

Mark nodded. "Would you like to meet them, Son?"

"Yes, Mark. I would. Very much," Trey said in a nervous voice that definitely held interest.

"Are you ready to introduce him, Kel?" Mark asked her in a loving tone.

"Yes, Mark. I'm more then ready."

"OK, then...," Mark said jumping out of his seat. "Come over here, Trey."

Trey got up slowly, and nervously stood next to Mark.

"Trey," Mark said in a warm, loving voice, "I'd like to introduce myself. My name is Mark Mitchell, and this here is Kelly, soon to be Mitchell."

"You guys?" Trey said staring at them in great shock.

427

"Would you like to be part of our family, Trey?" Mark asked in an inviting, loving tone. "Because, if you have any reservations, now is the time to speak up."

Tears started running down the fourteen-year-old boy's face. "I would like very much to be part of your family," Trey said looking from Mark to Kelly. "But," he asked hesitantly, "are you really sure that you want me?"

Kelly and Mark pulled Trey into a big, long hug. "Yes, Trey. We really want you."

Trey wept openly in their arms. He hadn't felt so loved since his Ma was around. "Thank you," he said looking gratefully at them both. "This is the best thing that ever happened to me."

"So, do you like the sound of Trey Mitchell?" Mark asked squeezing Trey's shoulders.

"Yes, I love it," Trey said confidently. "Thank you. Thank you so much."

Thirty-Three

Kelly and Mark watched Trey as he paced nervously in front of them. "I know that this is probably bad timing...I mean," he added sheepishly, "you're getting married in a few days, and all..." He stopped pacing, and looked at them directly. "Well, you said if I have any questions, I should come to you."

"What's on your mind, Trey?" Mark asked in a concerned voice.

"This!" His voice cracked in frustration. He had picked the Bible up off the table, and was holding it slightly toward them. "I've read this from cover to cover...and there's plenty that I don't understand...especially," Trey said rolling his eyes at them, "the book of Revelation. That's far out."

Trey sighed deeply, and then continued. "But, one concept that struck me over and over was God's love." Trey's voice had gotten soft now, and was barely above a whisper. "All He did for me..." the boy said shaking his head slowly, "I just don't get it."

"Trey," Mark said quietly, "God made you, and He loves you. Everything that God has done for you, and will do for you, is, because He loves you."

Trey nodded. "But I'm a sinner," he said hopelessly. "God and sin don't go together." Trey paused, and then said in an urgent tone, "I need God. I want God in my life...but I don't know how to ask Him. I don't have anything to offer Him. I feel as though I don't have the right to ask anything of God."

"Trey," Mark said in a gentle voice, "God loves you, and He wants to be part of your life. Just talk to Him, Trey. Talk to God like you're talking to me right now."

"Will you help me?" Trey asked with pleading eyes.

"Yes, Trey," Mark said lovingly. "Just tell God that you're sorry for your sins, and that you want Him to come into your life."

"That's it?" Trey asked skeptically.

Mark nodded and smiled at him. "Just talk to God, Trey. He already knows what's in your heart."

Trey dropped down on the end of the couch, and bowed his head.

"Please, Dear God," he said in a quiet, yet sincere voice, "I want you to come into my heart. I am so sorry for all of my sins. Please forgive me, and come into my life today."

Trey slowly raised his head, and looked over at Mark and Kelly. As he blinked his tears away, he smiled when he saw Mark and Kelly's tears. "Thank you," he said in a husky voice. "This past week-and-a-half have been unbelievable for me. I've gotten two new fathers, and a new mother, too." He paused, and then continued sincerely, "Thank you for everything. I have been given a new life. I can't begin to tell you how much that means to me. I don't think I can ever find the words to thank you for all you've done for me. I feel so overwhelmed. Two weeks ago I had nothing. Absolutely nothing. And now," Trey said through a choked up voice, "I have you guys and God." He wiped his eyes on the end of his shirt sleeves, and said in a low voice, drenched in emotion, "Now, I have everything. Absolutely everything."

Epilogue

Kelly's eyes clouded over with tears as she sat looking up at the stage.

She couldn't believe how quickly Trey had grown up. Before her was a young man who, at the age of twenty-three, had graduated from college with honors, and was graduating today from the Vermont State Police Academy.

As Kelly proudly admired Trey, she thought the young man before her looked handsome and brave in his navy blue officer's uniform. But what impressed Kelly even more was the heart of the young man before her. Trey was one in a million. His life had not been easy as a child, but with the Lord's help, he had risen above the pain from his past. He was one of the most sincere, giving individuals that Kelly had ever known, and she was proud beyond words that in just a few short days, Trey would join his father on the force of Sawyer's Crossing.

The squirming two year old in her lap drew her attention away, as he snuggled his head against her chest. Kelly gently kissed the top of the small boy's head, as she lovingly gazed at her children around her. Mark Jr., at eight years old, was the spitting imagine of Mark Sr. He had a tall, lanky frame, with thin blonde hair and deep blue eyes. His smile was warm and friendly, and needed little encouragement to spread across his face.

Rachel and Rebecca, six and four, looked more like Kelly. Their creamy white faces, with rosy checks, gave the girls a happy, healthy complexion. They both always wore their long blonde hair in ponytails, accessorized by either ribbons or bows.

Michael, the youngest of the bunch, was an energetic two-year-old, who seemed to be a curious combination of Mark and Kelly. In appearance, he resembled his father, but his mischievous smile and heart came straight from his mother. Kelly smiled at the boy in her lap, as she thought about Mark's threat that mischievous little Michael would never get a chance to drive until he was at least thirty. Mark could already see Michael's rocket-man potential, and it made the loving father reluctant to even put his youngest son on a bicycle.

"Mamma...," the little blonde imp in her lap said, "I see Dadda."

Kelly looked quickly to where the little pudgy hand was pointing. Mark, dressed in his formal, navy chief uniform, was just coming up on the stage. He was such a complete picture of a brave, all-American, trustworthy man, that Kelly couldn't help but smile proudly at him.

Mark returned her smile, and added a quick wink of his own. As Chief Mark Mitchell stood behind the podium, delivering the graduation speech, his presence was captivating and commanding, and Kelly knew he had the immediate respect of the audience.

Out of the corner of her eye, Kelly could see A.J., gazing up at Mark with open admiration. The nineteen-year-old young man's adoration of Mark was no secret to anyone. He loudly sang Mark's praises to anyone who would listen, and even to those who would rather not listen. Mark had gained an even higher status in

A.J.'s heart, when he custom-designed a job, filing reports at the police station, for the boy.

At the end of Mark's address, he presented Trey Mitchell with his Police Academy diploma. As father and son locked hands with each other, the proud, loving expressions that covered their faces spoke volumes of their true admiration for each other. Mark and Trey had grown closer than most fathers and sons. Their bond was special. Their bond was deep, and Kelly had no doubt that it would last a lifetime.

Mark had given Trey a rare and golden opportunity at a second chance at the life he deserved all along. Mark treated Trey as if he were his own birth son, giving the boy all the love he had in his heart. In return, Trey had quickly grown to love his new father, treasuring the father-son relationship that he had never had before.

God had blessed Kelly and Mark by bringing Trey into their lives.

When they opened their hearts to that fourteen-year-old boy nine years ago, they never, in their wildest imagination, could picture the wonderful blessings God had in store for them.

As Kelly eyed her family lovingly, she thanked God for the blessing of each one of them. After such a lonely childhood, God had blessed her with a wonderful, godly family of her own. Kelly's heart felt overwhelmed by God's goodness to her. God had taken the life of a little six-year-old orphan girl, and given her more than she could ever have dreamed possible. She had a relationship with her Heavenly Father, a wonderful godly husband, and five incredible children. Tears filled her eyes as she thought about that little orphan girl. She had finally been given a family. A family that she knew was hand-picked by her Heavenly Father above.

*Sugar Creek
Inn*

A New England Novel

Sharon Snow Sirois

Coming Soon
from
Lighthouse Publishing...

Sugar Creek Inn

Sugar Creek is a quiet New England town located on Eagle Lake in Maine. It is a beautiful, relaxing area that is frequented by tourists who enjoy a variety of outdoor activities, such as sailing, swimming, and skiing.

It is here on Eagle Lake that the Miller family runs The Sugar Creek Inn. There is never a dull moment between the four spirited sisters, the two elderly brothers who are permanent house guests, the boyfriend whom everyone loves, the boyfriend whom nobody likes, the regular house guests, and the Miller's two rowdy dogs.

And, when Matthew Bishop comes to Sugar Creek as the new pastor, things get very complicated for the youngest Miller daughter. Jacilyn Miller is engaged to marry her childhood friend, Bradley Clarke. The wedding plans have been made, invitations ordered, and

gowns picked out. Yet Jack's well-ordered world turns upside down as she finds herself attracted to the pastor who's supposed to marry her. The chemistry between Matthew and Jack is so strong it's electrifying. And the more Jack tries to stay away from the young pastor, the more they get thrown together.

Jack Miller struggles with her feelings and tries hard to rein in her spinning emotions. As she tries to honor promises made in the past, Matthew challenges her to honor God and His ways above anything else.

Preview

"*I* can't believe you guys won't tell me what the new pastor looks like," Jack complained quietly, as she fidgeted restlessly in the hard wooden pew seat. "You are all so mean!"

"We don't want to get you upset," Jay said in a matter-of-fact voice, as she causally glanced out the twelve-pane window she sat next to. "He kind of has the type of face that would be good for radio."

Jack's eyebrows shot up. "You're just saying that to get me upset," she whispered angrily. "You know I don't want anyone from the Munsters or Addams family marrying me."

"Maybe you should have a radio service," Jay said helpfully. "That could actually work well all the way around. No one would notice the new pastor's mug, and you wouldn't have to worry about spending a lot of money on your wedding outfits." Jay smiled at Jack enthusias-

tically. "This is going to be great! Leave the details to me."

"Go away...," Jack said in a low voice that was actually more of a growl. "I may kick you out of the wedding party."

"Don't do me any favors!" Jay said sarcastically, as she absent-mindedly dug the toe of her black shoe into the sanctuary's old maroon carpeting. "Besides," she said rolling her eyes at her engaged sister, "Mom would never let you. She's determined to see me dressed up in some flowery, ruffled, feminine-type getup. This whole thing is completely ridiculous, if you ask me."

"I wasn't asking you," Jack said in a tight voice, staring hard at her sister.

"I thought you'd want to know anyways...," Jay stated in an insulted tone, as she shrugged her shoulders indifferently.

Jack glared at her and then turned to her other sister. "Andy, you've got to help me out here," Jack begged in a distressed voice. "Tell me if he's really as bad as Jay is saying. I've got to know."

"No one," Andy said confidently, "is ever as bad as Jay says."

"That's true!" Jack said with instant relief washing over her. "That's definitely true!"

"He sort of looks similar to old Pastor Clayton," Andy said in a serious tone.

"What do you mean by 'sort of'?" Jack asked her older sister in an investigative tone. "That phrase worries me. It implies far too much freedom here."

"Well," Andy said playing with the hem on her floral spring dress, "what's to say? He's old, bald, and has huge bushy eyebrows on him, like he's got hedges glued to his forehead."

"And," Jay said leaning toward her sister, "a pot on the front of him that would make an old muddy pig proud."

"No way!" Jack said, completely horrified. "And this is the man who's going to marry Bradley and me?"

"Maybe it's not too late for you to join the Methodist Church on the other side of the lake," Jay said brightly "Their pastor's old, but he's taken care of himself well. And, since Bradley goes there, I bet they'd zip your membership right through."

A moment later Jack turned to her sister on her right. Sam was sixteen months older then Jack, yet the two of them were closer then two peas in a pod. "Sam," she whispered quietly, "what do you think of the new pastor?"

"You're going to like him, Jack," Sam said quickly. "He's very kind."

"Yeah, but Jay says he has a face made for radio," Jack said, struggling with the thought.

"You don't have to feature him in your wedding album," Sam said teasingly.

As Jack stared at the podium, for the first time she noticed a shiny black shoe. It belonged to someone who was hidden behind the podium. Jack turned and glanced at Andy for any clues, yet the eldest Miller girl just stared straight ahead. Whoever this man was, Jack thought curiously, he was so short that the podium was literally blocking him.

As her father finally introduced Pastor Matthew Bishop and he stood up and came forward, Jack's mouth dropped open so far it almost hit the floor. She quickly put a hand over the gaping hole, yet not before the young man at the podium noticed it. He paused, looked momentar-

ily at her, and then directed his attention to his new congregation and addressed them.

Jack kept her eyes glued to her hands in her lap. She knew from the heat that she felt on her checks, that her face must have looked red enough to explode. And, to make matters worse, she could hear the quiet yet steady laughter that her sisters were working hard to try to muffle. They had pulled a good one over on her, and they knew it. She would think of ways later to repay them for their *kindness*.

Matthew Bishop was not a balding, heavy old man. He was, in fact, gorgeous-looking, young and, had the most attractive, stunning smile that Jack had ever seen. And he was probably only a few years older then herself.

As Jack buried her embarrassment, she took a chance and slowly glanced up. Pastor Bishop stood in front of the podium, not behind it, and was talking with ease to the people. His voice was gentle and kind, and his expressive brown eyes were filled with tenderness and care. Jack could not tear herself away from those gentle brown eyes. They reeled her in, like a fish on a line. She found them intriguing, and yet at the

same time flooding over with a depth of love and compassion that she had never seen before. They stirred her to her very soul. As she continued to stare at his eyes, she soon found herself under his direct gaze. He was still preaching, and it panicked Jack a bit to think she couldn't recall a word of the subject that his sermon was on. The only thing that she could recall was the fact that this young, extremely good-looking pastor had incredible, luring brown eyes.

Again, Jack looked back down into her lap. She knew that he knew that she had been staring at him. Embarrassment flooded her face for the second time that morning. Jack slowly shook her head. What in the world was wrong with her. She was never one to gawk or stare at men, not to even mention that she was an engaged woman. Yet, for some reason, this man standing before her was a man she was finding it very difficult to take her eyes off of. It was very much out of character for her.

As she slowly lifted her eyes out of the safety of her lap, and back to the preacher, her heart stopped beating. He was looking at her so directly, it was as if he were simply waiting for her to bring her eyes back up to meet his. For when she did, he held her eyes with his own, just long enough for her to know that he was on to her game. A brief smile touched his lips, and he raised his eyebrows slightly, almost challengingly. Then, with full attention, he directed his energy back to his sermon.